<hr>

ANNA'S GUIDE TO GETTING EVEN

<hr>

LAURA HEFFERNAN

Anna's Guide
to
Getting Even

by
Laura Heffernan

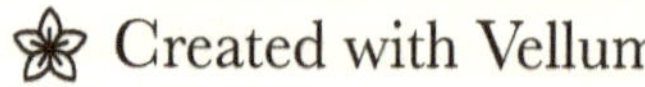 Created with Vellum

Part I

At the temple there is a poem called "Loss"
carved into the stone. It has three words, but the
poet has scratched them out. You cannot read loss,
only feel it.

Arthur Golden, *Memoirs of a Geisha*

My name is Anna. That's Ahn-a, not Ann-a. People hear my story, they say, "Oh, that's awful." They think it would never happen to them. I thought it would never happen to me, either.

But it did.

Chapter 1

November 10, 2018

The newscasters spent days repeating dire warnings most people ignored. After all, we'd made it through ninety-nine percent of hurricane season without any storms traveling anywhere near us. Early November wasn't exactly known for its tropical weather in the tristate area. Still, as Mamá used to say, it's better to be prepared *por si las moscas*, or just in case.

To avoid tempting fate, I stocked up on eggs, milk, and bread (as if I'd be making French toast in a storm), grabbed a box of strawberry-flavored toaster pastries for good measure, froze blocks of ice in plastic containers, and filled my bathtub with water. This basic nod at hurricane readiness seemed more than sufficient. It never occurred to me to cover the windows or anything like that.

When the storm hit, the entire northeastern seaboard realized the newscasters hadn't been overreacting for once. Winds howled and shrieked, shaking the house. Rain obliterated the satellite signal to my television early in the evening. Soon thereafter, I cowered in the basement of my three-bedroom house with a battery-powered lantern from an old camping trip and Hermione, my roommate's brown tabby cat.

The two of us huddled in the spot furthest from the row of tiny windows under a sea of blankets as the storm raged overhead. Not long after sunset, my house lost power. The dots of light provided by street lamps winked out at the same time. My phone provided a lifeline to the outer world for almost an hour before the service stopped working. At least the lantern gave off a steady glow.

Alone, scared, and bored, I unfairly cursed my roommate for not being with me. Tara was in the middle of nowhere, taking care of her sick mother. She lived in a tiny trailer with no TV, cell service, or Internet in one of those squarish-type states that started with a vowel. Tara probably would prefer to be with me, storm or no. If she even knew about the storm, isolated as she was.

Still, sitting alone in my basement listening to

rain beating against the windows was no fun. My boyfriend, Jay, got stuck working late. By the time he left the office, the Mayor of New York City asked all residents to remain home unless absolutely necessary, keeping the roads clear for emergency vehicles. The last time I talked to him, Jay was about to walk the twelve blocks home to his loft apartment through a downpour so thick he couldn't see five feet beyond the circle of his umbrella.

Thunder crashed overhead. A streak of lightning lit up the room before the roar ended. I shivered and rearranged my covers. Using my phone as a flashlight, I picked up one of about five dozen old copies of *Forbes* magazine stored in our basement. My own face smiled up at me from a sidebar on the cover. When the magazine ran its feature on "Up-and-Coming Executives Under Thirty-Five Years Old," I'd warned Tara that my friends and family would read it online, but she insisted on buying all the hard copies she could find. At least Tara's mother appreciated not having to drive thirty miles into town to read about me. The rest collected dust down here, in case the zombie apocalypse came and I needed a reminder of my old life or a way to start a fire.

The house shook, distracting me from reading about "No. 17: Katherine Ashcroft." A lovely woman, by all accounts. I saw her at a networking event a while back, but we didn't talk. To block out the storm, I sat trying to remember the name of her company. It worked until thunder crashed on top of me again. The rain hit the windows so forcefully, I double-checked the latches. Something banged against the roof. Cringing, I pressed my hands against my ears. The sounds of the storm grew louder, and Hermione squirmed closer against my chest, purring. The basement door rattled in its frame.

Another crash, followed by a bang. A siren wailed next to my ear. It took a moment to realize that the blaring sounded eerily like my car alarm. Uh-oh. Hopefully the wind, rather than a real problem.

I could turn the blasted thing off from where I sat. Except I'd left my car keys on the kitchen counter. Upstairs, beyond the safety of the basement.

For fifteen minutes, I sat listening, regretting my decision to pay for the extended battery. That thing would blast all night if no one shut it off. The salesman hadn't been exaggerating. Putting my hands over my ears was about as effective as trying to put out a forest fire with a Dixie cup of water.

Finally, I couldn't take it anymore. With a sigh, I threw off my blankets. Hermione glared at me before tearing off toward a pile of stuff in the far corner. For her sake, I hoped it was quieter under there. My legs tingled after so much time on the concrete floor. I rubbed them, one at a time, while I willed myself to go deaf. When the feeling returned to my lower limbs and the alarm still blared behind me, I drew a deep breath, pulled myself upright, and told myself there was no reason not to venture into the house for a minute or two. I'd be perfectly safe.

My prosthetic left foot sat against the wall where I'd left it when Hermione and I settled in for the night. It wouldn't take long to strap it on, but I couldn't stand the thought of another single second listening to that siren. I'd hopped up the basement stairs before, I could do it again. The kitchen lay directly across from the basement door. Less than twenty feet of open space separated me from silence. Lots of windows, lots of potential for broken glass up there, but I had no choice. My shoes were also in the kitchen. Perhaps I should've shown the newscasters a little more respect.

A sturdy banister helped me to the top of the stairs. The basement door stuck, especially on humid days. Apparently, "humid" applied to hurricanes. I shoved with all my might. The wood didn't budge. I tried again, with the same lack of results. On the third attempt, I braced my shoulder against the door, rested the bottom of my calf against the step, and slammed my full weight against the wood. The door opened—and whipped away from me. Without the support, I stumbled out into the hall, tripping over the top step. My palms and knees slammed against the ground, knocking the wind out of me.

The kitchen wasn't overly large, and my keys hung from a hook between the French patio doors and the door to the garage. I braced myself against the gusts, wondering how many windows broke to create this wind tunnel in my hallway. Still, I needed to move forward. Either I turned that alarm off, or I'd lose my mind by morning. With a deep breath, I started across the kitchen floor as quickly as I could.

Before I made it two feet into the room, I came to a dead stop.

"*¡Dios mio!*"

The wind slapped my face, tearing the words from my mouth. Water drenched my hair and clothes. Shivers immediately followed. Surprised, I glanced toward the glass doors. The panes weren't broken. They weren't there at all. Neither were the doors. Or the walls, or the kitchen, or the roof. I stood, shivering, in the middle of the storm, sur-rounded by granite countertops, peering through the sheets of rain at our beautiful old oak tree, which lay across my newly topless Infiniti, alarm still blaring.

BY THE TIME the winds died down and the rain slowed, my phone's battery had long since crapped out. The moon finally peeked through the clouds, sending streaks of white light through the miraculously-still-intact basement windows. I lay huddled in the blankets, wishing for the warmth of the traitor cat that still lurked somewhere in the depths of the basement. I managed a couple of hours of fitful sleep by the time the sun peeked over the horizon.

My first hysterical thought upon opening my eyes was, "I'm going to be late for work." Of course I was. I also wasn't likely to make it at all, since the storm smashed the roof of my car in and whisked away my kitchen. I didn't even know if the house still contained my closet. If not, the only thing I had to wear, other than my navy blue sweatpants and Yankees t-shirt, sat folded in a box of Halloween costumes we stored in the basement. The idea of showing up at work dressed as Slutty Cop brought a ghost of a smile to my lips.

Ugh.

I forced myself to sit up and reached for my prosthetic.

"Mwar?"

"Hey, sweetie." Now that the danger passed, Hermione was more than happy to rub against my legs and accept petting until I remembered my obligation to feed her. One problem: we stored the cat food in the kitchen. Which could be somewhere over the rainbow by now.

I picked her up and rubbed my face against her soft fur. She purred. An answering rumble from my stomach reminded me that I hadn't eaten, either. "Let's see if Mother Nature left us anything in the fridge. Or a fridge."

Talking to the cat soothed me. I kept up a constant stream of chatter while I found my phone in the tangle of blankets, plugged it in, confirmed that the power remained out, and headed upstairs to assess the damage.

"Well, Hermione, it appears that we lost the kitchen. Luckily, we still have a fridge." It lay on its side, and the cord dangled uselessly down the back, plug no longer attached, but I did *have* a refrigerator. "You like three-day-old burrito, right?"

"Mwar?"

Gingerly, I opened the door, thankful at least that the side with the handle landed on top. A tangle of condiments lay against the far wall, most of the containers still intact. On the top shelf, several plastic containers created a haphazard pyramid. Grabbing the top one, I pulled out a chunk of ground beef, wiped off the rice, and offered it to the cat while I kept digging. "Old lunch meat?"

She stood on her back legs when I opened the

package, so I dropped a slice on the floor and grabbed a second for myself while I explored the rest of the house to assess the damage. The spare room, naturally, seemed more or less untouched.

Pretending I wandered someone else's home was the only thing holding me together at the moment, so I held my head high and tried to imagine an invisible realtor leading me on a tour…of a very water-logged house owned by a messy homeowner.

Not much happened to the bathroom, other than a pile of broken glass in the tub and the complete lack of hot water. I shrugged and shut the door to keep Hermione out before moving on. Then I stood for a long time, surveying Tara's room, delaying the moment before facing my own. I refused to allow myself to think about what I might find behind my closed door.

My best friend's room always looked like a hurricane hit it. Truly, I couldn't tell the difference until I spotted the puddles. Or, I wouldn't have, if the roof had been attached. Instead, sunlight streamed into every corner of the room as if mocking Tara for spending three hundred dollars on blackout curtains she never opened. My lips twitched upward when I realized the curtains themselves still lay perfectly in place, not even ruffled by the winds. Too bad she wasn't here. She'd appreciate the irony.

Finally, I turned to my room, on the same side of the house as the kitchen. As the missing pantry. The bedroom window five feet from my smashed car.

The door wouldn't open. With one shoulder braced against the wood, my hand tightened on the knob. I shoved as hard as I could. For my efforts, the door moved an inch. Something brushed against my face. I screamed and jumped before realizing it was only a tree branch. A branch with no business in my bedroom. Wonderful.

The door wasn't budging, so I abandoned my bedroom and continued my exploration. I felt nothing. Somewhere, deep inside, shock numbed my emotions, kept me from feeling the brunt of the pain.

My feet carried me from one room to the next as my eyes took in damage that my mind refused to process. Shattered windows. Shards of broken glass everywhere. Plaster coating every surface. A soaked couch in the dining room. Something soggy touched my right foot. I jumped, then realized it was a scrap of paper.

Thick, heavy paper, part of something once much larger. The letters on the front now spelled "Colum—." This could be either my diploma or Tara's. It didn't matter. Below it, I found a soggy mass of blue and red fabric. It took a minute to realize this wad of filthy sateen used to be horseback riding ribbons from my childhood. Shaking my head to ward off the onrush of emotions, I dropped everything into the rubble and continued picking my way toward the door.

Outside, movement caught my eye. Hermione dashed across the lawn, chasing a squirrel or something. Oh, no. I should've locked her in her carrier before doing this. Assuming I could find her carrier, which in my defense, was a pretty big assumption.

A wave of despair welled in my chest. A familiar old emotion I thought I'd long since conquered. I needed to get out of here.

If only I'd been wearing shoes when I went to hide in the basement the night before, escape would've been easier. I poked along the floor the best I could, trying not to step on nails or broken glass until I got to my "picking up the mail" slippers near the front hall. I slid on sunglasses I found dangling off the chandelier in the dining room, a pair Tara lost before she left. She'd be glad to know I finally found them. With a deep breath, I headed outside to assess the rest of the damage. I just needed a plan. First a plan, then I could be sad.

One glance at the trunk of my shiny red Infiniti sticking out from under a tree broke through my emotional barriers. I blinked back tears as if when I hit the hundredth blink, my car would magically be restored. My pride and joy was a total steal at seventy-two payments of four hundred fifty dollars. Two payments down, only seventy to go.

Random stuff covered the lawn: the lid to my cast iron skillet, what looked like an old prescription pill bottle, the remote for a window air conditioner I'd recycled years ago. Not knowing where to start, I bit my lip and forced my gaze toward the curb.

Across the street, the house belonging to my favorite elderly couple mirrored mine—half the front room lay in ruins, the garage decimated, but the other side more or less intact. Thankfully, my neighbors already left for Florida for the winter, so they would be fine, but I needed to call when the networks cleared to let them know. They unfortunately didn't know how to text and didn't want to learn.

No one else was in sight, but I called out, looking for anyone trapped inside their homes or needing an extra pair of hands. Only my voice broke the eerie silence.

Downed power lines to the east and the storm-created swimming pool next door in what used to be Mrs. Everling's living room persuaded me to head west, up the hill, toward a gas station on the corner. Walking past the house to the west, I marveled at the lack of damage. One front window was broken, the hole shaped suspiciously like a baseball.

The shouting match that had carried across the yard the day before and the sulking teenage boy who'd offered to mow my lawn for twenty dollars suggested the storm had little to do with the damage to my next-door neighbor's house. That conversation felt like a lifetime ago.

Most of the other houses on this end of the street were fine, untouched. The sun still hovered near the horizon, filling the air with tinges of color. If I didn't turn around, only the eerie stillness would give any indication a storm occurred. I couldn't think about that. Focusing on the road ahead helped staunch the rising panic in my chest.

A week ago, the fact that the gas station owner still maintained a working payphone had been a running joke throughout Red Bank. Now, the archaic device reeled me in like a lifeline. Me and half the town, apparently. I stood in line with neighbors I'd seen a million times and never spoken to. Everybody wore the same sunken-eyed, slack-jawed expression on their faces. If I'd possessed a mirror, I suspected the same dead eyes would peer back at me. We were haunted. No one spoke above a whisper.

The woman behind me poked something in my back. I whirled around before realizing she held a crumpled granola bar. "You hungry, honey?"

My stomach rumbled, but the thought of eating didn't appeal to me at the moment. I shook my head.

She shoved it into my hand. "I walked by your house, your kitchen's gone. Take it for later."

The woman's sincerity touched me, even as I struggled to remember how she knew me. Finally, it hit me: a week after I bought the house, her dog got loose. We'd met when I returned him, exchanged pleasantries, and not spoken since. "Thank you. Are you okay?"

She laughed. "Ain't nobody okay 'round here, but I'll live. I'm doing better than you, I think."

The sun rose higher. Our voices dropped away as we each processed the extent of the storm. I inched closer to the phone, wondering if anyone was trying to reach me.

When I finally reached the booth, my fingers fumbled for a minute. Change. How had I forgotten I needed change? Once upon a time, Mamá made me memorize her calling card number for an emergency such as this one. If someone asked me two days ago, I'd have been hard-pressed to recall what a calling card was.

A voice rumbled behind me. "Make a call or get out of line, sweetie."

I didn't acknowledge them. Instead, I grasped

at a distant memory and dialed the operator. "I'd like to make a collect call, please."

Less than a minute later, my boyfriend's voice filled my ear. "Anna, thank God! Are you okay?"

"I'm fine, but the house is a total wreck. No electricity or hot water. My car's smashed. Phone's dead. I can't possibly get to work today. Or all week, probably. I can't even get to my clothes."

"Don't worry about that. My place is fine; the storm passed right over it. I'll come pick you up, we'll pack your stuff together, and you can stay with me until you get everything settled."

A three-thousand-pound weight lifted off my shoulders. "Thanks, Jay."

"Where are you calling from? I'm on my way."

"Just come to the house. I'll be sifting through the rubble." I thanked him again and hung up.

My homeowner's policy could be anywhere on the East Coast by now. The spare was in my office at work, currently unavailable to me. Not knowing what else to do, I trudged back home. The insurance company would send people to help with clean-up eventually, but I needed to do something to keep busy. I couldn't just sit here and stare at the mess. The scope of the damage overwhelmed me. For a long time, I stood in the kitchen doorway, just staring and hoping Hermione would bound across the lawn.

Deep breaths, Anna. One thing at a time. Just do one little thing. Then do one more little thing. That was manageable.

All those leftover magazines from the basement turned out to be useful, after all: I used them to divert water away from the main hallway, back into what used to be the kitchen. I spent several seconds watching the water seep into my image on the cover before flipping the top one over and dumping more slick pages on top. Not quite as good as a door, but at least Hermione could hop over the stacks when she returned to get into the house. My treasured ribbons, memories of a lost youth, went into a trash bag with chunks of plaster, broken picture frames, and something furry that might've been a drowned rat. Sniffling, I added the now-beheaded, one-legged ceramic horse Tara made me when I gave up riding to the trash pile.

I wiped my eyes. "Goodbye, Sir Maxwell."

The last time I saw the horse was twenty years ago, and I hadn't been in a saddle since. But saying good-bye to the figurine hit me almost as hard as the day I quit. Tears flowed freely down my cheeks. Ignoring them, I continued to sift through the rubble, looking for anything that could be salvaged. Tara's favorite Blu-ray, our picture from prom, both of us sporting "the Rachel".

I sniffled again, wondering if a bit of music could lift my spirits.

The lack of a phone, computer, router, or electricity made streaming music impossible, but I rooted around in the basement until I found an old battery-operated CD player with my other camping stuff, along with some tarps that could come in handy.

"Hello? Anna?" Jay's voice emanated from the general direction of what used to be the kitchen.

The moment I saw him, my facade of bravery broke. An armload of tarps tumbled to the ground. My chin quivered, and a sob escaped me. He held me, the boom box cradled awkwardly between us, for a long time. "I'm so sorry. It's okay. We'll rebuild together."

"Thanks," I sniffled. "How did you get here? And what time is it?"

"I borrowed a scooter from my neighbor. I couldn't leave you to deal with this alone. Traffic is backed up all the way into the city. You don't want to go out there if you don't have to. Trees blocking lanes, power lines down, flooding everywhere. About three blocks over, water's up to people's doorsteps. But I'm here now."

I smiled up at him and leaned forward to kiss him, drawing strength from the touch. "Thank you. *Te amo, mi vida.*"

"I love you, too. Let's get to work."

Eventually, everything would need to come out while contractors did the repairs, but at least I could try to avoid more water damage until I got a truck and a storage unit. I turned on the boom box while we got to work. We needed to move as many of my belongings as possible to the basement, since I could lock that door. Tarps would hopefully protect things we couldn't move and what used to be the kitchen entrance from the elements for a few days. At least we might be able to keep out the local wildlife, although I hoped Hermione would come back.

"Just out of curiosity," Jay said as Ace of Base filled the room, "When was the last time you listened to your boom box?"

I thought for a minute. "A little over a year ago, maybe? Tara and I went camping around the time I met you."

"Not that I don't love 'The Sign,' but do you have anything more recent than, say, 1993?"

"Nope," I shot back. "When was the last time you bought a CD?"

"Touché. I don't even own any CDs anymore. Donated 'em all years ago."

I gestured toward my room, swallowing a lump in my throat. "I had some yesterday."

A heartbeat later, Jay wrapped his arms around me. "Hey, it'll be okay. I'm here with you. We'll both take a couple of days off work to clean this mess up. They'll manage without us. The whole office is closed. You can stay with me until this place is rebuilt. A few weeks, several months, it doesn't matter. Okay?"

I nodded, trying to quell the growing panic inside me. Everything I lost was stuff. It wasn't me. Stuff could be replaced. Breathe in, breathe out. "Thanks."

We moved to the living room and sat on the couch. From this angle, with the wall blocking my view of the blue tarp, I could almost pretend things were normal if I didn't let my eyes wander toward the pile of debris Jay'd swept into one corner. Perhaps any light in the room would've helped the illusion. Or maybe it would've made everything worse.

No puedes tapar el sol con un dedo, as Mamá used to say. *You can't cover the sun with one finger.*

Unfortunately, now I possessed a perfect view of the mantel. The empty mantel where Tara and I once displayed our favorite pictures.

I got up and sifted through the stuff on the floor.

"Ahn? What are you doing?"

Ignoring him, I kept digging until I found what I wanted—the only gold-framed picture in the room. Mamá always hated silver, thought it looked cheap. Inside the frame, she and I stood before the house, with our identical long dark hair and smiles. Her white sundress made her seem half her age; I wore a light blue cap and gown. Glass showered onto the floor when I lifted the frame. Dirt and gook streaked our clothes and faces. We gave the impression less of mother and daughter at college graduation, more like survivors of a disaster movie.

"This is the last picture of us together." My voice cracked. "Now it's gone, too."

A tear dropped off my nose, making a clean spot on the snapshot.

"It's going to be okay. Your dad probably took a hundred pictures that day, right?"

I nodded.

"We'll call him when we leave here, tell him you're okay, ask him to send you another one. Good?"

It wasn't good. We hadn't owned a digital camera back then, and Papá probably didn't keep the negatives. Still, I nodded, knowing if I didn't put on a brave face, I'd never get through the rest of the house. "Okay. Thanks."

When the waning light made further work impossible, we walked into town to see if any place serving food was open. One of the sagging power lines had given way under the weight of a tree during the afternoon, blocking access via the route I followed earlier. Jay and I picked our way through fallen trees, soggy leaves, broken glass, and puddles until we reached the end of the street. The bistro at the corner now offered outdoor seating in the back, but I suspected the owners would've preferred to build a patio over losing the rear walls. Employees milled around, moving chairs and boarding up the broken windows. I waved, offered condolences, and kept moving.

We weren't picky: restaurants, fast food, a gas station. Since my stove was in the kitchen, and the kitchen was no longer attached to the house, all foods requiring any preparation whatsoever were out of the question. Luckily, the nearby pizza shop used a wood-burning oven and a back-up generator. The line stretched for a couple of blocks around the corner, out of sight.

Jay pointed at a bench across the street, partially hidden from view by a green Acura stopped in traffic. "You've been on your feet all day. Do you want to rest?"

I hesitated. As much as I hated to show weakness, my left leg throbbed where the end connected with my prosthetic. The only thing I wanted more than my bed and my house back was to sit and remove the device. Jay touched my chin, forcing my gaze back to him. "Hey. You've had a rough day. There's no shame in sitting down."

Puddles littered the path between me and the

debris-covered bench. Still, sitting seemed more appealing than standing in line. My heart warmed at his thoughtfulness. "You're right, thanks. I'll take—whatever they have, honestly."

About an hour later, Jay returned with a large pepperoni pizza. Although the wind carried a bite, we ate on the bench, as if this were an ordinary day and we were just another couple enjoying a pizza for dinner in the middle of a disaster zone. We shared a tender, cheesy kiss under the stars.

Cars packed the center of town. As we tried to decide whether we wanted to fight traffic to get back to Jay's, I realized the green Acura I'd walked past to get to the bench still idled at the end of the street, waiting to turn onto the main road. If this tiny town was gridlocked, trying to get to Jay's house in midtown would take hours at best. Considering the amount of work left to us the following morning, we decided to unpack the rest of the camping gear and spread it out in the basement.

We picked our way up the hill, detouring around more tree branches. Two college-aged guys in a raft offered to take us up one of the side streets, but the road to my house wasn't underwater, so we declined and gave them each a slice of leftover pizza.

Emergency crews hadn't made it anywhere near my neighborhood yet. Between the rubble, the flooded areas, and the lack of street lights, walking home took nearly twice as long as the trip into town.

On the way back, I insisted we knock on a couple of doors to see how the neighbors were faring. The only one who answered seemed more concerned with feeding me than the tree lying across her living room. I asked her to keep an eye out for Hermione and convinced her that we had enough food for the night.

Although part of me wanted to take the scooter back to Jay's, I hoped the cat would return if I stayed. On top of everything else, I couldn't stomach telling Tara I lost her beloved pet. I couldn't even call her with the news about the hurricane until Hermione was safe. Jay put bowls of food and water on what used to be the back porch while I scoured the house for usable pillows and blankets.

The next day passed in much the same way, except we finished securing the house before dark. Hermione remained out of sight. News reports told me that traffic into the city had lightened up, so I went to a neighbor whose house was mostly okay and offered him some free samples of our new product line in exchange for borrowing his truck. He agreed and even helped me load up a few boxes.

"You ready?" Jay asked after he loaded the last of the stuff.

I shook my head. "I can't leave without Hermione."

"I'm sure she's fine. You know how cats love to hide."

"I do," I said, "and she's probably in the basement. But I'm not going anywhere until I'm sure."

Jay surveyed the resolute line of my mouth, the determination in my eyes. He'd seen it before at many a board meeting, and he knew what it meant. After a long moment, he sighed. "I'll pack up the food and kitty litter, then find the carrier. Check the basement again, and if you don't see her by the time I'm done, we'll go for a walk."

"Thank you. I really appreciate it."

He nodded and disappeared into the house. After a moment, I followed. Hermione did love to hide in the basement when Tara or I opened the door to do laundry. With luck, I'd find her squished behind the water heater.

Ten minutes later, I'd scoured the entire basement and determined that if the cat hid there, I would never figure out where. With a sigh, I grabbed a bag of cat treats from a drawer in what used to be the pantry and went outside. Jay and I walked up and down the block, shaking the treats and calling her name. Finally, a meow answered us.

"Hermoine?"

The fat cat bounded out of the bushes, absolutely soaked, and catapulted into my arms. I'd never been so happy to see another living creature. I snuggled against her, cooing until Jay pointed out that it was dark and we'd need close to an hour to get home.

We didn't have a towel, so I dried Hermione off as best I could with my sweater before bundling her into the carrier for the trip into the city.

By the time we reached Jay's apartment, I barely had the presence of mind to plug my phone into the wall before I collapsed into his bed, exhausted. Nearly three days of emails, texts, and unanswered calls awaited, and I didn't possess the strength to even turn the device on. It could wait until I got to work the next morning. Even Tara didn't need an immediate call. She shouldn't have heard about the hurricane, tucked away at her mom's, and I'd better be able to convince her everything was okay in the morning once I believed it myself.

A good night's sleep did wonders for my health and mental well-being. Jay and I arrived at the office in high spirits. I was halfway through the door of the ladies' room before I remembered my phone had been off for almost three days. Funny how, after years of treating the phone as an extension of my hand, a few days without power or service made me almost forget it existed.

When I turned the phone on and finally got my three days of messages, I wished I'd never remembered it. A flurry of notifications flashed across the screen, blurring together. My voicemail beeped, and then a text popped up on top of everything.

Slut.

Chapter 2

Slut.

I gazed at the text unblinking, trying to figure out how I'd offended the sender. Maybe a wrong number? With a tap of my thumb, I sent it to the trash. The next message popped up.

Ur hot. I'd fuck u, even if ur illegal.

My heart rose into my throat as I stared at the words. Tears welled in my eyes. My parents both naturalized decades ago, and I was a natural-born American citizen. But whoever this person was, they wouldn't care. Nothing I could say would matter more than the color of my skin. I stabbed at the block button and moved to the next message.

Whore.

I gasped. What was going on? How could this be happening to me?

Gonna make u cum so hard, *sucia*.

When I could breathe again, I blocked that one, too. And the next. The red indicator reported more than three hundred messages. That must be a mistake. Three. Hundred. Twenty-seven. Messages? All since I'd last checked my phone. But it wasn't a mistake. There they were, in black and white on my screen. More kept popping up while I read. Strange number after strange number appeared on the list. I scrolled, not reading, scanning for any message from anyone I knew. Any hint as to what happened. Four more messages came in while I swiped upward. Word fragments popped out at me, all bad. Racial slurs, anti-female statements, both. The words blurred together.

My mind raced as I tried to figure out what happened. Our company released a new line of shoes, but this outrage didn't seem consistent with the public not liking a product for three-year-olds.

Oh, God. What if the rubber melted or something and fused some poor kid's shoes together? Our testing hadn't indicated any risk, but mistakes happened. Nothing else I could think of explained the vitriol exploding across my phone, unless a few hundred people confused my number with someone else's.

Before opening my email, I splashed cold

water on my face and took a deep breath. Maybe one of my zillion messages at least gave me a clue as to the problem. It might be worth reading the insults if I could find out some information.

Wrong. Scrolling through my email was even worse than reading the text. There were thousands of messages, most with subject lines following the same themes: YOU'RE A SLUT. YOU SHOULD DIE. I'D FUCK YOU. GO BACK TO MEXICO.

My heart pounded against my ribcage. This couldn't possibly be about issues with our new product or the hurricane. My brain fought to make sense of the pieces, but finally, I dropped the phone. It skittered across the turquoise tile, coming to rest against the drain. A pit opened in my stomach. I slumped against the sink. Afraid I might lose consciousness, I shoved my face under the tap and hit the faucet a second time. The rush of water jerked me out of my stupor.

But still, I had no idea what happened or why. Was this how people treated hurricane victims? Had the fabric in one of our shirts turned out to be flammable? How did all these people get my email address and phone number?

I shoved my phone into my pocket, straightened my shoulders, and headed back to my office to see if I could make any sense out of things.

As I passed Jay's office, his voice stopped me. "Anna."

His tone told me we had a serious problem. I gulped and closed my eyes, steeling myself for the news. If the stock price dropped, my job could be in jeopardy, girlfriend of the boss's son or not. With another deep breath, I entered the office.

Despite my anxiety, I instinctively relaxed at the sight of my boyfriend. Whatever happened, we'd get through it, and the company would be stronger than ever. Jay probably already knew how to spin whatever disaster occurred to the company's advantage. At the thought, more tension drained from my shoulders, and I smiled at him.

My smile died when he glanced up from his computer monitor with storm clouds on his face. "Close the door."

Uh-oh. I shut the door and settled into the plush cream and gold striped chair across from his desk.

"What's wrong? Is there a problem with one of our products? Did Jasper from PR drunk tweet again?"

"No. This is... It's bad. And... oh, hell. You don't know, do you?"

"Know what?"

"Did you get any strange messages this morning? Emails from people you don't know? Phone calls or texts?"

In response, I held up my phone. The device still lit up every couple of seconds, despite my muting it. "Constant calls, emails, texts. Each weirder than the last. I was headed back to my office to try to figure out what happened when you called me in here."

"Do not Google your name, sweetheart. Whatever you do, don't do that."

This was getting ridiculous. What the hell was going on? My jaw clenched. "Why? What caused this? Is someone harassing people listed as displaced hurricane victims? That's fucking low."

"No. Someone's harassing you." Jay tapped his fingers together, one at a time.

I took deep breaths while I waited to quell the onrush of panic, like my old therapist taught me. If only I hadn't forgotten to go to yoga for the past... thirty-four years, it would've been much easier to relax. I couldn't believe any of this was happening. What could I possibly have done to make people respond so cruelly? Parts of the country had shown themselves to be increasingly racist over the past few years, but usually, some event brought people into their crosshairs.

Finally, my sadness turned to frustration. I'd dealt with trolls before, and I could do it again. "C'mon, Jay. I'm trying very hard not to freak out, but the longer we sit here, the harder it gets. What's going on?"

When he finally dragged his attention from his fingertips and met my eyes, tears streamed down his face. A shudder ran down my back. My boyfriend rarely got upset, and he was unflappable when in lawyer mode.

"Okay, I'm sorry. I'll tell you." The words rushed out of him like air deflating from a balloon. "I don't know what happened, but there are these naked pictures of you all over the internet. Someone posted them with your real name and address and our company's name. They say you'll have sex with anyone for money. I've been getting calls and emails all morning—"

The world around me collapsed into Jay's moving lips. I couldn't see anything else. His words went right through me, stabbing me in the gut. It had to be a mistake. This couldn't be happening. A strangled sound reached my ears, a high-pitched keening.

Jay's lips stopped moving, and I realized vaguely that the horrible noise must've come from me.

A moment later, he crouched in front of me, pulling me into his arms. I let out a sob, crying for everything that happened in the last two days.

When I finally pulled back, Jay looked as sad as I felt. "I'm so sorry, Anna. Are these pictures real?"

"Does it matter?"

He hesitated for just a second too long. "Of course not. This whole thing threw me for a loop.

The shareholders are already calling to complain, and Father's called a meeting of the board of directors. You know there's a morality clause in your contract, right?"

Unable to speak, I nodded. The exact language of the full clause escaped me, but the words "appearance of impropriety" sat clearly at the forefront of my memory. We'd let another board member go for racking up excessive gambling debts a couple of months ago. Probably, the board would think offering to trade sex for money suggested improper conduct more than throwing away money on Yankee games. A horrible thought, and yet, my mind was all over the place. I couldn't control the things flooding through my brain.

I gasped for breath, choking on nothing. Nude pictures? Oh, God. Who would do that? Reputation in this business was everything. Especially now that we'd recently launched a huge new product. No one wanted their kids wearing light-up shoes made by someone who posted naked pictures on the internet or prostituted herself. Worse, of everyone at the company, my face was the most recognizable. Thanks to those *Forbes* articles and the rarity of Latina females in US executive positions, people all over the world knew me.

"Obviously, we all know you're not a hooker, but the pictures present a real problem. They're probably going to call for your resignation. I convinced Father to let you take a leave of absence until things cool down. Paid of course, but at least for a month. We canceled your flight tomorrow—Tom will go instead. I'm going, too, so the investors don't think they got shunted to some kid they don't know."

No one knew my second-in-command. He worked behind the scenes to make everything run seamlessly. He was both priceless and underpaid. If he became the face of the new product, we'd lose him to a larger company in a matter of weeks. And then I'd be out my assistant when I came back to work, on top of everything else. What a nightmare.

Words escaped me. I stared straight ahead, as if my eyes could bore through the back of the computer to whatever Jay saw. He stood, coming around the desk to wrap me in a hug. My head leaned against his chest, inhaling his usually comforting odors of milk and honey body wash and his laughably expensive deodorant. Scents I would henceforth associate with a still-vibrating phone in my lap, a forced leave of absence from work, and the whole world seeing me naked. I'd done dozens of magazine articles and interviews, but I'd never been more exposed.

Hysterical laughter bubbled forth.

"Do yourself a favor. Don't pull up the pictures. Absolutely do not read the comments. Go home, okay?"

For a brief second, I'd forgotten about the hurricane. What on earth was I supposed to do? "I don't have a home right now."

"A minor blessing. At least no one can harass you there," he said. "I sent a moving crew over to get the rest of your stuff. This should all blow over by the time you get back home. They're saying on the news that it could be months, or longer, before contractors finish repairing all the hurricane damage."

When I opened and closed my mouth but no sound came out, Jay stroked my hair. He took a deep breath and kissed my forehead. I was afraid to ask what else was on his mind, but it was clear he had something else to say. How could this morning possibly get worse?

Stupid question.

"There's more. Father is insisting we take a break from our public relationship. I know I said you could stay with me until your house got fixed, but you can't." He shifted in his seat, the chair creaking loudly. "I'm so sorry, honey. I wish there were a way to make things better."

"You're throwing me out?" Unbelievable. My lower lip trembled, and I willed myself not to cry. Again. This was ridiculous. I never cried. I was a hard-as-nails junior executive, the face of

Forbes magazine. And I was about to lose everything.

"No, of course not. I'm giving you a quiet place to regroup, where no one will look for you. You can stay at any hotel you want. I'll expense it."

A hotel. All alone. And the hits just kept on coming.

"Don't worry about it. My homeowner's insurance will cover the room. I wouldn't want to inconvenience *your father* anymore with my personal crisis." If Jay noticed the sarcasm in my voice, he wisely ignored it.

"Do you have any idea who did this? Who would hate you this much?"

The thought had yet to enter my mind in all the horror and frustration. Still, a picture formed immediately in my mind, as crystal clear as if he stood before me.

"Eric."

He pressed his lips together. "I was afraid you'd say that."

"I guess he's finally back on the grid." Our eyes met, and I forced air into my lungs. "Fuck."

JAY LIVED two miles from the office. I wasn't supposed to walk that far, but the thought of getting onto the subway, being packed in with strangers, wondering if any of them saw the photos, made me hyperventilate. Instead, I covered my face with large sunglasses, wrapped a scarf over my head, and trudged toward the apartment to gather my stuff. Lead filled my legs. Every movement required too much effort.

On the way, I scrolled through the early texts, replying to the only one that mattered. HI, PAPÁ. I'M FINE. THE HOUSE IS GONE, BUT TARA'S IN OK W/ HER MOM, AND I'VE GOT INSURANCE. WE'RE FINE. PHONE LINES BUSY, TEXT BETTER.

No need to bother him with the other stuff. A few clicks set Papá to VIP status so the phone would notify me if he responded while ignoring everyone else. Before I finished, I had his reply.

Papá: GLAD YOU'RE MANAGING. WHAT ON EARTH IS ADELE DOING IN THE MIDWEST?

Me: SHE MET SOME CONSPIRACY THEORIST HANDING OUT FLIERS IN TIMES SQUARE AND FOLLOWED HIM. THEY'RE LIVING OFF THE GRID, WAITING FOR THE APOCALYPSE WITHOUT THE DISTRACTION OF MODERN CONVENIENCES LIKE PHONES.

My phone buzzed again. NO PHONES? NO INTERNET. NOTHING BUT CONSPIRACY THEORISTS? POOR TARA.

His words made me chuckle, but I'd reached Jay's apartment, so the phone went into my pocket. A heavy sigh escaped me when I unlocked the door and stepped into the entry.

I hadn't even managed to unpack yet. Battered cardboard boxes stood stacked in the living room, silently mocking me. I ignored them while I gathered the few items I used the previous night. Items that all seemed so important less than twenty-four hours ago. Now, I'd leave all my stuff there without a second thought if it meant going back in time and undoing this nightmare. I still couldn't believe what happened.

A label on one of the boxes reminded me to call my neighbors about their house. The call was relatively brief and painless: I tried not to sound robotic, and the answering machine at their winter home understood that these things happen. I left them the name of the hotel where I'd be staying in case they needed anything.

Just as I hung up, the phone rang again. The number showed as unavailable, but I figured one of them was calling me back.

"Hello?"

"Hello, my name is Detective Gretchen Stern with the NYPD. I—"

"Oh, thank goodness you called." My entire body relaxed. Jay must've filed a police report for me. "Yes, I'd love to give a statement. How soon can you be here?"

"Ma'am, are you Anna—?"

"Yes, that's me. I'm leaving soon, but I'll wait for you." I rattled off the address, thanked her, and hung up the phone.

Ten minutes later, I'd finished packing, requested a car, set my suitcase and purse in the entry, and started pacing the front hall. Finally, someone knocked.

When I opened the door, a tall, sturdy woman in her forties spoke first. I would hate to face her in a dark alley. "Good afternoon. I'm Detective Stern. We spoke on the phone."

She didn't introduce her partner, a well-muscled, dark-haired man in his mid-to-late thirties, probably a couple of years older than me. Something about the firmness of Detective Stern's mouth, the set of her shoulders, told me that many a criminal suspect knew her as Bad Cop. Her younger partner's dancing eyes and a hint of dimples suggested he preferred the role of Good Cop.

In the back of my mind, Tara's voice suggested that she'd happily let him handcuff her for being naughty. I shook my head. Even when she wasn't around, my best friend could make me smile.

I led the officers into the living room and motioned for them to sit on the couch. They declined coffee, so I perched on the armchair beside them.

"I'm so glad you're here. I was about to call when my phone rang. Someone stole—"

"Ma'am, we're not here to take a report for you. We're investigating allegations of trespassing, public obscenity, and vandalism." My heart sank as Detective Stern consulted her phone. "It says here that you unlawfully entered private property and posted nude pictures of yourself on several prominent billboards between the Upper West Side and the New Jersey state line."

The whole world faded away. My ears roared; the world past my nose dropped out of my vision. What on earth was happening to me? My breath came in short gasps.

A clap brought me back to reality. My vision cleared on a square-cut diamond ring and mauve fingernails accenting pale, wrinkled hands. "Ma'am? Some of the billboards are around this very building. You must be aware of them."

I shook my head, as if my unwillingness to accept her words would make this entire nightmare go away. Then I actually pinched myself. Nothing happened. Of course it didn't. That never worked in living nightmares.

Detective Stern rattled off a couple of addresses. "Have you been in either of these locations recently?"

I answered robotically, no longer recognizing the voice coming out of my mouth. "The first one is my house. It's gone. I left a couple of days after the hurricane. It'll be a long time before it's ready for me to go back."

Beside Detective Stern, the other officer clucked a sympathetic sound. This, they were sorry for? They didn't care that I was being set up, that half the city—hell, half the world—saw me naked? I shot him a dirty look.

"And the other?" Detective Stern asked.

"The second address is near my office. I was there this morning. I don't really notice the billboards. There's a big one on the way to the subway, but I walked here."

Out of the side of her mouth, she said to Good Cop, "So she admits being there."

"Being where? Yes, I go to my own home and my own office. Don't you want to talk about the naked pictures?"

"So you admit that you've been distributing naked pictures?"

"What? Are you serious?"

"Excuse me, ma'am." Finally, Good Cop spoke. He cast a sidelong glance at his partner as if asking for permission. When she didn't move, he continued, "There seems to be some confusion about what we're doing here. Last night, someone visited those three intersections and covered existing billboards with full-sized nude pictures. The woman in the pictures looks identical to you. The billboards say, 'Call Anna,' and they list the phone number Detective Stern dialed earlier, which you answered."

The blood drained from my face, leaving me light-headed. "I didn't do that. Oh, God. Please tell me that's not true."

"It's true. Why did you think we were here?" His eyes softened, as if for the first time he realized I wasn't a hooker and now I deserved sympathy.

"The pictures online. The threatening and harassing phone calls, emails, and texts I've been getting all morning. My boyfriend said…, well, I thought he called you for me." It occurred to me that I probably should have called myself, but I'd had quite a lot on my mind what with becoming homeless for the second time in twenty-four hours and being sent home from work. I would've thought of it eventually.

Detective Stern toyed with her phone for a moment, searching for something instead of meeting my eyes. "The reports we've received about you this morning all involve indignant advertisers and parents who take their children to schools by walking under those ads."

"Oh, no." Hermione jumped into my lap, and I stroked her back without thinking. The gesture calmed me somewhat.

The detective shoved something under my

nose. I blinked several times before the image cleared. There it was: the picture Jay told me not to seek out. My face, my naked body. Every inch of my mahogany flesh. Long, dark hair not really covering my nipples. Come-hither brown eyes, head tilted, red lips pouting. Arms twisted to hide the faint lines on the inside of each wrist, barely visible scars after all these years, but which stood out like a brand in my mind's eye.

"You think I posted those pictures? That I invited all of New York City to ogle my naked body? I've been featured in *Forbes* twice. My salary is well into the six figures, and I'm projected to step into my boss's job within the next five years. Why on earth would I ruin everything?"

"All we know, ma'am, is that you answered when we called the number." Detective Stern said. "And you're clearly the woman in the pictures, so we have to investigate the possibility that you're the one who posted the ads. It's not our job to figure out why you did it."

My knuckles turned white. Warm, wet liquid trickled onto my fingertips where my nails met my palms. Trembling, I pulled myself to my feet and pointed one finger at the front door. "Get the fuck out of my apartment."

"You don't live here, ma'am. You stated that you live in New Jersey."

My mouth opened and closed, but at that

point, I couldn't even speak. I kept waiting for Ashton Kutcher or the guy from *Totally Hidden Video* to show up. This couldn't be real.

"How did you lose your foot?" she asked.

Horseback riding accident, but no way she needed to know. "I slutted it off," I snapped. "Yup, that's a verb. I slutted around until my foot fell off. Now leave."

Good Cop cleared his throat. I still didn't know his name.

"We should go," he said quietly. Without another word, the detective turned and headed for the door. After a long, sweeping glance up and down my body that made me choke on my rage, Detective Stern followed.

"We'll be in touch," she called over her shoulder. "I wouldn't leave town if I were you."

In response, I slammed the door so hard, it bounced back, nearly hitting me in the face. Awesome. A black eye was all I needed. I leaned against the door, still shaking.

Why was this happening? How could anyone do this to me? How could police ignore all the facts and threaten to charge me, the victim, with a crime? Tears of humiliation slid down my face.

Down the hall, the elevator dinged. A second later, someone tapped on the other side of the door.

"No. No more." I muttered.

The knocking sounded again, slightly louder, so I deigned to twist around and check the peephole. Good Cop.

No, no, no, no, no. Were they back to arrest me?

"Go away," I choked through the door.

"Ms. Guerra? I want to apologize for my partner. Please open the door."

I opened the door approximately two millimeters. "Is she gone? Or waiting in the hall to attack me again?"

"No, she took the elevator. I always take the stairs down."

"We're on the seventeenth floor."

His lips twitched. "If she were your partner, wouldn't you want an excuse to spend a few minutes away from her?"

Under other circumstances, I would've laughed. Now, I relaxed my death grip on the door, opening the gap to about three inches. My expression didn't change; I gazed at him coolly.

"She can be overly judgmental. What can I say? She still thinks Obama was born in Africa." I smiled, letting the door open all the way. "I'm sorry. I can only imagine how upsetting this all must be for you. Any idiot can see you didn't post those billboards. I wanted to tell you not to worry. We're not going to charge you with any crimes." He pulled a small rectangle from the front pocket of his shirt. "If you think of any information that might help us find the person who did this, any known enemies, anything at all, please call me."

Was this all some trick to get me to incriminate myself? I wanted to believe him, but after my morning, it was impossible.

He leaned closer, warm brown eyes searching my face. "Do I know you from somewhere?"

"Astute deduction, Detective. Perhaps you know me because my face is plastered on every corner of the internet, or you've spent the morning looking at billboards purporting to prostitute me?"

A flush colored his golden skin. He ducked his head before grinning up at me. "That's not what I meant. I feel like I've met you somewhere else. Did you grow up around here? I was born in Brooklyn, but my family moved to Connecticut when my mom remarried."

"New Jersey. I've never set foot in Connecticut. But I was listed in the March and July issues of *Forbes* this year—one of the 'Up-and-Coming Executives Under Thirty-Five-Years Old' and one-half of 'Manhattan's Top Twenty Power Couples.'" I glanced around the apartment behind me. "We've got copies here somewhere if you want to see them."

"No, that's okay. I can pull them up online."

"I highly recommend you not do a Google search for my name, Detective."

"I've seen you somewhere else. I'm sure I'll figure it out. I'm pretty good at what I do." He turned to leave, then looked back over his shoulder. "I meant what I said, Ms. Guerra. If you need anything, anything at all, please call me."

"All I need right now is some time alone." He shook his head, and I relented. "But I'll think about it. Thanks, Detective."

"You're welcome. Call me if Detective Stern starts to bug you. I can help you."

"She's already started to bug me, but I'll keep that in mind." I shut the door and let the card flutter to the ground without looking at it. It was clear the police wouldn't be able to help me.

Chapter 3

On the way to the hotel, I paid the cab driver a hundred bucks to stop at a wireless store and wait for me. My phone was still buzzing constantly when I went in, but eventually I left with a scrubbed phone, a new number, and renewed hope. I'd suffered worse than a couple of naked pictures, and I'd come out okay.

Under ordinary circumstances, I'd have appreciated the suite Jay booked for me, with plush carpets, a mattress that sank beneath my fingertips, the walk-in shower with a stool and detachable showerhead, whirlpool tub, and floor-to-ceiling windows pointed at Times Square. Today, none of that mattered. I texted him a quick thank you, then told him to use the new number. He texted back that my stuff would be delivered later. I had no idea if he'd arrive with the boxes or if I might see him before he left for China in the morning on what should've been my flight. It didn't matter. My heart ached so much already, I lacked the ability to worry about anything else. The boyfriend who fired me and rendered me homeless for the second time in two days didn't seem terribly important.

The six-hundred thread count Egyptian cotton sheets could've been tweed for all I cared. I would've slept on a bed of nails. All I wanted was to crawl into bed and never get up. I pulled the curtains shut and sat on the edge of the bed to remove the prosthetic that finally started to irritate my left leg. Then, I fell sideways onto the mattress, buried my face in a pillow, and let the tears flow until merciful sleep claimed me.

When I woke up, I spent several minutes contemplating the ceiling. The weight of the world pressed down on me. Standing and getting out of bed seemed as impossible as sprouting wings and flying out the window. Who did this? It could be a random attack, but somehow, I doubted it. The inclusion of my name and address, the billboards near my home and office, the emails and texts specific to Jay all felt personal.

Would hackers go to the extra trouble to make sure I knew what they did? Maybe I took everything more personally because it happened to me, but I didn't think so.

When Jay asked earlier, my mind went immediately to Eric. As much as I resisted wrapping my mind around my ex-boyfriend doing something so malicious, I'd be hard-pressed to come up with anyone else who possessed the resources and the residual anger. To think, near the end, I was so sure he didn't care anymore.

El mayor aborrecimiento, en el amor tiene su cimiento, as Mamá used to say. The greatest hate springs from the greatest love.

As if Eric loved anything other than himself, his reputation, and his money.

Being a public figure often included damage control. I kept a tight rein on what information about me leaked, and I lived a generally clean life, but sometimes things went wrong. Li'l Tots retained a public relations company to deal with this sort of nightmare. We would fix this. Deep breaths. All I had to do was pull out my laptop, set it on the desk, and open it. The shock had frayed my nerves, but I forced myself to pull it together. Several more slow inhalations, then I made myself sit up. Another deep sigh and I managed to stand and drag myself to the computer.

Before I did anything else, I set up a new email account. The old one was useless—it would be impossible to sift through all the spam and death threats to find any messages from friends or family. Then again, most of my friends were work acquaintances who'd drop me like a hot potato. Working long hours to get to the top wasn't conducive to finding besties. Thank goodness for Tara. Which reminded me that I needed a new account so I could email her.

To: Jay
From: Anna
Date: Nov. 12, 2018, 11:46 a.m.
Hey Jay,
I set up a new email address. My work email's as flooded with crap messages as Gmail. You may want to suspend it if you haven't already. Send me the login info for the new account? I did some research, and we need to start sending takedown notices to these porn sites ASAP. Can you give me the number for Mary at our PR firm? All my contacts are somewhere in the East River by now.

Love,
Me

While I waited, I sent a quick message to Tara to tell her where I booked a room and to use my new email and phone number from now on. She didn't need the details.

Everyone else in my life could wait. I didn't know what to say to all of my co-workers, my other friends...*dios mio*. Papá.

What if my dad saw the pictures? What if

someone told him that people thought I prostituted myself? I wanted to think he wouldn't believe the lies, but I'd also thought he'd have given me a chance to say good-bye to my mother before she died, and that didn't happen. He didn't spend a lot of time online, but this thing turned out to be bigger than I thought. Someone might find his name and address. He might hear about it from someone else.

Just as I teetered on the verge of hyperventilation and despair, a new message appeared in my inbox.

To: Anna

From: Jay

Date: Nov. 12, 2018, 12:03 p.m.

Hey Sweetie,

Mary isn't allowed to help you. Father is worried about what our shareholders would say. I'm working on him, but Li'l Tots can't officially defend you. We need to protect the company first. Unofficially, Mary gave me a copy of the takedown notice they typically send on behalf of clients. I hope it helps.

I'm headed to a lunch meeting with Tom to prep him for the trip, but I'll call you as soon as I can. I'm so sorry.

All the best,

Jay

What? My own boyfriend wouldn't even help

me. My company was shutting me out. What the hell? And what was up with the super-formal sign-off? He'd started signing emails "love" about two months after we'd started dating. Even emails on the work account only used formal language if they copied a third party.

Warning bells jingled at the back of my mind. He was backing away when I most needed him. His first thought had been for the company, not for me. My boyfriend didn't care about me anymore, couldn't have cared much at all if he'd distance himself this quickly.

I laid my head on the desk's cool wooden surface for a minute and let my mind go free. A tear trickled onto the surface, then another, creating a pool under my face. Why did terrible things always happen to me? My left foot got amputated, I had to give up horses, my mom died, and now all this.

Before I even managed to come up with anything to say, any idea what to do next, the computer dinged to alert me of another message. Since only two people had this email address, I forced myself to sit up and read the email.

To: Anna

From: Jay

Date: Nov. 12, 2018, 12:04 p.m.

I hate to put more on your plate right now, but you've been hacked. I checked my personal email once I got in the car, and I just got a crazy message from your old account. My Facebook notifications are blowing up. Someone's posting as you. You need to shut it down ASAP. Good luck. Talk soon.

Oh, no.

My fingers shook as I pulled up my social media profiles.

Password incorrect. Please try again.

No. No. No. I typed again.

Password incorrect. Please click to email a new password.

I clicked the link before I wondered if I wanted to wade back into the cesspool of my email address. I didn't, but there was no other option: my social media passwords didn't work. A code texted to my cancelled old number seemed less than helpful. It might be better to let the account die and make a new one.

At least my Facebook profile was private, right? Whatever people said about me, only a few people would read it? I had less than a hundred Facebook friends. None of them would think I intentionally plastered my own naked body all over the internet. But anyone could see profile and cover photos.

My phone buzzed with a text. Jay again. Ahn? Call your father. Call him now.

Uh-oh. I was going to have to say something

to him. He must be so ashamed of me. More than anything, I hated knowing that Eric managed to hurt Papá.

Before picking up the phone, I navigated to my Facebook page. All I should've been able to see was the profile picture, which used to be an inspirational quote. Today, it was a zoomed-in picture of a flower—except on closer inspection.

No, no, no, no.

Whoever hacked my account changed my status to, "I am so dirty, I want you to fuck me so hard. I love it when men cum on my face. Please leave me a message and tell me what you're going to do to me. Love, Anna Guerra." My home address, phone number, and email address were all public. They'd opened up the wall to public posts. I scrolled through the comments for about thirteen seconds before a wave of nausea hit me. I minimized the window, chest heaving. Tears splattered onto the keyboard.

My phone buzzed again. Another text from Jay. *Do you ever use your LinkedIn?*

Fuck. Fuck, fuck, fuck. A junior executive for an international corporation that sells children's clothing can't post naked pictures on her LinkedIn profile. Especially if her company is launching a line of Bible-themed products in the next six months and the first set of Noah's deck shoes are already on the market. Not if she ever wants to work again outside the porn industry.

My fingers flew over the keyboard. I'd never established a LinkedIn account. That didn't stop whoever created my profile and resume. "I am skilled at sucking cock so hard your eyes roll back in your head. I can swallow buckets of cum. My objective is to find the biggest cock I've ever seen to fuck me until I can barely walk. My skills include double anal."

Darkness swam before my eyes as the reality of my situation hit me. Someone was out to get me. The police refused to help. I didn't know who was doing it or why, but I did know one thing. This was personal, and I was in hell.

THE LIST of people who might want to ruin my life was short. The list of people who had nude pictures of me was even shorter, although my email—or his—could've been hacked. After searching for answers on the ceiling for a long time, I logged into my old email account and typed a message.

To: Eric

From: Anna

Date: Nov. 13, 2018, 2:03 p.m.

What the fuck do you think you're doing? This is my life, asshole.

No, that wouldn't work. The cursor moved backward, eating my words. It blinked at me for a long time before I started typing again.

Look, you absolute piece of human garbage. Why don't you launch yourself into outer space?

Delete.

Dear Eric,

How could you do this to me?

Nope, nope, nope.

I stood in front of the window. Human ants buzzed around on the sidewalk below. What on earth would I possibly say? What could an email accomplish? Sure, it might lift my spirits a notch, but Eric wasn't going to apologize and undo the damage. Besides, I had no way of knowing if he used the same email address these days, I refused to give him my new email address, and my existing account received more messages every second. If he bothered to reply at all, the onrush would bury the message in a matter of minutes. Poking the tiger might also result in a fresh posting of the photographs or some new and more inventive form of torture.

On top of everything else, I'd look like the biggest jerk in the world if I sent a nasty email, and it turned out that someone hacked one of us to steal the pictures.

But what to do instead?

My old SIM card was long gone, but I could make a call through my computer. Once again, I found myself at a loss for words. How to talk to the type of person who would do this? What to say?

When my leg ached from standing in one place for so long, I flopped into a chair and leaned back, fingers tapping against the arms. My brain still refused to grasp what happened, and without that comprehension, I couldn't formulate a plan.

With a sigh, I reached over and grabbed the laptop sitting on the table, then pulled it onto my lap. I steeled myself, then typed "Anna Guerra" into the search bar. Nearly a full minute passed before my fingers directed the trackpad to the search button.

My image filled the screen, in all its glory. Brown eyes looked out over full, pouting lips. My skin gleamed against the navy sheets in the background. Eric's sheets. With the full-body view, the double Ds, and the left leg ending above the ankle, no one who'd met me could doubt the identity of the person in this picture. Even if my name and personal contact information hadn't been displayed beneath the image.

With a click, a second picture filled the screen. This time I knelt on the bed, peering back over my right shoulder, giving the entire world a view no one other than my gynecologist needed. Again there could be no doubt I'd posed for these.

Every parent who'd ever bought clothing from our company would see these pictures. Their kids were too young to use the internet, but still: I'd never work with children again. Never be allowed to hold focus groups. The job I loved would never be the same. My heart sank even further.

I groaned and shut the screen. Seeing was believing, but viewing the websites didn't tell me what to do next. Beside me, the phone buzzed with a text from Jay. ARE YOU OK? DID YOU CALL YOUR DAD YET? I'M SERIOUS. HE'S FREAKING OUT.

Shit. Just what I needed.

SORRY, I FORGOT. GIVE ME TEN MORE MINUTES.

Before I could begin to explain to my conservative father why his little girl was plastered all over the internet without clothes, I needed a drink. Or several. I chugged all the wine in the mini-bar, called for room service, and changed into the softest robe I'd ever touched before picking up the phone.

Before the first ring finished, Papá answered. "Anna. What is going on?"

Before picking up the phone I'd carefully planned what to say about family and overcoming differences during hard times. Things had been awkward ever since Mamá died. We didn't know how to talk to each other anymore. I wanted to remind him of how close we were when I was a kid, suggest we work harder to regain our old relationship. After all, he was all I had.

Instead of the speech, a wail escaped me. Five words from my father, and I wasn't a successful, thirty-four-year-old career woman. I was that recently-injured thirteen-year-old girl who lacked the will to go on living in a world of two-footed people. But when he spoke, the wall I'd built between us evaporated.

"I'm so sorry, Papá," I sniffled. "I don't know what happened."

"I don't blame you, sweetheart. People get new technology, it's exciting, they don't think. They lose all respect for one another. Someone gets mad, they think it gives them the right to ruin lives. No one ever asks for this."

A smile broke through the tears. "If you're not mad at me, what's wrong? Jay said you're freaking out."

"My phone is ringing off the hook. I call your phone, it goes straight to voicemail! You text me earlier and you forget to mention this? Your father worries, Muñeca. The church thinks my daughter is a prostitute."

Of course. He didn't care about me. He cared what the church thought. Typical.

"I changed my number. Now you have the

new one. Save it, but don't give it to anyone else. Ever. I'll send you my new email address later. Guard it with your life."

"Give me Jay's number. I can't believe you moved in with him already. Do my words mean nothing to you? He'll never buy the cow if you give away the milk for free. Look what happened with Eric."

My jaw clenched at the reminder of why we only spoke on Christmas and Mamá's birthday. "No, I'm staying at a hotel until things blow over. I'll email you the information."

He cleared his throat. "There's no easy way to ask this, but…" Oh, dear. Here we go. Now he can pretend he cares what happens to me. "…you're not going to do anything drastic, are you?"

Like it would matter to him if I did. I snorted. "I'm not thirteen anymore, Papá. I've been off the meds for more than fifteen years, and I'm fine."

"I know, and I trust you. Just…if you need anything, call me, okay?"

"Believe me, I just want things to get back to normal. Once this dies down, I can find a new job, rebuild the house, and move on with my life."

"You shouldn't be surrounded by strangers. Come home, be with your family."

Since Mamá died, my former home felt empty, lifeless. I preferred to have Papá visit me rather than going to North Carolina. Still, what did they say about family? When you have to return home, they have to take you in? Maybe Papá had a point.

Thanks to Eric, family was one of the few things I had left.

<hr>

LESS THAN A DAY after I checked into the hotel, the front desk called to say a reporter from the *New York Post* stood in the lobby, requesting an interview. I told them to hold all calls to my room, refuse all visitors and hung up. There wasn't a soul I wanted to see or talk to.

By the end of the day, I received a second call that the lobby was packed and, should I wish to leave, I might prefer to contact the front desk for an escort out the maintenance entrance. If only I'd realized sooner how well-known I was, maybe it would've been time to leverage my "celebrity" status into a raise by interviewing at some other companies.

Days passed in a haze. At first, I researched revenge porn, returning to the same conclusion over and over: there weren't many options. Copies of the takedown notice Jay had forwarded me went to dozens of sites, but the internet is forever. Even if they were deleted from these particular sites, there was no way to ensure they wouldn't come back. Nothing to stop people who'd down-loaded the pictures from sharing them elsewhere other than a sense of decency I couldn't count on.

Jay didn't contact me. I didn't reach out to him, either. I couldn't be with someone who abandoned me in my time of need. A relationship without trust and respect stood without foundation. Yes, the company needed someone to go to China; it didn't have to be Jay. Even though I understood his need to protect the business, his choice to leave me, on top of everything else, was too much. Part of me hoped he didn't call, didn't ask to see me. If he did, I'd break up with him, and it was easier to let our relationship slip away. Like everything else good in my life.

After about a week, the walls of the beautiful, impersonal hotel suite started to close in around me. I lost the will to binge-watch *Telemundo* soap operas, which never seemed possible. Self-imposed solitude wasn't improving my situation or my outlook on life. But I still didn't want to leave the suite, especially when some of the smaller tabloids still lurked outside the building after being banned from the lobby. Poor schmucks. Who did these reporters piss off to get stuck on "sit in the hotel lobby hoping for a glimpse of a disgraced junior executive" duty? Talk about a slow news day.

Finally, I pulled out my makeup, determined to transform my face. Better or worse, it didn't matter, as long as even my best friend would hesitate before recognizing me. Highlighter raised my cheekbones, eyeliner accentuated my eyes, making them seem larger, further apart. I silently thanked my mother for insisting I learn all this in high school, although I usually preferred a more natural look.

Once I changed my appearance as much as possible, I used the hotel scissors to cut a fringe across my forehead, removed my contacts, and put on glasses never, ever worn in public. There. Even Tara would do a double-take.

Instead of attaching my prosthetic foot, I pulled out the canes I rarely used. People typically moved out of the way, avoided my eyes when they saw the metal devices.

The hotel bar was perfect for blending in, with high-backed booths and shadowy corners. I tucked myself into a seat facing the rear of the room and ordered a whiskey sour. "Keep 'em coming, and I'll double the tab for you."

A few businessmen sat at the bar. A well-dressed couple flirted at one of the tables near the front. Three women with spray tans and Southern accents laughed loudly about their day waiting in line for the ferry at Battery Park. When one of them caught me looking, I redirected my gaze—and found my eyes resting directly on Jay's face.

Not in the flesh. The televisions displayed

around the bar were tuned to some news channel. On the screen, my former boyfriend laughed, one arm around a stunning brunette who looked oddly familiar. I leaned forward, but the laughing Texans behind me obliterated the sound of the TV. After a moment, I gave the bartender ten bucks to turn on the captioning. Part of me insisted that I close my eyes and run, but I needed to see what was happening. My heart refused to believe he moved on so soon. My brain wanted more evidence.

"...the daughter of British tycoon Percy Ashcroft," the captioning said.

Ah, okay. Li'l Tots Corp. had been trying to get Mr. Ashcroft to invest for months. He must have sent his daughter over for negotiations. We'd spoken on the phone and via email but never met. I hoped things were going well.

I almost finished convincing myself before the next line of captioning popped up. "Ms. Ashcroft and Mr. Epstein were reportedly seen together in Beijing on Thursday. A spokesperson for Li'l Tots claims they were there on business, but the photos we saw looked pretty friendly. Viewers may recognize Epstein as the boyfriend of disgraced former executive Anna Guerra."

My heart leapt into my throat.

"After nude photographs purporting to be Ms. Guerra appeared on the internet, the once up-

and-coming junior executive vanished. Epstein refused to comment on Ms. Guerra's whereabouts but insists the pair are no longer together. The company issued a statement that it lacked any knowledge of the photographs before they surfaced. Neither Ms. Ashcroft nor Mr. Epstein commented on the nature of their relationship."

Without thinking, I picked up a handful of popcorn from a bowl on the table and hurled it at the screen. The kernels barely cleared the other side of the booth. Then I buried my face in my hands. I wasn't even important enough for Jay to tell me he was breaking up with me. I'd lifted so easily out of his life, like I didn't matter. I could fade away, and no one would notice. Just like when I was a kid.

I needed to get out of there. I didn't have anywhere to go. The thought of heading back upstairs was too depressing to contemplate, and a handful of members of the media still maintained their camp in the lobby.

Frozen with indecision, I hid under the curtain of my hair until I heard a glass being set on the table. One hand touched my shoulder, and I flinched.

"Hey," a voice said.

The bartender stood in front of me, a white-haired man gazing at me over horn-rimmed glasses. "Here's another one for you, on the house.

I changed the TV to the Broadway channel. Financial news bores the tourists, you know."

My disguise apparently wasn't terribly effective. At least the bartender's blue eyes brimmed with concern rather than scorn. I squeezed his hand briefly. "Thank you."

"Don't mention it," he said. "My daughter is about your age, and when I think about something like this happening to her…Keep your chin up, dear. But keep your head down until the reporter in the corner booth leaves."

He returned to the bar, and I held my drink, staring at the wall. Jay was already dating someone else. Possibly. Probably. Katherine Ashcroft. Katie to her friends.

A little more than a week ago, I'd been reading about her in *Forbes* while waiting out a storm in my basement. Her background was impeccable. Born with money, attended all the best schools, private tutors, passed everything with flying colors. She'd been trained to take over her father's empire practically since she learned to walk. Plus, she was smart, elegant, perfectly composed at all times, quick as a whip, and once dated some cousin of the royal family. She could be the poster child for the British upper class, if they ever stooped to something as déclassé as posters.

I didn't know how long I sat there before a stranger slid into the seat across from me, with close-cropped black curls and browns eyes that wrinkled in the corners. A tan line on his left hand told me he was married but didn't want me to know. It didn't matter; I wasn't looking to hook up.

"Mind if I sit?" he asked. "There's a woman at the bar who keeps eyeing me over her date's shoulder, and I'm worried she's going to get me involved in a bar fight."

"Well, I don't know. It's been a rough day. A bar fight might provide a nice distraction." I smiled and tipped my drink at him to let him know I was kidding.

My new friend motioned at the bartender. "Another two of whatever she's having." To me, he said, "I'm Ted."

The name stumbled on his tongue, revealing the lie. It didn't matter. "So, I know why I'm sitting alone in a bar in the middle of New York City. What about you?"

The way his gaze lingered on my chest made his intentions pretty clear. I wondered how easy I looked. But I was drunk and depressed and Fox-News just informed me that my boyfriend broke up with me. Talking to this guy couldn't possibly make things worse.

I shrugged. "Doesn't matter. You're not here to listen to my sad stories. Tell me something funny."

"I'm not the funniest guy," Ted said. "I sell life insurance."

"Then make something up. Please." I tossed back the rest of my drink and signaled for another. Jay seemed a million miles away. "I've had an awful couple of weeks."

He reached forward and squeezed my hand where my fingers drew patterns in the condensation rings on the table. A shiver ran down my spine. "Want to talk about it?"

"No," I said, meeting his eyes. His pupils dilated, and something flared within me, the first hint of real emotion in weeks. All I wanted was to hold onto that flicker. The liquor gave me courage. "Look, I appreciate the effort, but I'm not in the mood to go home with anyone."

"I could fix that for you. Buy you another drink?"

Ew. My upper lip curled at that. "You're asking me if I want you to get me drunk so I'll sleep with you after I already said no?"

"When you put it that way, it sounds so unseemly."

"Yes. It really does." I widened my eyes and smiled broadly at him, blinking in a faux expression of innocence until he sighed.

"Fine, whatever. Be alone."

"Thanks, I will!" I called after him. Then I signaled the bartender. "Keep an eye on him. And any woman he talks to."

The man nodded. "Sure thing. Thanks for the heads up. Want another?"

"Yes, please."

I possessed no memory of the next drink arriving, or the check, or of leaving the bar. The next thing I knew, sunlight streamed through the window. I squinted and shaded my eyes, cursing myself for not drawing the blinds before I'd left.

I remembered telling the bartender to keep my glass full. The throbbing in my temples suggested he'd earned his tip. I remembered someone sitting across from me. Right. "Ted." He did not appreciate me telling him no. Jerk. Double jerk, since he was also married. I wished I could call his wife and tell her what her husband did while presumably traveling on business.

Whatever. He wasn't worth a second thought. Moaning, I pulled myself up and found a bottle of painkillers on the dresser. A minute later, I stood in the suite's enormous shower, letting hot water pound against my back while I struggled with what I'd seen on the news, the information that led me to drink until I couldn't remember how I got back to my suite.

I should call Jay, ask if the news finally got something right. No, I shouldn't. Yes, I should. No, I should call my old therapist and make an appointment. She could help. Except she couldn't make this go away, and I think she retired, and I hated her when I was thirteen. No, I'd made it through Mamá's death on my own, and I'd make it through this. I was fine.

Closure would make me feel better. I just needed to talk to Jay. Unless that would make me feel worse. Water sluiced down my face while indecision seized me. Paralysis glued me to the beige tiles until my fingers turned to prunes.

A FEW HOURS LATER, my phone rang. I froze. When I finally picked it up, the display showed an unfamiliar number.

Dios mio, Eric found me.

My heart stopped at the thought. Maybe, somehow, Eric figured out my new telephone number and posted it online. Was the flood of texts about to start again? Should I turn my phone to Do Not Disturb again? Or was I freaking out over a wrong number?

Struggling to keep my voice steady, I answered on the fourth ring. "Hello?"

"Hello, is this Ms. Guerra?" A woman's voice, unfamiliar. Both men and women had expressed what they thought of my naked form, so the caller's gender did nothing to reassure me.

"May I ask who's calling, please?"

"Yes, this is Bettina with New Jersey Mutual Insurance. I'm calling about your property claim."

My entire body sighed with relief. "Hi, Bettina. Yes, that's me. Did the adjuster finish the estimate?"

"We sent a crew out last week. The 'good' news, as it is, is that you're one hundred percent fully covered for everything. The contractor thinks it'll cost about four hundred thousand dollars to rebuild the house, and your policy covers you for up to half a million."

"Does that include the appliances and stuff?"

"It does. Your policy also covers the contents. You'll have almost a hundred thousand dollars left to replace your personal belongings after the house is rebuilt, as long everything goes smoothly."

Truly, things in my life couldn't possibly be going less smoothly, but it was time I caught a break. "So, how does it work? You pay the contractors?"

"Since you own the house outright, it's pretty simple. The contractor bills you, we send the checks. You'll sign the back, and the contractor cashes them. Once the work is done and everything's been inspected, we'll send a check for the remaining balance so you can replace your personal items. Or not—the money is yours to do what you want. Meanwhile, we'll need a list of everything in the house. How soon do you think you can send it to me?"

I thought for a minute. "There's an inventory on my laptop. It'll take me about ten minutes once we get off the phone to review it, update, and send."

"Great! If any issues pop up, give me a call." She gave me her email address and direct line. "Meanwhile, if you need a few things, to replace your work wardrobe or whatever, I can authorize a small check of up to a couple thousand dollars to cover you. It'll be deducted from the total, though. If construction costs go over the limit on your coverage, you may have to cover some of the bills yourself."

My work wardrobe. Ha. "That shouldn't be a problem. The storm mostly destroyed my furniture and books and stuff."

"Excellent!" Did she understand the meaning of that word? In the background, her keyboard clacked. "Send me your list, and I'll have our contractors reach out to you."

"Do you have any idea how long it'll take to get my life... I mean, my house back?" A Freudian slip. Going home could be a big step toward feeling like myself again.

On the other hand, Eric knew my old address. Would moving back home give him more ammunition in the war against me? I should sell the place and move to a small island nation where they hadn't discovered the internet, smartphones, or electricity. Maybe I should move in with Tara's mom.

"I wish I could answer that for you, but the hurricane destroyed half the Jersey Coast, most of Staten Island and large portions of Long Island. It's going to come down to whether you know a good contractor who's prepared to make you a priority and how long it takes to get the materials."

My neighbor did construction. That didn't necessarily mean he'd make me a priority, but it couldn't hurt to ask.

"I might know someone. How long do I have to get the work done?"

"It takes as long as it takes. You made the claim right away, which is the most important part. But if you start to run out of time, you can always cash out the policy. I don't think it'll take much to convince my supervisor you've lost at least the policy limits, based on the adjustor's pictures and nearby real estate listings."

"I guess that's both good and bad news, huh?"

She chuckled. "I guess so. Say, are you by any chance the same Anna—?"

"Nope, not me. Sorry." My voice trembled, betraying the lie. "Just a coincidence."

"Oh, well. I was going to say, if you were, I'm sorry for this horrible thing that happened. An ex sent nude pictures to my father once. Not the same scale, of course, but still terrible."

"That's awful. I'm so sorry to hear that."

"Yeah, well, I got through it. So will… the other Anna Guerra. Have a good day. We'll be in touch."

After Bettina hung up, I considered her words. Things would be okay. I just needed to keep moving. Yes, what happened to me was horrible. It happened to other women in the past, it would happen to more in the future. Unless one of us fought back.

Chapter 4

Time dragged until I couldn't even remember the day of the week without turning on the television to see the shows on primetime. It took all my effort to get out of bed each morning. Being alone in a strange place on top of everything else just left me utterly miserable. Other than calling contractors and making arrangements for movers to take everything salvageable to a storage unit, my days were empty.

My neighbor agreed to do what he could to push my repairs through faster, keeping in mind the time needed to fight other contractors for materials and available subcontractors. I told him not to prioritize me over the families in the area. Everyone needed to rebuild. Taking care of kids was difficult enough without having to live out of a suitcase. I'd be fine, here by myself.

Tara was blissfully unaware of what happened and probably would be for quite some time. She texted me when she could, but I hadn't been exaggerating when I texted my dad: Mrs. Fisher and her boyfriend lived entirely off the grid these days. Hopefully by the time they found out the extent of the damage, Hurricane Harriet would be old news. I couldn't bring myself to burden her with my problems when she couldn't do anything to help. Foolishly, I hoped everything with the pictures would blow over before she returned.

Résumé after résumé went out. Phone calls to my business contacts bore rotten fruit. I quickly discovered that being named one of *Forbes*'s "Up-and-Coming Executives Under 35" and one-half of "Manhattan's Top Twenty Power Couples" meant little when every company in the tristate area received nude pictures of me attached to a résumé offering sexual favors. I didn't even know where to begin trying to fix my life, unless I changed my name.

The money wasn't a huge issue. Since I didn't have a house payment and insurance was paying for the hotel, my savings would support me for a long time. But sitting around in a hotel all day with nothing to do made me stir crazy. Other than chatting with the room service staff, I was alone.

And bored. Working long hours wasn't conducive to cultivating friendships with people who weren't co-workers, and I no longer had co-workers.

After weeks of hearing absolutely nothing, when a Mr. Turner offered me an interview as an office manager at a small shipping company, I jumped at the opportunity. I'd never heard of the company, and the annual pay wasn't much more than I could get flipping burgers, but I needed something to keep me busy, and beggars couldn't be choosers. The longer I was out of work, the bleaker everything seemed. A person could only spend so much time sitting in their hotel room watching reruns of a reality show about people living in a giant fishbowl before wanting to climb the walls.

Preparing for the interview turned into a comedy of errors. My hairdryer died. Of course it did. I called Housekeeping for a new one, stressing the importance of it arriving as soon as possible. The cleaners hadn't managed to get a stain out of my favorite suit after the storm, and I hadn't spotted the coffee-colored splotch earlier. After spending half an hour waiting for the iron to heat up so I could get the wrinkles out of my second-favorite suit, I realized that the light switch for the socket had been turned into the off position. Par for the course, everything just kept going wrong. All I wanted was to cancel and crawl back into bed, but I needed this job to feel better about myself. Finally, I made it out the door in one piece.

Half an hour later, when my taxi stopped before a rundown building, I immediately realized my mistake. Several of the units in the office appeared to be vacant. Threadbare carpet beneath my feet led me down a poorly lit hallway to a door covered with signs advertising services for "Western Union," "Cash Checks Here" and "LOTTO!", plus a few others. My suit cost a thousand dollars; I didn't belong here.

It took three deep breaths and a stern talk about snobbiness to get myself through that door. Every instinct in my body screamed to run away, but a job was a job. It would take time to work my way back up to where I'd started. Besides, I reminded myself, how was judging this opportunity based on the outside of the building any better than people sending me death threats because nude pictures of me appeared online? Steeling myself, I turned the knob.

A sweaty, pungent man sat behind the desk. He wore a wife-beater and a pair of ripped jeans, topped by a gray comb-over that was about as effective as hiding a basketball under a shoelace.

"My, my. Aren't we fancy?" he said. "You in the wrong place?"

Inwardly, I cringed, but I summoned my inner

executive. "Mr. Turner? It's nice to meet you. I'm Anna Guerra."

"Naw, I'm not the boss man. He's in the back. I'm Jimmy." He jerked a thumb at a closed door behind him, then turned and bellowed. "Turner? There's a broad here to meet you."

Run, Anna. This is not the job for you.

Sheer stubbornness kept me from walking out.

The door opened, and Mr. Turner appeared. At least he wore a collared shirt, although it was a polo. Unlike Jimmy, he appeared to have showered sometime this month. His clothes were clean, his smile friendly. I decided to at least go through the motions of an interview before racing back to the hotel.

"Nice to meet you," I said, "I'm Anna."

His hand grasped mine firmly, a good handshake. "Welcome, Anna. Come into my office."

"Thank you for meeting with me today," I said. "I have extensive experience running a much larger operation than this—"

He waved one hand. "It doesn't matter. You're way hotter than Jimmy. I need a pretty face to get people in the door. And with those tits, aw, man!" He punctuated those appalling words with a sigh that sent a shiver of revulsion down my spine.

"Wait. What?" I swallowed. This was the strangest job interview imaginable. "I'm here for the office manager position."

"Oh, I know you. I saw your pictures. Do you know the cachet of having a porn star in this office? Men will flock here to cash their paychecks here instead of the cheaper place down the block."

Bile rose in my throat, and I struggled to maintain my composure. "That's not exactly the type of job—"

"Oh, sure, you think you're better than us, in your expensive suit and carrying that fancy briefcase. But once you strip everyone down, we're all the same, right?" He glanced up and down my body in a way that told me in no uncertain terms he was picturing me naked. When the tip of his tongue darted out, I stood and headed for the door.

"Anna, wait. You're what this office needs." I'll never know why I paused and looked back at him. "And if you ever need to make a little extra, I can certainly help you out." One hand drifted toward his crotch and the unmistakable sound of a zipper cut the silence.

I ran.

My face burned. Fury fueled my steps. I should sue that asshole for sexual harassment.

Lost in thought, I stepped off the curb without paying attention. Tires squealed, a horn honked. Hands scrambled at my elbow, gripped my upper arm. Something dragged me backward. My right heel hit the back of the curb and I stumbled, sitting hard on the pavement.

A taxi flew by, the driver waving a fist and screaming obscenities through the window. "Fuck you, lady! Why don't you watch where you're going?"

Once, those words would've jarred me. Now, hysterically, I thought about forwarding this cabbie some of the emails I'd gotten recently to improve his vocabulary. I had an inbox full of "slut," racial slurs, and my personal favorite, "cum-guzzling fuck whore." I'd been called things I'd never heard of and things I didn't think were possible.

A voice jarred me from my reveries. "Are you all right, ma'am?"

Ma'am. That was something no one had called me in a long time. I forced my gaze upward, toward the man who prevented me from becoming a stain on the asphalt.

And further upward. My neck craned until my gaze rested on the face of the man who probably thought he'd done me a huge favor. Once again, a man made a decision for me, exercised control over my body. I didn't want to be saved. Getting hit by a taxi would be the best thing that happened to me since before Hurricane Harriet.

Closely cropped dark hair framed a handsome face. The hint of crow's feet at the corners of his brown eyes suggested he possessed a few years more years than I did. The insignia on his chest identified him as a corporal. My lower lip trembled. I couldn't speak.

"Is everything okay? You walked right out into traffic." His eyes searched my face probably seeking gratitude or awareness that he'd saved me. "You could've been killed."

The words were supposed to scare me. Instead, a sinking black hole opened in my chest. Ignoring the hand he offered, I pushed myself onto my feet.

"I could've been killed," I repeated mechanically. "And you stopped me? Why would you do that to me? Why not let me die?"

Shock slashed his handsome features. Then his face softened with concern. "Is there anything I can do to help you, ma'am?"

I barked out a hysterical laugh. With a sob, I shoved at the center of his chest. The marine stumbled backward. Then I turned and I ran. I ran and ran and ran, not knowing or caring where I wound up. When my prosthetic started to make my lower calf ache, I slowed. I trudged down the street, not even sure where I was, staring with unseeing eyes at the sidewalk, wondering what my life had become. Why I even bothered anymore.

Every step seemed an effort. Cotton stuffed my head, blocking rational thought. No matter what I did, I found myself swimming upward through quicksand with my arms behind my back. Could nothing ever go right? When was the last time I hadn't felt numb and broken?

Losing everything left a gaping hole inside me, as if Eric ripped out my soul. It wasn't just the pictures: No house, no job, no friends, no hope. I didn't know how to fill the void. This wasn't me. This couldn't be my life. I'd been floating along, and I needed to take control.

Thunder cracked overhead, and the clouds opened. I glanced up, earning myself a face full of water. "You're kidding me, right?"

The skies didn't answer. I ducked under an awning, weighing my options. The thought of spending another dreary day locked in an impersonal hotel suite…No. My instinct whenever I felt down was still to call Mamá, even after all these years. Unfortunately, I lacked a connection to the afterlife.

Papá and I never had the kind of relationship where I turned to him with my problems, even before she died. More than anything, I hated the thought of disappointing him. I could never forget the look on his face the day I woke up in the hospital when I was thirteen, and I never wanted to see it again.

Still, there was one person I'd always been able to call for help. One person who stood by me after my accident and my depression and visited every day until my parents moved us to North Carolina. Years later when I moved back, she was at my side within hours.

For the first time since all of this started, I called Tara. I didn't want to burden her while her mom was sick, but I needed her. Not surprisingly, it rolled straight to voicemail. When choosing cell phone providers, Tara hadn't cared whether service was available in the middle of nowhere. She only managed to call me twice since she'd left, both times from the phone at the General Store.

I missed my best friend. It was selfish to resent her mother for getting sick at the worst possible time for me. Still, I couldn't staunch the flood of negative emotions.

There wasn't anyone else I could call, anyone to talk to. With a sigh, I stepped out of the awning, into the rain. My whole body was numb. I'd been too numb, for too long. Ever since the hurricane. Since the moment messages from strangers flooded my phone and my inbox. Since forever. Those weeks might as well have been eons. I just wanted to feel something, anything other than this emptiness.

Chapter 5

Later that night, music filled the air around me. Bodies danced on the floor, pulsing and grinding. I sat, staring into my glass. What a terrible idea. I'd needed to get out of the hotel, away from Manhattan, but maybe getting off the subway randomly and walking into the first place selling alcohol wasn't the solution. Now I sat alone, surrounded by college students practically having sex on the dance floor. Being miserable in a club didn't improve my overall outlook on life. Nothing did anymore.

"What on earth is such a hot thing like you doing looking so sad in a place like this?"

A guy stood next to my table. He seemed young, probably in his early twenties. Too young for me, but cute. "Sorry. Long day. Well, long month. I should go."

He slid into the seat next to me, took my hand. "What if I told you there's a way to make things better?"

I chuckled. "I would not believe you, my friend. But thanks for the laugh."

He leaned over until his lips touched my ear. "I've got some happy pills. You'll feel awesome in about half an hour. Scout's honor."

Although I'd never taken drugs in my life, a pill to make me happy sounded pretty good. He probably wasn't talking about Prozac. Most of the drug users I'd known in college seemed pretty happy. What could it hurt?

My eyes met his. "Sounds wonderful."

My new friend squeezed my hand under the table, pressing a pill into my palm. I pretended to yawn and tossed it back without even looking at it, not much caring what the drug did. "Is it working?"

He chuckled. "You have to give it some time. Let me buy you another drink, and then we'll dance."

I tipped my full glass at him. "I'm good with this one. But please, join me. When this doesn't work, I want to be able to say 'I told you so.'"

He smiled, rubbed my knee. A shiver went

down my spine. I thought about asking his name, realized I didn't care. On the dance floor, a mass of bodies writhed to the pulse of the music. The beat filled me, and I rocked back and forth in my chair.

When we finished our drinks, my friend pulled me out onto the dance floor. We danced for an eternity. In time, we mostly swayed, rubbing against each other, savoring the touch of each other. Multi-colored lights danced overhead. The music throbbed through my veins; angels singing with my entire body. I wanted to stay there forever.

When we took a break to finish our drinks, my new friend spoke. Such a lovely voice. "C'mon. Let's go to my place. It's a few blocks away. My roommate's there, but he won't mind."

I beamed up at him. He appeared cuter by the second. "Works for me."

We walked in silence up one street, down the next. I didn't pay much attention to where we went. It didn't matter. The rain had washed away the suffocating thickness in the air.

When we got to his building, my friend led me up the stairs and down a wide, well-lit hallway. We left our shoes inside the front door. I shuffled across the cool, smooth mahogany floor. The planks urged me to lie down and press my whole body against them, but my friend led me into the kitchen.

"Get on your knees. Keep your head down."

I obeyed without hesitation. The wavy lines etched on the tile dug into my knees. Wanting more of it against my skin, I leaned down and pressed it with my hands. Pretty tile, pretty lines, rough caulk between each. So weird. So cool. I liked it.

"Mmmmm. I love that Latina booty. Shake it for me, baby."

My hips wiggled as if of their own accord. Part of me felt suspended in reality, watching these events unfold in horror. I couldn't stop the things I was doing, didn't know why I was doing them. The man groaned, and the person I barely recognized as myself beamed up at him.

A fly unzipped, and seconds later, a pale penis poked out at me from the slit in a pair of tightie whites. Skinny penis.

Something a friend once said flitted through my mind. "No point hitting the bottom of the barrel if you can't scrape the sides." My new friend wouldn't be scraping any sides.

The drugs took over, and I giggled. It would get bigger. Straight, dark pubic hair prickled my face when I leaned forward and licked his cock. My friend moaned. The dick became longer, harder, easier to grip between my fingers. Not thicker, though. My fingers burned where I touched him. I gazed up at my friend, smiled. He should feel as good as this pill made me feel. Yay for pills!

My hand ran up and down his length, and I licked the tip a second time. A drop of moisture appeared. A hand trailed down my back, landing on my ass. I shivered, leaning into it before I wondered how my friend grew a third arm. I froze. Oh, yeah. Roommate. Roommates are nice. I missed my roommate. Maybe this roommate is cool, like Tara. Tara makes me pancakes in the mornings sometimes.

Why hadn't I discovered happy pills sooner? I nuzzled backward, into this unseen person. He stroked my ass. Not like Tara, then. But everything felt so nice.

"Dude, she's only got one foot." A new voice. Deeper, rougher.

As if I couldn't hear them. Like I wasn't even there. Maybe I wasn't. Maybe this was all a dream. The air moved like molasses in dreams, right? An awesome dream.

The voice wavered. "Is this okay?"

Everything felt so wonderful. These guys were amazing. Such lovely sensations. Maybe two friends could give me double the pleasure. Like Doublemint gum! I nodded, and my hips thrust backward in invitation. A condom rolled down the shaft in front of me. It smelled like balloons. Balloons were fun. They made balloon animals. I giggled, seeing a neon balloon snake made out of glow-in-the-dark condoms.

Rough, plump fingers pulled at my panties. The contrast of callouses against my sensitive flesh made me shiver. Then nothing mattered but me, this moment, and the euphoria coursing through my veins.

***

WHEN I AWOKE on the floor later, the world did not shine nearly so brightly. The second I realized what I'd done, humiliation flooded me. I grabbed my clothes and bolted from the apartment, thankful not to see anyone. In trying to block out the pain, I'd turned into exactly what Eric said. Once I got out the door, I slowed, all desire to move quickly gone.

The world around me blurred before I even made it out of the elevator into what I now realized was a posh lobby. My shoe squeaked on the marble floor, drawing the gaze of the concierge. Through the open buttons of my coat, he took in the top barely covering my breasts and the skirt I still struggled to smooth into place, disapproval etched into his features. I avoided his eyes.

Outside, the honking and sirens and buzzing voices of city life dimmed until I blotted out everything but my heartbeat. Without the false joy that sustained me earlier, once again I was cold inside. I moved woodenly through the crowd, seeing nothing, acknowledging no one.

The numbness was worse than the pain. I wanted to make it stop. Wanted to make everything stop. It was all too much. There wasn't any way to make it better.

After tossing and turning for a few hours, I gave up and got out of bed, looking for anything to ease the tsunami of emotions warring inside me. Once the effects of the "happy pill" wore off, everything became a hundred times worse.

When I looked in the mirror, empty eyes and a slack jaw gazed back at me. I didn't even recognize the person I'd become. Once I'd walked with confidence, knowing I'd clawed my way to the top of the world. But that was before everything got ripped away, before the gremlins in my brain returned to whisper that nothing I ever did could be good enough. Now, resignation and depression seeped from my pores, clouding the air around me. With a heavy sigh, I grabbed my cane and trudged into the living room. All of my careful plans for my life, gone. Everything I'd ever done, meaningless. There was no point in doing anything.

Sipping my drink, I listened to the early morning traffic a while before ordering room service. Morning sunlight barely filled the room when a knock sounded at the door. I woke up feeling as if a stampede of elephants ran over my body. The banging made my head throb, and I winced. Ice cubes clinked together as I set my drink on the table. It hadn't made me feel much better, but the morning was young.

"Coming!" I called. The sound of my own voice echoing in my head made me wince.

Room service knew by now not to leave my trays outside the door, but I still needed to open the deadbolt before they entered. "You're earl..." The words died in my throat as the door swung open.

Jay stood on the threshold. "Early? Were you expecting someone?"

Words. Needed. What? "Hello, Jason."

He flinched at my use of his full name. "I know this is a surprise. Can I come in?"

Still unable to speak, I tilted my head up and down a fraction and let the door swing open. Jay moved past me into the sitting area.

"If you're expecting company, I won't stay long."

"Huh?" My brain wasn't quite up to snuff yet. "Room service. What are you doing here?"

He sank onto the couch and motioned for me to do the same. Not wanting to be next to him, I stumbled toward the armchair beside him. "I just need a few minutes. I wanted to see how you're doing."

A bitter laugh escaped me. "Oh, that's rich. I'm *increíble*. How are you? Would you care for some tea?"

"I know you're going through a hard time." Jay glanced at the uncapped bottle of whiskey sitting on the table but didn't comment.

"Congratulations! You won the Understatement of the Year award! That's quite the coup on top of the World's Crappiest Boyfriend award. I thought Eric was a shoo-in, but you managed to edge him out in the end."

"You never gave me a chance to explain—"

"You never tried. You sent me away, told me to move out of your apartment, stopped texting, left the country, and I didn't hear from you for… God, I don't even know how long. It doesn't matter. I've moved on." A tear slid down my cheek, betraying the lie. "I don't need you. I've got Jim and Jack to keep me company."

"Who?"

"My new boyfriends: Jim Beam and Jack Daniels."

Jay wrinkled his brow, then glanced back at the coffee table. "Are you drunk? Anna, it's nine o'clock in the morning."

"Is it? Huh."

Time was irrelevant. Days of the week and

dates were irrelevant. Everything blurred together. Jay seemed as out of place in my world now as if my dead mother dropped by to say hello. Of course, I'd have been delighted to see Mamá.

He picked up the glass on the table and sniffed before setting it back down. "Anna, I'm here because I'm worried about you."

White-hot pokers of irritation jabbed at me. "Oh, are you? That's lovely. You know what would've been a perfect time to be worried about me? Before you abandoned me during the worst thing that's ever happened to me. This coming from someone who has literally been dismembered."

"I'm sorry. I didn't have any choice."

"That's bullshit. You could've chosen to stand by me. Hillary Clinton stood by Bill."

"That was different." He shifted, and something on the couch crinkled.

"You're right, it was. Bill actually did something wrong."

He raked one hand through his hair and sighed. "I know you didn't do anything wrong. But the answer isn't to lock yourself in a hotel room and drink your life away."

"Oh, yeah? Well, if you're so perfect, Jay, tell me how you'd handle having your entire life ripped out from under you. Would you throw a party? Jaunt off around the world? Fly to China?

We don't all own a private jet, you know." He opened his mouth, but all my frustration and anger came rushing out. "Do you even care what it's been like? The horror of reading hundreds, no thousands, of messages, calling you a slut, a whore, saying you should die? Imagine three thousand punches to the gut in the row. Do you know how it feels to have your trust violated? To have your clothes ripped off and everything exposed to the entire world? Of course you don't. I don't have a life left to drink away. Everything's been taken from me."

"There's something I need to tell you, and I want you to hear it from me first."

The pity crossing on his face told me exactly what he was about to say. Darkness and despair threatened to overwhelm me, but I used the remnants of my rage to shove them back.

"I know about your new girlfriend," I spit out. "I've been watching the news."

He blanched. "I'm sorry. I wanted to be the one to tell you. We met—"

I put up one hand. "I do not want the details, and if you say another word about the girl you dumped me for while I was lying in a hotel bed staring at the walls in a pit of despair…"

There were no more words. I couldn't even finish my sentence, but Jay's face told me I'd gotten my point across. Snot tickled the inside of my nose. I refused to sniffle, to let him see me cry. Instead, I swirled my glass, staring at the ice cubes, wishing he would leave. "Was there something else you needed?"

"I need to know you're all right. That you forgive me."

"Then you're going to be here a very long time. Want a drink?"

"Anna, this isn't you. What are you doing to yourself?"

"Get the fuck out of my hotel room."

"I'm sorry. This isn't why I came here." He shook his head and started to leave. "The board held a meeting yesterday afternoon. We sent a notice, but you didn't show up. They took an official vote, Anna. They've terminated your contract. You're getting one hell of a severance package if you sign a document agreeing not to sue the company. I did the best I could for you, and I think anyone would agree it's fair. I'll email the documents over later. Talk to your lawyer and let me know."

The door closing behind him was punctuated by glass shattering against it. The wall shook.

His voice traveled back through the door. "I'm sorry, Anna. Happy Thanksgiving."

I hadn't even been aware of the holiday. All of November, gone in a blur of pain and misery. How had I lost an entire month?

My head fell into my hands, and I sobbed. No job, no hope of a job. No boyfriend. No friends. No one to stand by me. Everything I worked for, gone in an instant of someone else's petulance and revenge. Blackness pushed at the corners of my mind, overtaking everything. I didn't know who I was anymore. Fragments from the prior evening flashed before my eyes: Unknown hands touching me, the humiliation, the cries of ecstasy.

Having Jay witness my destruction made everything worse. If only I didn't care what he thought, what everyone thought.

My heart pounded in my ears. Air moved in and out of my lungs in great gasps. I couldn't breathe. I didn't want to breathe anymore. All I wanted was to make everything go away. Anna Guerra was dead. My life was over. Why was I still here? Why couldn't my being vanish into the night as quickly and effortlessly as my reputation, my dreams, my life?

The darkness seemed so inviting. If only I could slide into it. Just slip away.

I always carried a bottle of over-the-counter painkillers in my purse for my leg, although I rarely took them. With shaking hands, I pulled my bag into my lap and started digging. A nearly-full, relatively new bottle awaited me.

Just enough to make the pain stop. There were

two hundred pills in the bottle. Would that make me feel better?

Broken glass blocked my path into the kitchen, so I picked up the bottle of whiskey and shook five pain killers out into my palm. I tossed them into my mouth, took a swig from the bottle.

So much pain.

More pills. Another swig. Again, and again. Again.

Just enough to make it stop.

Part II

We've got this gift of love, but love is like a pre-cious plant. You can't just accept it and leave it in the cupboard or just think it's going to get on by itself. You've got to keep watering it.

You've got to really look after it and nurture it.

- John Lennon

Chapter 6

September 2015

A hunky, blue-eyed blond whose muscles and too-tanned skin suggested he spent a lot of time at the local gym entered the tiny elevator behind me. He glanced from my second-hand black pin-striped Armani suit to the red leather portfolio I clutched with white knuckles and offered me a smile.

"Interview?"

"Yeah." My eyes remained glued to the numbers increasing at an agonizingly slow rate as I continued to run through my resume in my head. When I was twenty-five years old, I started working in research and development for a corporation that manufactured and sold diapers. Over the next six years, I'd worked my way up the rungs until I landed a junior management position. Not long after I started that job, a headhunter invited me to interview for a much higher paid mid-level position, working on children's socks, shoes, and accessories.

Now in the elevator, I focused on my breathing. No matter how confident I grew in my abilities, trying to sell myself always felt too much like public speaking, which terrified me.

"Can I offer you some friendly advice?"

I dragged my gaze away from the shining "18" and took in his dark suit, shiny loafers, and new haircut. "What? You going to tell me you got the job all locked up and I shouldn't bother?"

"Something like that." He chuckled and offered a hand. "I'm Eric."

"Ahn-a. Spelled like Ann-a."

When our hands met, a jolt passed through me. Not from the touch, but from the elevator.

A horrible screech penetrated the metal floor. The tiny space tilted, and I thudded into the wall. The elevator ground to a halt. The ticker at top paused halfway between "19" and "20." Lights flickered before the tiny steel cage plunged into darkness. A siren wailed.

Bands squeezed my chest. I opened my mouth, but no air entered my lungs. My carefully constructed portfolio crashed to the ground. A sound mortifyingly like a whimper escaped me.

"Anna, are you okay?"

The words didn't penetrate my panic. More voices sounded in the world beyond the doors, but I couldn't make out the words.

A hand touched my back. A horrible stench filled my nostrils.

I jerked back, gagging. "What are you doing?"

"Sorry. I needed a way to snap you out of your fear. I was looking for something with a strong odor, and all I had was this blue cheese I'm bringing to my father. The more it stinks, the better it tastes, you know."

"Gross." My nose wrinkled as if trying to expel the odor. For the first time, I registered alarm bells in the distance.

"Yeah, I know. Are you okay?" Something touched my hand. I started before realizing it was him. Warm fingers curled around my clammy palm.

"I'll be fine. I'm not a fan of dark, enclosed spaces, that's all."

"Yeah, me, neither. Weird that there aren't any emergency lights in here."

Now that we'd been in the dark a few minutes, my eyes were adjusting to the gloom. Tiny bits of light filtered in through the cracks around the door. A rectangle of light flared from Eric's hand, reminding me my cell phone also worked as a flashlight. Pulling it out and gulping in the light made the elevator stop spinning.

Eric set both phones on the floor, and a shaft of light bathed me. The walls returned to their normal position. I took a deep breath, willing the metal bands in my chest to loosen.

"Here." He tugged on my arm. "Why don't you sit in the corner until someone comes to let us out. The fire department could get here in five minutes, but with these old buildings, we still might be stuck here for hours."

"Awesome," I said, staring at the "NO SER-VICE" warning on my phone. "Nothing says professional like being late to a job interview."

The banshee shriek of metal against metal filled the air. The floor rolled beneath me, and my breakfast climbed from my stomach into my chest. I swallowed hard, my gaze moving expectantly from the doors to the numbers above to the key-pad. We didn't move. One hand sat on my chest, willing my breakfast burrito not to make an appearance on my expensive interview suit.

Eric squeezed my hand before filling the silence. "You're still going to the interview?"

"Of course I am! Aren't you?"

"Absolutely. I can't cancel due to getting stuck in an elevator and be shown up by you acing everything."

He was goading me to keep my fear at bay.

His transparent plan worked, so I let him continue needling me. Also, every little jab carried a flash of gorgeous, straight white teeth and dimples. Dimples never failed to make my knees weak. If I hadn't been sitting, this conversation may have knocked me off my feet. Confidence and dimples: my dating kryptonite.

"I plan to ace everything whether I show up three seconds after leaving the elevator or next week. Just so you know."

"Oh, yeah? Then maybe this would be a good time to tell you that my father's best friend owns the company."

"Yeah, well my father's brother's nephew's cousin's former roommate works in the cafeteria."

He chuckled. "You a *Spaceballs* fan?"

"Isn't everyone?"

"Touché."

Banging outside the elevator muted our conversation temporarily. Eric stood, banging on the doors. "We're in here! Help!"

Finally, the elevator lurched upward, sending another blast of my breakfast up through my throat practically into my nose. I coughed to cover a gag. The doors slid open and I launched myself out onto the twentieth floor.

Behind me, Eric spoke. "I thought you were still going to the interview." He hung out the doorway, holding my portfolio in one hand.

I grinned as I took it. "I am—but I'm taking the stairs."

"Well, in that case, let me come with you."

"It's a free stairway, right?" I shrugged. "Just don't think I'm giving you interview tips on the way up."

When we reached the twenty-fourth floor, Eric stopped, his hand on the door. "It was very nice to meet you, Anna. There's no one I'd rather be stuck in an elevator with."

"Nice to meet you, too. There's no one I'd rather beat for a job."

He pulled a card out of his wallet, then hesitated. "I have a confession to make."

My eyebrows raised, and I glanced at my watch pointedly. The interview started in six minutes. "Are you trying to make me late?"

"No, I—" He swallowed. "My company's on the fifth floor. I said I was interviewing too so I'd have a reason to keep talking to you."

A smile spread across my face. No one had ever ridden up an extra nineteen floors in an elevator just to spend time with me before. I'd never been the kind of woman men crossed rooms to meet. "I'm glad you did. Otherwise, I'd have been alone when the elevator got stuck. You saved me from a full-blown panic attack."

"You'd have been fine. But I'm glad I could be

there." Eric gestured with the card again. "Call me?"

Finally, I reached for it. My fingertips lingered on his as I took the card. Lightning bolts shot up my arm.

The name on the card startled me. Eric Rutherford, III. As in, Rutherford Communications. Son of Eric Rutherford, II and presumably heir to more money than a person could spend in several lifetimes.

Trying not to let him know I recognized the name, I took a pen from my purse and scribbled on the back of the card before handing it back. "I never call men first. But if you call me, I'll buy you dinner. You have to let me thank you. I'd never have gotten through that without you distracting me."

"I'd love to." He flashed a wolfish grin before opening a door off the hallway and motioning inside. "Now go knock 'em dead."

Later that night, Eric called to see how I was doing after my panic attack in the elevator. We chatted for three hours. Flowers appeared the next morning with a note saying he hoped I felt better. Two days later, Eric invited me out to dinner to celebrate getting the job. I didn't hesitate before saying yes.

TEN MINUTES before I expected my date to arrive, I stood in my room, putting the finishing touches on my makeup, when Tara poked her head around the door. "Hey, did you call the Secret Service?"

"What?"

"There's a creepy-ass car sitting in front of our house. Tinted windows, driver wearing a little hat. Totally looks like Secret Service. Hey, your new job isn't with the NSA is it?"

I laughed. "Nope. That must be my date. He said he'd pick me up."

"In a car service?" Tara wrinkled her nose. "He couldn't be bothered to drive to pick you up, so he sent a car like you're at his beck and call?"

The eyelash curler interfered with my attempt to give her the stink eye. "Well, we planned a date, so I technically am at his beck and call for the next few hours. But he's probably *in* the car. Did you think about opening the door to let him in?"

As if on cue, the doorbell rang. Tara huffed but raced down the hall. Hopefully she'd let him over the threshold.

Leaving Eric on the doorstep wouldn't be the first time my fiercely protective best friend decided to test the mettle of one of my dates. A couple of years ago, she greeted a guy with a story about the time she won a sharpshooting championship. She failed to mention that she'd been in the fifth grade. Since her heart was in the right place, I found it more touching than annoying when she pretended to be my father. Mostly.

My makeup was nearly complete when the first burst of laughter traveled down the hall. Female first, followed by male. Good. Eric passed the first test. I couldn't date a guy that didn't get along with my friends.

On the dot of seven-thirty, I emerged from my room to greet my date. He sat on the couch, Hermione perched on his lap, sniffing his face. One hand held a red, white, and green bouquet out to the side, away from the cat's questing nose.

"Sorry to keep you waiting," I said. "If I'd known what she was doing to you out here…"

"Hey," Tara said, "I offered to take the flowers. Dude said he needed to give them to you himself." She shooed the cat away, and I offered Eric a hand so he could rise from the quagmire of our old, sunken couch.

"Never apologize for looking that beautiful," he said. It was obviously a line, but I smiled despite myself. "These are for you."

I took the bouquet and inhaled the sweet scent. "Thank you! I love roses."

Tara took the arrangement and put them in a vase on the coffee table while I got my coat. "Shall we?"

"Your carriage awaits," Eric replied with an exaggerated bow.

On the way out the door, I turned back to exchange a grin with my roommate. She winked and flashed two thumbs up.

When we reached the walkway, Eric cast an appraising glance back at the house. "Nice place you got. How's the landlord?"

"Oh, it's mine," I said. "Tara and I found it after college. I don't need a roommate anymore, but I like having the company."

"You been friends a long time?"

"Forever," I said. "Since junior high." No need to mention that she was the only friend who stood by me after my accident.

He held the door open for me, and I slid into the plush leather seats. The inside of the car oozed money. My parents had done well for themselves, provided me with a very nice upbringing but they also gave a lot back to the community. They never frittered money away on designer clothes or personal drivers. This car belonged to a guy who'd been handed everything in life. I wondered what Eric would think if he knew I'd worked for everything I had, that the money for my nice clothes and my fancy education and the house came from a settlement, not from my parents. Just plain bad luck, a society mother who'd do anything to help her daughter win a stupid horseback riding competition, and a jury's artificial estimate of the value of a left foot.

I never let myself think about how much I'd loved riding, loved working in the stables to earn my keep. The house and the education would never compare to the feeling of showing off flawless tack to an unsmiling judge or nailing a jump before a crowd. Which was a very different feeling from falling in front of a crowd.

Eric settled beside me on the seat. His scent, cedar and some spice I couldn't identify, drove those thoughts out of my head. I inhaled deeply. A moment later, Eric spoke, his lips hovering inches from my ear. His hot breath against my neck made me shiver. "What's that building over there?"

As we drove around, Eric asked questions, and I pointed out some of my favorite spots. By the time we crossed into the city, I'd nearly forgotten that I was on a date with a multimillionaire. It was just me and Eric, the smart, funny guy who helped me through a tough situation in the elevator. Excitement slowly replaced my nerves.

Chapter 7

In all my years of dating, I'd never been out with a guy who screamed money from head-to-toe. The nervousness that nearly evaporated in the car returned full-scale when we arrived at the restaurant. The dark-paneled walls and candlelit room were far ritzier than where I ate with my friends. Even business meetings at my level didn't happen in places like this. The forty-seven-dollar chicken on the menu made me wonder if it came with a foot massage.

After the hostess placed a linen napkin on each of our laps, an awkward silence descended. Despite our marathon conversation the other day, I couldn't think of a single thing to say.

I studied the menu like there would be a quiz later. When I accidentally sloshed water all over the table, I jumped. This was the most awkward first date ever.

"I'm sorry," I said.

"Don't worry about it." Eric smiled at me. "Hey, I come here all the time. The chef's awesome. Why don't I ask him to make something special for us? I promise, it'll be delicious. The sommelier can pick the wine. Just sit back, relax, and tell me about your new job."

I nodded, and he relayed the request to the waiter. Then we were quiet again, and I began to twist my napkin in my lap. Why was I so nervous? Was it just that he was the type of guy I'd always thought out of my league, or was it because I really liked him? All of a sudden, fear that he might not like me when he found out I wasn't "whole" made my mouth paper dry and my palms sweat. I couldn't talk.

"…my nose until it bleeds."

For a second, I thought my date was sitting across the table talking about picking his nose. But then I realized, in the quiet restaurant, a high-pitched masculine voice carried to us from the next table. I snuck a peek through a veil of my long hair to see a girl dressed much as I in black dress pants, a form-fitting V-neck sweater, and high heels (hers bright red, a brilliant detail I wished I'd thought of) across from a guy who suffered from diarrhea of the mouth.

"That's…something." The girl said.

I clapped my hands over my mouth to avoid laughing, but then a soft snort drifted across the table. My eyes met Eric's, and he tilted his head at the other table. With his knife, he mimed picking his nose, and I smothered a burst of laughter with my hands.

At the other table Nose Picker, for some unfathomable reason, continued the conversation. It was like a car accident, but I couldn't stop peeking out of the corner of my eye, especially since Eric's eyes were also glued to them. "Yeah, didn't stop until I was twelve. My mom took me to a special doctor."

"Huh," the girl said. Her eyes darted around the room as if she plotted an escape.

Eric reached into his pocket and pulled out his phone. Wonderful. I was boring him so much, he wanted to talk to someone else. Then he gestured at my purse, sitting on the table and tilted his head. He typed furiously while horror and embarrassment warred inside me. Then my purse started buzzing and realization dawned.

A text popped up on the front of the screen. I MAY NOT BE THE MOST BRILLIANT FIRST DATE CONVERSATIONALIST, BUT I NEVER PICKED MY NOSE UNTIL IT BLED.

HA!, I typed. I'M NOT SURPRISED. YOU LOOK MORE LIKE A BEDWETTER. ;-)

Eric: :-P

Me: THAT POOR GIRL. SHOULD WE CALL THE MAITRE D' AND PRETEND THERE'S AN EMERGENCY FOR HER?

At that moment, the waiter arrived to pour our wine. Eric motioned him closer and quietly relayed a request to deliver a bottle to the couple at the next table. Then he asked about my job interview.

The ice finally broken, I sipped my wine. "It won't be official until we sign the paperwork next week, but the company makes toddler clothing, and they're hiring a junior executive. It's similar to what I've been doing for my old company, which made cloth diapers. I've been telling everyone how excited I am to finally get out of diapers now that I'm thirty-one."

Eric chuckled.

Another snippet of conversation drifted over from the Disastrous Date table. "What if humans ate their vomit like dogs do?"

"What about you?" I asked, trying to refrain from listening for her answer.

My date glanced over as if he also wondered, but answered my question. "Right now, I'm working as Operations Officer at my father's company. He had a heart attack a couple of years ago. He's fine, but he wants me to learn the ropes, just in case. Ideally, I'll take the things I learn and move on to make my own fortune, the way he did."

We had a lot in common. We both got our undergraduate degrees at Columbia, although Eric graduated three years ahead of me. Our paths never crossed. We'd both gone on to get M.B.A.s, mine at Columbia, his at Wharton. We both dreamed of running large corporations someday.

After the Disastrous Date Couple left, I laid my hand on the table, stretched across toward the middle. He gripped it gently for a moment, holding my gaze with his.

"Thank you for making this such a painless first date," he said. "I know that sounds like a line, but this has been so easy. And you didn't talk about picking your nose once, so that's a bonus."

"I know what you mean. I could talk to you forever." I blushed. "I mean, well, I like talking to you."

"Me, too." He smiled, and my stomach did flip-flops.

By the time dessert came, we ate slowly, lingering over each bite to stretch the date out as long as possible. My right foot brushed his left calf under the table, sending tingles down my spine. Our eyes locked, and my mouth went dry at the naked desire etched into his face. When his thumb flickered across my palm, my breath caught.

The waiter arrived to ask if we wanted anything else, ending the moment. I shook my head, thinking about how I didn't want the evening to end. After leaving the restaurant, Eric and I strolled around Central Park. We wound up at the duck pond. As the day's light fell behind the trees, orangey-pink light illuminated the water.

"It's beautiful," I said.

"Yes, it is." His eyes never left my face.

I leaned forward and kissed him lightly. "Thank you for a lovely evening."

Eric gestured at a nearby hotdog vendor. "Want me to get some buns so we can feed the ducks?"

I hesitated. It was in my nature not to correct people I wanted to like me, but… "Let's just sit. Research shows that bread is really bad for ducks. It could make them sick."

"Really?"

Holding my breath, I nodded.

"Fascinating." His face broke into a smile, and I relaxed. "You're even smarter than I thought, Anna Guerra."

We found a bench and looked out across the water. Few ducks remained on the pond, but we sat in silence, enjoying the stillness. Our hands almost touched.

"You come here often?"

"It's one of my favorite places in the city. This

is where I go when I want to be alone with my thoughts."

The idea of him taking me to his alone place seemed unlikely. "I bet that's what you tell all your first dates."

He turned toward me, touched my face. "I've never brought a first date here, but I'm comfortable with you. Maybe it was because you let me see you so vulnerable in the elevator."

"That wasn't exactly intentional on my part," I pointed out.

"I know, but after sharing that experience with you, I can be myself. There's no need to hide who I am, because you've shown me who you are. You don't seem like you'd judge me for opening up to you."

Not even the skeptic in me could stop the flush of pleasure that comment brought to my face. Our lips met again, and I moved my hands into his hair, holding him close. For a heart-stopping moment, ducks, vulnerability, and the fact that we were in public were forgotten.

Then, a blaring filled the air. Eric jumped back. "Sorry, that's my phone."

"Your ringtone is a fire alarm?"

He fumbled in his pocket. "Only when my father calls. I'm so sorry, I have to take this."

As he walked toward the trees, I reapplied my lipstick, fixed my hair, then shot off a quick text to

Tara with several fireworks emojis. Even accounting for the interruption, I couldn't remember the last time a first date went so well.

A family meandered off the path toward my spot, and I scooted to the end of the bench to make room for them. Across the pond, my attention was drawn by a red-haired woman being walked by five spaniels. I marveled that she could control them all: even though they were small dogs, she was a tiny woman. Their collective weight must've matched hers.

"Mac! What are you doing?"

A gasp drew my attention back to the family. Seeking the source, I instead found a tow-headed boy leaning against the bench, so close he almost touched me. He couldn't be older than two or three. A leash extended from the red harness around the boy's midsection, stretched taut to a woman about ten feet away who must be his mother. Glancing down, I realized the toddler perched his full weight on my left shoe.

"I want doggies!"

The mother tugged on the leash while juggling a baby in her arms. When the boy didn't move, a black-haired man with streaks of gray at the temples rushed forward.

"I'm so sorry. Mac, get over here." He took the child's hand and led him away, right as Eric reemerged from the trees. The boy wailed and ran behind the bench, hiding his face. The mother rushed to comfort him and the toddler while I dealt with the stricken man in front of me.

"It's absolutely fine."

"Is everything okay?" Eric ran to my side and dropped to his knees beside me.

I put one hand on his chest, pushing him back a step. "Absolutely. Everything's great."

The man said, "I glanced away from my son for two seconds, and the next thing I know, he shoved your girlfriend out of the way to climb down the bench. I don't know what gets into him."

"He didn't push me. It's fine," I said. "He accidentally stepped on my shoe."

"Well, he practically climbed into your lap. I'm surprised you didn't say anything."

"It's fine. I'm just sorry he's so upset."

"He's mad that you were where he wanted to be. He'll get over it. Let me—"

The father continued to try to apologize, but I brushed him off. Eric tilted his head at me and raised his eyebrows, but waited to speak until they'd all moved closer to the pond, out of earshot.

"Why didn't you say anything to the little boy when he climbed on you?"

"I didn't notice," I said.

"What do you mean?"

I shrugged.

He persisted. "That doesn't make any sense. How can you not feel thirty pounds standing on your foot?"

Here it was: the moment of truth. When I was in college, too many potential hookups either freaked out at my prosthetic foot or reacted like "bang a disabled chick" was on their bucket list under "do a Latina," and they'd gotten twice as lucky as they thought. Both reactions were unacceptable: I'd spent many unscheduled nights at home alone as a result of my disability.

Then again, better to know sooner if my date was a douche-canoe, so there were some benefits to ripping off the Band-Aid quickly. I probably should've told him at dinner, but it was tough when all I wanted was to continue this evening.

I leaned back against the bench, staring across the water while working my lower lip between my teeth.

"What's wrong?" Eric asked. "I thought we were having a good time."

"We were. I mean, we are." Time to put my big girl pants on. "I hoped to get to know you a little before this came up. It's no big deal, but my left foot is fake. I wear a prosthetic."

"No shit? Like the Six Million Dollar Man?"

I laughed. "Not a bionic foot. Just a prosthetic. I lost it in an accident when I was a teenager."

His expression softened. "Do you want to talk about it?"

I shook my head. "It's not a first date story."

"I understand. Still, it must've been hard for you." He took my hand and helped me to my feet. Instead of releasing me, he turned me toward where we entered the park. "Guess it's a good thing I called a car after talking to my dad, huh?"

"I can walk a couple of miles before my leg starts to bother me. I can run short distances if I have to. But I may not always realize when I step in a mud puddle."

"Don't worry. I'll tell you." Eric leaned forward and kissed me gently. "I like you, Anna. I don't care if you have one foot, no feet, or three feet. I want to spend more time with you. Don't think you have to hide anything from me."

My resolve to keep my distance until the third date melted, and I sank into his arms.

Chapter 8

March 2016

"You can't leave me," Tara said. She stood in the doorway to my room, watching me scribble illegible labels on boxes of clothes. "For one thing, you won't be able to raid Eric's closet when you need something to wear."

Her last-ditch effort to get me to change my mind about moving in with my boyfriend came as no surprise. Our entire adult lives, lovers had come and gone, but neither of us had ever lived with anyone else. Tara was the closest thing to a sister I'd ever had—and I couldn't quite convince her that she wasn't losing me.

For the hundredth time, I reminded myself that Tara's worries were rooted in love for me, not anything against my boyfriend. After the move, we'd keep hanging out, and she'd see that everything was better than ever. Plus, she got to double her closet space.

"Between the two of us, I think Eric and I can afford our own clothes." I hugged her. "But don't worry, I'll come back once in a while to make sure someone is watering the plants."

"You're not taking your plants? No way. Deal's off. You have to stay."

The doorbell rang.

"Would you please let Eric in while I finish up in here?"

"Do I have to? Can't the prince open the door himself?"

"Probably, but I never gave him a key. You didn't want me to, remember?"

She stuck her tongue out at me before disappearing. "Fine."

A moment later, Eric appeared in the doorway, holding a tray of Styrofoam cups. "Good morning, beautiful."

"Hey, handsome. What'd you bring me?"

"Well, Tara commandeered the caramel latte and the jelly doughnut, but I can offer you this churro and an espresso."

My favorites, both of them. Churros from the bakery down the street weren't as good as the ones Mamá used to make, but I loved them. "Thanks for bringing her coffee, too."

"No problem. I will kill her with kindness. Someday she'll realize she adores me."

As he walked toward me, Hermione rose from her spot at the end of my bed, stretched, and hissed at him. Then, tail held high, she leaped onto the floor and trotted out of the room. "And her little cat, too."

"Hermione is just cranky because I'm leaving and you didn't bring her anything."

"Says who? There's catnip in my pocket."

Our lips met. "Thank you. Tara will come around eventually. She's not thrilled that she has to find another roommate. Plus, she's worried I'm going to sell, and she doesn't want to move."

"Are you thinking about selling?"

My complete inability to believe my good luck at finding a guy like Eric completely overruled any financial benefits from selling the house. I wanted a place to return if the fairy tale bubble burst. But there was no reason to tell him that.

"Maybe, but not in this market. She doesn't have anything to worry about until the value of the house increases a bit. At that point, I'd probably give her first shot at buying it."

"That's smart," he said, nodding in approval. "I was worried you were throwing money away because she's your friend."

I sipped my espresso, watching a bird fly outside the window. Time for a subject change. "Tara will come around. She's worried things are moving too fast. When she realizes that you both love me and want what's best for me, she'll thaw out."

"Glad to hear it. I'd hate to have to make you choose." I chuckled, but he gulped his coffee and set the cup on the windowsill. "Let's get moving."

He grabbed a box of books and started down the hall. For a moment, I wanted to call him back. Would my boyfriend make me choose between him and my best friend of twenty years? The friend who stood by me when I lost everything? I loved Eric, but that would be such a short conversation, and he wouldn't like how it ended. He must've been joking.

A couple of hours later, we arrived at Eric's apartment—our apartment. We worked quickly, unloading my clothes, breakables, and other personal items I didn't want to trust to the movers. To minimize my walking, my boyfriend offered to circle the block and find parking while Tara and I carried the last load of stuff up in the elevator.

When I was halfway up the stairs leading to the upper part of the loft, my phone vibrated, clattering against the kitchen counter. No one ever called instead of texting, but maybe it was Eric. I turned to go back down so I could answer the call.

The box in my arms caught against the railing, and I stumbled. Everything tilted. I swore under my breath, struggling not to drop my antique jewelry box—and all of its contents—through the gaps in the iron steps. Leaning forward, I set the box on the railing and huffed, trying to get my arms under it.

"Tara! Help!"

Feet pattered against the marble tile. "What's wrong?"

"Phone's ringing in the kitchen. Grab it? It could be Eric."

"No problem." Her feet moved away, echoing across the floor.

Sweat trickled down my back. The day was unseasonably warm, and the humidity made my lungs ache. I prayed for rain. My clammy hands slipped on the box. Resting my chin on the top, I wiped one hand, then the other, on my yoga pants. The box teetered. I took a deep breath, shoved my arms under the box, and yanked upward with all my strength. The motion brought my back against the other railing, but at least I was upright.

A minute later, the box thudded onto the parquet floors of the loft. I swiped a lock of hair off my forehead and headed back down the stairs.

"Was it him?"

Tara shushed me, still holding the phone. A shrill female voice emanated from the device. I strained, but I couldn't make out the words.

Before I could move closer, a voice rang out behind me. "Honey, I'm home!" Eric appeared in the doorway. When he spotted Tara, the smile slid off his face. "Why's she on my phone?"

"Hold on a sec." Tara put one hand over the device and held it out. "Eric, I thought this was Anna's phone, but it's some woman saying you hit her car or something? I'm sorry."

Thunder clouded Eric's face. "Never, ever touch my phone." He grabbed it so fast, she winced. Into the phone, he said, "I told you never to call me again. We're done."

The phone slammed onto the counter. Tara and I gaped at him.

"I'm sorry," I said. "I thought it was my—"

"Riiiiiight. Tara can't tell your iPhone from my Android?"

His attitude made no sense. Who was on the phone?

"Eric, why is some woman calling you asking for money?" Tara asked.

"Don't worry about my business." To me, he said, "You don't need to touch my phone, either."

His words slapped me in the face. "The phone was ringing. I asked—"

"She can speak for herself, right?"

Fuming, I glanced at Tara, who had smoke coming out of her ears.

"Look, Eric," she said, "I'm sorry. The phone

rang, I ran to catch it before it rolled to voice mail. It didn't even register that it wasn't Anna's phone. It won't happen again."

"You're overreacting," I said. "Why don't we finish unloading, order some sushi, and open a bottle of wine? I want to enjoy our first night together in our new home."

Eric glanced from me to Tara, and the anger drained from him as quickly as if he'd flipped a switch. "You're right. I'm sorry, Tara. It's just that this woman's crazy. She's been hounding me for months. We went out for a few weeks, ages ago. Then she met someone else—I didn't even think we were exclusive, so it was no big deal. Anyway, I guess someone vandalized her car or something after it ended, and she swears I did it. I can't get her to go away, and I refuse to pay her off. The thought that her lies got to you made me a little crazy."

"You poor thing. I'm so sorry." I wrapped my arms around his waist, and he rested his chin on the top of my head. "I'd never believe you vandalized some girl's car because she broke up with you. That's outrageous."

Tara said nothing for a minute before pulling out her phone. I could tell she wasn't all that comfortable with Eric's explanation. "It's later than I thought, so I can help you unpack your closet real quick if you want, but then I gotta go."

The two of us returned to work quietly, unloading the suitcases with my work clothes into one of the walk-in closets attached to the upstairs loft. Below, Eric took my mother's china to the kitchen to get set up. Before long, he came upstairs to shower, and I walked Tara to the door.

"I don't trust him," Tara whispered, with a glance at the stairway. "Way too weird about his phone. He's hiding something."

"He's fine," I insisted. "Moving is stressful, parking in New York City is stressful, and it's a hot day. Stay, go out to dinner with us, and you'll see that everything's fine."

"Can't. I've got a date. Next week, let's hang out, okay? I need a pedicure."

"Absolutely. Let's do Saturday at three." I hugged Tara, and she headed off down the hall. After she left, I remembered Tara hated pedicures. She never wore open-toed shoes. Whenever I got one, she said I was wasting money. Was she trying to impress someone, or did she intentionally choose an activity where I couldn't invite Eric?

The issues brewing beneath the surface came to a head on my thirty-second birthday.

Since the house had more space and many of my friends still lived in Jersey, Eric begrudgingly agreed to let Tara host the fiesta. Besides, she knew all my favorite recipes.

We arrived to find the party in full swing: Music filled the living room, people packed the dance area, and a gorgeous array on the buffet table filled the room with the tantalizing aromas of fried food, cumin, and chili powder.

Eric seemed quieter than usual, sipping his drinks, picking at his food. But it was nearly an hour into the party before he finally told me what was on his mind.

"That explains everything." He nodded toward Tara, sharing a kiss with her date over by the buffet table. "Why didn't you tell me?"

"Tell you what?"

He replied with a phrase that would've made Mamá scrub my mouth out with soap.

In my mind's eye, for just a second, my drink drenched him from head to toe. But I resisted, although the slur made me wince. "One, because that's an extremely offensive term, two, it's none of your business." With effort, I kept my voice steady. "Tara's bisexual. What does that explain?"

"Why she hates me so much. Tara's in love with you!"

I choked on my empanada. "How much did you drink?"

"I'm not drunk. I see the way she looks at you, and I know she hates us together. I can't help thinking it's because she wishes she were the one sleeping next to you."

"That's completely ridiculous. And lower your voice," I hissed.

"What do I have to be quiet about?" Eric turned and gestured to the room, sloshing liquid onto the wooden floors. "Everyone knows she hates me. Maybe they're wondering why, too."

I grabbed his arm and pulled him toward the corner. "It's not about her. You're embarrassing me. Tara's not in love with me. We're practically sisters. What is wrong with you?"

"Fine, whatever. But look, babe, you're either for us or against us. Tara's against us. I don't know why, but she's not your friend. If she were, she'd want what's best for you."

"You think you know what's best for me?" Words crashed onto the floor like falling icicles. "Tara. Is. My. Best. Friend. I've known her for twenty years. She——"

"People grow and change. Maybe you've out-grown each other."

"You need to sober up before you say something we're both going to regret. Go get some water. Eat a roll or something. Splash some water on your face. Then maybe you'll still have a girlfriend when you get back."

After a moment, he stumbled off in the direction of the kitchen. I had zero interest in following him. My blood boiling, I spun around to find my best friend.

"Everything okay?" Tara appeared at my elbow the moment he vanished, as if she'd been waiting for him to leave the room.

"Not really. I'm so sorry. I had no idea he couldn't hold his liquor—or what he would turn into when he overdid it. This isn't the Eric I fell in love with." This also wasn't an Eric I wanted to spend any time with in the future.

"Some people are mean drunks. Hopefully he doesn't get shit-faced often."

"He drinks, but never this much. We order wine with dinner or a drink at the club, but I've never seen him so trashed."

"Just keep an eye on him. If things get worse, you call me. Don't let Eric turn you into my mother." Tara's father had spent most of our childhood in and out of prison on petty theft and domestic violence charges before Mrs. Fisher eventually divorced him, and a judge forced him to get sober by ordering a nice, long stint in Sing-Sing after he moved on up to mugging people in Central Park.

I smiled at her. "Thanks. I'll be careful."

"You better. If he hurts you, I'll kill him, and I don't know enough about the law yet to get myself off." She sipped her drink.

"I'm sorry, Tara. He's never been like this. Something must be going on. I'll take him home." I glanced toward the kitchen. "What's taking him so long?"

"Maybe he went to the bathroom?"

"I guess." I twirled a lock of hair around one finger. "What got into him?"

She sipped her wine. "It's fine. I don't like him; he doesn't like me. I don't need to be best friends with everyone you date. Maybe he's threatened because we're so close? I'm sure when you've been together longer, and he sees that I'm not trying to come between you, he'll be fine. Meanwhile, I'll drown my loneliness in wine, empanadas, and our favorite *Telemundo* shows. Sitting in my empty house. Without you." Her lower lip extended in an exaggerated pout. Her loud sniffle made me laugh and hug her.

"Uh-huh. You'll just sit alone and devour all of my favorite things?" Her head moved up and down emphatically. "You're not trying to tempt me into staying?"

Back and forth, her hair swished with her movement. "I would never do such a thing!"

"As Mamá used to say, *ni tu memo te lo creen*," I said. "Not even you believe what you're saying. You'll continue having a vibrant social life, and we'll talk every day. We'll hang out when we want, and he can deal with it."

"Deal with what?" Eric draped one arm across my shoulders. His hot breath stunk of whiskey. "Ready to go, babe? I called for the town car while I was waiting for the bathroom."

As much as I didn't want to go anywhere with Eric at that moment, someone needed to make sure he got home okay. Besides, the things I needed to say to him would be much better said in private. Confronting him here would make everything worse.

"Sure, we'll go." My eyes begged Tara to forgive me for having to leave my own party early. "I'll call you tomorrow? We should hang out next week. Thank you so much for everything."

She hugged me. "You're welcome. I love you. Happy birthday."

As soon as our driver pulled away from the curb, Eric started giggling hysterically.

"Are you okay?"

"Yeah, I'm great. But someone else isn't going to be." His face turned nearly purple with badly contained mirth.

I had no idea what he found amusing. "What are you talking about?"

Laughter punctuated his response. "Tara...hot sauce... toilet...OMG, it's going to be epic!"

"Whoa. Hold on." I couldn't have heard him correctly over the street noise. I forced him to meet my eyes. When he realized I wasn't laughing, he calmed slightly. "Wait. Eric, stop. Start over. You did what?"

"When you were saying good-bye, I took a bunch of hot sauce packets from the kitchen and put them under the toilet seat in her bathroom. When she sits down, Tara's in for a big surprise." His chuckle morphed into such full laughs, I wondered if he might fall off the seat. Or if I might push him.

Horrified, I scrambled in my phone for my bag. "Eric, that's not funny. You can't do that."

"C'mon. People do stuff like that all the time. It's a prank. Pranks are funny. We used to do it in college. She'll think it's hilarious."

"She will not find it hilarious that you ruined her three-hundred-dollar pants." My fingers closed around the smooth surface of my phone, but Eric swatted at my bag. Everything tumbled to the floor.

I swore, then leaned forward and banged on the partition separating us from the driver. "Stop the car. I'm getting out."

"What? No!" Suddenly, Eric didn't find the situation so amusing. The car slowed, and he grabbed my hands. "I'm so sorry, babe. I got upset because she doesn't support our relationship. You understand, right? If she doesn't like me, then she might convince you not to like me, and then I'll lose you. I don't want to lose you. I'm sorry about the hot sauce. It seemed funny at the time. I drank way too much."

The car halted. In the back of my mind, I wondered if he was stalling so she'd use the bathroom before I managed to warn her. I scooped my bag off the floor of the car and opened the door.

"It's fine, Eric. I forgot my sweater. I'm going to get it. Go home and sleep it off. I'll be there soon."

Ignoring his protests, I climbed out of the car and directed the driver to continue to our address. As the sedan pulled away, Eric's head poked out of the window. "I love you, babe!!!!"

I didn't respond. I'd never seen him drunk in the several months we'd been together. Had he just been on his best behavior? What if he usually got trashed at parties? Was this how he behaved when he was drunk? How had I not known this before we moved in together? Because this guy was not the Eric I knew and loved. With a sigh, I texted Tara to tell her what happened, then turned around and walked back to the house. Better to sleep on the couch for one night than share a bed with an angry drunk.

The next morning, I awoke to sunlight streaming in the window, Hermione curled up next to my head, and a ringing doorbell. After months of living with Eric, it took me a minute to figure out why I was lying on my old couch. The doorbell rang again, the notes repeating over and over.

Grumbling about needing time to put myself together, I used the couch to get to a standing position, then hopped to the front door, one hand along the wall.

A wall of red and white flowers filled the doorway. Only the hands wrapped around the vase warned me of a person on the other side.

"Hello?"

The flowers shifted, and a clipboard appeared. A moment later, a head poked through the massive bouquet. "I've got a delivery here for Ann-a Guerra."

"Ahn-A," I corrected. "That's me."

"Uh-huh. Whatever." He thrust the clipboard at me. "Sign here."

With an apologetic smile, I gestured at the air

beneath my left calf. "I'm sorry. Would you mind carrying them inside for me?"

The delivery man flushed. "Sure thing." He took the clipboard back and I led the way to the living room, where he set the flowers on the table. "Someone sure is sorry."

At least three dozen fire and ice roses—my favorite—mixed in with some baby's breath, sitting in a crystal vase. The envelope on the front said, "I'm an ass."

A smile crossed my face. "Yeah. Well, he should be."

"Good for you. Give him hell." The driver chuckled while I signed my name and returned the clipboard. I waited for him to leave before sinking on the couch to read the inside of the card.

I'm so sorry about last night. I don't know why I drank so much. I never want to wake up alone again. Please forgive me.

Forever Yours,

Eric

For a long time, I sat on the couch, thinking. Remembering the Eric that rode up nineteen extra floors to talk to me when we met. Thinking about the sweet, funny guy who made me laugh and anticipated my every need. The Eric I loved. Then I considered the sloppy drunk, the guy who insulted my friends and embarrassed me in public. Versus the guy who sent me flowers.

I still hadn't reached a decision when my phone rang. Hesitantly, I accepted the call and lifted the device to my ear, without saying anything.

"Anna? You there?"

I let out a breath. "I'm here. I just don't know what to say."

"Don't say anything. I'm so sorry about last night. In college, I had a drinking problem, and I swore I'd never touch hard liquor again. I don't know what came over me. I wanted us to enjoy your special night, but I ruined everything."

Words continued to escape me, so I waited.

"I've been drinking a lot, not letting you see. I've gotten pretty good at hiding when I'm drunk, usually. But last night, I lost it. That was the last straw." He took a deep breath. "My dad pulled some strings, and I'm checking into a treatment facility for a couple of weeks. I love you, and I miss you, and I hope you'll be here when I get back."

"No more drinking?" For the first time since the party, I started to feel hopeful.

"None. I don't like who I am when I get like this."

"I don't, either. He's not someone I want to be with."

"You know I would never soberly hurt you, Anna. I need you. Please come home."

The pleading in his voice tugged at my heartstrings. He seemed so contrite, and I believed he would control himself in the future. Before the party, everything was wonderful. He just made a mistake, probably because he was nervous to be around so many of my friends all at once. A mistake he was taking steps to fix.

"I love you, too," I said. "I'm going to have breakfast with Tara, but I'll see you in a couple of hours."

"Thank you. We can work through this."

Chapter 1

September 2016

The day before our one-year anniversary, Eric dropped by my office. Since he usually texted or emailed, I was surprised when I looked up from my quarterly expense reports to find him standing in the doorway.

"To what do I owe this pleasure?" I asked with a smile. "Do you want to go get coffee?"

"No, I can't stay long. I was in the neighborhood, so I thought I'd stop in." He moved around my desk to kiss the corner of my mouth. "As you may or may not be aware, tomorrow is a special day."

"You're kidding! Is it National Pancake Day already?"

A low chuckle usually reserved for in the bedroom gave me goosebumps. "So close! I made reservations for dinner tomorrow night. We're going somewhere swanky."

"Somewhere 'swanky,' huh? The good IHOP?"

"Ha! No, a real restaurant with cloth napkins and an hour wait for your food and everything. We're both so busy, we're two ships passing in the night."

A pang hit me. Over the past few months, I'd been working toward a huge promotion. Eric spent three weeks "in Europe finding himself" (translation: getting treatment) before pouring a hundred hours a week into a new job. Our weekly dinners out had turned into grabbing eggs together Saturday mornings before I went to work. I tried to remember the last time we'd had sex and drew a blank.

"I know, and I'm sorry. I keep hoping once I get this promotion and your company takes off—"

"Actually, I have some news about that. It's one of the things I wanted to talk to you about tomorrow."

"One of the things?" Unbidden, a picture of a diamond ring swam before my eyes. To be specific, it was the picture of the platinum, two-carat, square-cut diamond ring I'd bookmarked six months ago, "accidentally" marked in a catalog and left sitting on the coffee table three weeks before my birthday. The ring sold by a jewelry store not two blocks from my office.

I'd gotten an espresso maker. The fancy kind that costs nearly as much as a ring, but alas, no proposal came with it. It made delicious lattes, though.

I shoved those thoughts aside, realizing Eric still waited for me to answer. "I already cleared my entire schedule for tomorrow evening. My calendar has a big 'Do Not Disturb' from four o'clock until Wednesday morning. I wanted to be sure we get some quality time together."

The smile that split his face in two made me glad I'd made the effort. "Sounds great. I can't wait. I'll be working late tonight, so I may crash at the office, but I'll absolutely be home tomorrow by six so we can go to dinner."

"Then I'm doubly glad you dropped by. Have a good night."

"You, too. I love you." He kissed me again briefly, then headed for the door.

A new email dropped into my inbox, and I resumed work mode. My fingers typed out a response before Eric disappeared from the doorway.

Without any thought on my part, the email signoff read, "Mrs. Eric Rutherford."

Shaking my head, I deleted the line. That probably wasn't even what he wanted to talk about. Last time Eric got all excited about a "big surprise," it was getting on the list for a Tesla.

Enough stalling. Back to work.

The next day, I managed to tear myself out of the office by four-twenty-three p.m. Being less than half an hour late was a bit of a record for me. I hailed a cab, hoping to make it to our loft before Eric realized I'd gotten held up.

When I arrived at home, the place was empty, quiet. My takeout containers from last night's midnight dinner still sat on the counter. The hall light I never remembered to turn off on my way out shone brightly in the waning afternoon light. He hadn't even been home yet. I rushed to get ready before the car arrived, making it to the lobby of our building at five minutes until six.

The doorman whistled.

Dropping a slight curtsy, I beamed at him. "Thank you."

I did look pretty killer, if I said so myself. After all, if we were about to post engagement photos on Facebook, I needed to bring my A-game. My red and white silk dress hugged all my curves in the right places before the skirt trumpeted out, skimming the ground. I wore a simple gold hoop necklace and matching earrings—nothing to compete with the ring, once I got it. Styling my hair had never been my strong suit, but I'd managed to tame some of the natural frizz and pull it back out of my face.

"Going somewhere special tonight?"

At that moment, a black town car pulled up outside, and Eric stepped out of the back. I flashed a giant smile on my way out the door. "It's our one-year anniversary."

"Well, happy anniversary!"

Eric waved at him over my shoulder. "Thanks, Raul! Have a good night!"

"You, too, Eric. Have a good night, Anna."

"Oh, we will."

The doorman caught my eye and winked.

I couldn't contain my excitement on the way to the restaurant, but Eric ignored the questions I pelted him with: Where we were going? What was his big surprise? Was it bigger than a breadbox? He seemed tense, probably nervous about proposing. I wondered if I should give him hints that I planned to say yes.

We could have a long engagement, right? To get us through this rocky patch, get our careers on firmer footing. It would be nice to be able to take time off for a honeymoon. I fell into silence and let my thoughts occupy me as the car navigated the busy streets.

Fifteen minutes later, we pulled up in front of one of those super trendy, incredibly upscale restaurants that no one ever mentioned was essentially Olive Garden-quality food at five times the price. Half the trendy restaurant industry in New York City was a food version of "The Emperor's New Clothes." As soon as someone realized the Emperor was naked, the place vanished, to be replaced by another one days later. This particular unnecessary establishment was called "Sunflower."

Still, seeing and being seen in the right places was important to Eric, so I didn't say anything as a waiter wearing a neon-yellow unitard led us to a table and left a bowl of sunflower seeds instead of bread. I pictured someone buttering a tiny seed and hid a giggle behind my menu.

My boyfriend fidgeted from the moment we sat down. His hand shook so hard, he slopped water all over his bread plate, or sunflower seed plate, as it were. He bit into a seed and somehow sent a shell shooting out of his mouth onto the table.

"Sorry," he said, flushing.

"Are you okay?"

"Yeah. Long day. Sorry."

I played along, assuming he'd tell me what was going on in his own time, but our conversation felt disjointed.

When I asked what he had planned for the following day and he said, "Mother is fine, thanks," I'd had enough.

I snapped my fingers. "Earth to Eric. Can you even hear me?"

He blinked, shook his head, and sipped his wine. "I'm sorry, Anna. I've just got something on my mind."

"I can see that." Across the table, I gave him a smile I hoped was open and encouraging. "You can tell me anything. Just say whatever it is."

"Okay, I'm sorry. This is a good thing." Eric leaned forward and grasped my hands. I smiled up at him. "There's something I need to tell you. You know I love you, right?"

"Of course. I love you, too."

"And you know I want us to be together."

A fluttering hit my heart, but it was accompanied by a sinking sensation in my belly. Somehow, this moment didn't feel like the beginning of the rest of my life. "We haven't really talked about the future, but yes, that was the impression I got. Things seem to be moving in the right direction."

His eyes caught mine, and I knew with one hundred percent certainty that the next words out of his mouth weren't going to be a proposal.

"I'm moving to Tegucigalpa."

"Gesundheit."

"No, it's the capital of Honduras. I'm moving to Honduras. In two weeks."

A sunflower seed caught in my throat. I

coughed until Eric came helpfully around the table to pound on my back. Sipping my water, I blinked repeatedly. No words came to mind. Several long seconds after setting the glass back on the table, I realized my mouth hung open. When I was a kid and got flustered, Spanish and English ran together in my head. I hadn't been that gobsmacked in ages.

"*Lo siento,* I must have misheard you. *¿Que? ¿Por que?* Ummm… what?"

He reached for me across the table, but my hands went to my face instead. They felt like giant, five-fingered ice cubes.

When he finally spoke, the words tumbled out of his mouth. "Now, listen, I'm not saying I want to break up or anything, because I don't. But the new company went belly-up, and I don't have a job anymore."

"What?"

"That's why I've been working so many hours —trying to keep everything afloat. I know I should've told you sooner, but I kept hoping we wouldn't fail. Anyway, my dad won't release my trust fund until I show him I'm giving back to the less fortunate. I've got my regular allowance, but that's it. I don't get the rest until I'm forty, not unless I can convince Dad to give it to me. And if I can't, he'll cut me off."

I nodded, trying to process the words as they

hit me. "I'm sorry, Eric. But you don't have to leave the country. My salary is en—"

"You don't understand. I'm talking about forty million dollars."

My mouth dropped. I'd known Eric came from money, but we never talked about the specifics. Wow.

He said, "I'm signing up to do a stint with Habitat for Humanity. They build houses in Central America for people who need them."

"Do you want me to go with you? Have someone by your side who's fluent in Spanish? I can take a leave—"

"No. I need to go alone. I should only be gone for a few months. You can stay in the apartment—it's all paid for, and I wouldn't let it go when I'm only away for a couple of months. This doesn't have to change our relationship. I'll be back before you know it."

So many words, all at once. I understood the meaning of each individually, but when I put them together, nothing made any sense. I thrust my chair away from the table. Eric stood, too, but I waved him into his seat. "I'm going for some air. You stay here. Order a bottle of wine. I'll be back in a few minutes."

Outside, I paced in the frigid air, too thrown by his revelation to even grab a coat. Inside the door, the maitre d' fidgeted as if he couldn't decide whether to call a cab, find my coat, or check to see if the Latina runner paid for her meal.

Finally, a coherent thought rose to the surface. *I don't have to decide anything right away. I can keep working on my promotion, and I'll barely notice he's gone. We're talking about forty million dollars for a few months apart.*

My spirits lightened considerably. Maybe some time was exactly what we both needed to decide what each of us wanted from this relationship. I'd get my raise and my promotion and when he came back, he'd have a new lease on life. We could create a plan for the future together.

* * *

THREE WEEKS LATER, Eric's voice against my ear painted vivid pictures. I remembered the feel of his flesh against mine as I traced my nipples with my fingers. The phone sat cradled between my ear and shoulder. I panted, imagining him caressing me, kissing me. One hand clutched the vibrator between my legs so hard the plastic might leave imprints on my fingers.

"Oh, God, Eric. That feels sooooooooo gooo-ahhhhhh." A moan cut off my word as I climbed the peak higher and higher. "I'm riding up and down on your cock. One hand squeezes my breasts as the other slips between my legs, touching the spot where our bodies meet."

I clicked a button, and the intensity of the vibrations increased. I moaned, my hips pulsating frantically back and forth as I imagined Eric's cock inside me.

"Anna. Oh, Anna. You feel so warm, so wet. So tight. Oh, God."

The button clicked again, and the vibrations increased to the point where my eyes rolled back in my head. I rode the crest, savoring the journey toward what promised to be a spectacular orgasm.

"I'm gonna come so hard."

My response came in pants. "Me. Too. Oh. My. God."

An electric shock hit my nether regions. No, not the good kind. A literal electric shock. My moan of pleasure turned to a shriek in a heartbeat. My entire body jerked about three feet, and the vibrator slid out of my grip. As I jumped off the bed, the phone slipped from my shoulder and clattered onto the ground.

"What the fuck?"

The pain shooting through my lower limbs made it difficult to process what happened. The pleasant hum of my vibrator had stopped, yet I hadn't turned it off. Hadn't planned on turning it off for about ten minutes or three orgasms. Long-distance dating was hard. The smooth plastic device lay on the bedspread, smoking. I yanked the cord, and the plug shot out of the wall, smacking onto the phone.

"Fuck fuck fuck fuck?"

From the floor, a tiny voice emanated from my phone. "Anna? Are you okay? What's wrong?"

I plucked the phone off the ground. "My vibrator just attacked me."

"What do you mean?"

"It's dead. Went out in a blaze of glory, shocking me as it went. Holy fuck that hurts."

"Oh, shit. You forgot to change the batteries?"

"No, I got the one that plugs into the wall before you left. I think we wore the motor out."

"I'm so sorry, sweetheart." After a moment, he chuckled. "I guess it wasn't designed for three months of extensive use, huh?"

"Apparently not. Stupid cheap electronics."

I threw the danged contraption. It bounced off the wall, sent the lamp crashing to the floor, then landed on top of it with a decidedly unsatisfying thud.

"Are you okay?"

"Fine," I grumbled. "But I'm afraid I'm not going to be able to finish our lovely fantasy. Hope I didn't ruin things for you."

On the dresser, I spotted the King Dong vibrator Tara presented me with as a joke at Eric's going away party. The damn thing was bigger than my entire torso. With a sigh, I sat up and threw my legs over the bed, then headed toward the kitchen.

"I'll be fine. You don't have anything else near to *hand*?"

I snickered while scouring for anything to relieve the new and different fire between my legs. Somehow, I didn't think this was what the romance novels meant when they talked about "burning loins." I grabbed a bag of peas and stuffed it between my legs before waddling toward my desk.

"*Lo siento, Amorcito*. The electric shock to my clit kind of killed the mood. Plus, there's now a bag of frozen vegetables between my legs." I lowered my voice as I sat at my computer. "But, I've got something for you, if you're still, um, well, standing at attention."

"Oh, yeah? What's that?"

My fingers clicked the mouse to bring up a surprise I'd created for him a few days earlier. A photographer came to the apartment, set everything up. The first photographs were tastefully done, a preview. The second set was…less so. But I wanted to remind my boyfriend what he was missing while he was gone.

"Anna? Are you there?"

"Yup. Just looking. Give me one minute." I flipped through the pictures again before attaching a few of the shots. In one, my face shone bright red and I'd had to peep through my fingers at the camera. In another, I peeked up from under the sheets. The lens picked up a bottle of wine on the nightstand. I called it "Preparation." It only took a minute to create an email with the subject **"PRIVATE AND CONFIDENTIAL"** and hit "send."

"There's a surprise coming at you."

Chapter 2

June 2017

"A few months" passed, but Eric didn't return.

At first, things were fine. The loft was lonely without him, but Tara had a late class on Friday nights, so she'd come over after. We ate cookie dough and talked until the sun came up, like when we were in college. Video chat was spotty due to unreliable internet, but Eric and I agreed to a weekly phone call—most of which avoided disastrous results. Long emails flew back and forth across the equator. Work filled my days, dreams of the future filled the nights.

When I got my promotion, Tara and I celebrated at the site of Sunflower. As expected, that ridiculous restaurant had closed and been replaced by a spot that specialized in savory cupcakes. We got super dirty looks for calling them "meat pies". The two of us were having a blast, but I missed Eric.

Finally, finally, his stint in Honduras came to an end. Eric emailed me pictures of the completed work, which looked great. He'd met a lot of people from different walks of life down there, and he did seem more mature when we talked. Maybe Mr. Rutherford had been onto something, insisting Eric help the less fortunate.

I greedily anticipated the email bringing me a date and time to meet my boyfriend at the airport. Then he could find a new job, and we could start our future.

To: Anna

From: Eric

Date: June 3, 2017, 11:17 p.m.

Dear Anna,

Sorry I couldn't call, but things are crazy here. We finished the houses in Honduras, and one of the guys heard about a similar project in Argentina. I'm at an internet café now, hoping I can manage to send this message.

I think I'm going to go, Ahn. I'm sorry I'm not coming home yet, but it's only another three months. Cell phone coverage will be spotty, but I'll send you the number for the house where we'll be staying. I'll hit up a better internet café as soon as

I can to see if I can get Skype to load so I can see your beautiful face.

Meanwhile, we can send letters! How romantic is that?

Love,

Eric

Tears of disappointment and frustration blurred the last lines of the email. Nine months was a long time to stay with an absentee boyfriend. Another three would be excruciating. Nights without Eric were lonely.

The lack of human contact was starting to get to me. Old, familiar depression I thought I'd beaten lurked around the edges of my mind. Some days, only the promise he'd be home soon gave me the strength I needed to get out of bed. Sure, we were three-quarters of the way to the end of his trip, but… With a sigh, I cut off the thought, forcing myself to repeat the first words over and over. *We're three-quarters of the way there. Only three months left. We'll be together soon.*

Another, more traitorous voice spoke up. The voice that haunted me late at night. *If he loved you, wouldn't he come home now? It's all a lie. No one will ever love you.*

I shoved the thought away. Eric loved me, I knew he did. This was the best relationship I'd ever had, hands down. Sure, it sucked that we had to be apart, but it wasn't forever. My doubts here were stemming from so much time apart, without even a weekend together. Maybe I should take some time off work, fly down to surprise him.

Images of all the things I'd planned for the summer passed before my eyes. New York City stuff I hadn't done since college. Things I'd enjoyed at the time, but would be more fun with a partner. Shakespeare in the Park. Picnics. Watching the ducks, which was never the same. I couldn't lecture myself on the dangers of feeding them bread. Going to see the shows. Coney Island. Dumb tourist stuff I'd had years to do but never gotten around to, like meeting at the top of the Empire State Building or going to see the Statue of Liberty and holding hands while walking up the staircase. I didn't even know if the last one was still possible. I'd missed my chance by never finding a relation—

WE'RE ALMOST THERE! Mentally, I shouted down the little voice in my head and forced my attention away from the images of me, alone in the city. *WE'LL BE TOGETHER SOON.*

My eyes fluttered shut. Breathe in. *We're three-quarters of the way there.* Breathe out. *We'll be together before long.*

The mantra sustained me for several agonizing moments. When I opened my eyes, things looked brighter.

Finally, I forced my fingers to type out words

significantly more upbeat than the emotions swirling in my chest.

To: Eric

From: Anna

Date: June 4, 2017, 7:03 p.m.

Another three months? Guess I better buy a new vibrator. Or not. I'm still a little gun shy. I do like the idea of letters, though. Very Victorian. I can't wait to tell my friends. "Forsooth! My beau hath sent me a letter from yonder, where he toils in earth all day to create new hope for the poor and the hopeless. Bless his Christian soul, and I will pray daily until the day comes that we meet again!" *hand to forehead* *letter to bosom* *swoon*

:-P

Amor y besos,

Me

P.S. I went to our spot today to see the ducks, but it just wasn't the same without you. Hurry home, or there won't be anyone at the pond to stop the tourists from feeding them.

My eyes traced the words over and over until I started to believe everything would be okay. It didn't take long for a new message to appear in my inbox.

To: Anna

From: Eric

Date: June 4, 2017, 7:05 p.m.

Glad to see you're taking things so well. Why on earth did you go into business instead of creative writing?

His words made me smile. Together, we could get through this. Our love could survive a bit of time apart. All we needed was to keep in contact, and then he'd be home in another three months.

To: Eric

From: Anna

Date: June 12, 2017 4:23 p.m.

Well, I started out preparing press releases and marketing copy. Those basically are creative writing, right?

THE LIGHT TONE of the messages finally lifted my mood. I reminded myself for at least the five hundreth time that Eric hadn't exactly abandoned me to go out drinking and hiring hookers. He was living in a third-world country, without his expensive aftershave and fancy loft and stainless steel appliances that practically prepared the food for us, no driver or expense account. He'd gone out in the world, helping provide houses to people who made less in a year than he made in a single day. Or used to make, before he left.

To: Anna

From: Eric

Date: June 21, 2017, 6:32 a.m.

Touché. I'll call as soon as I can. I miss you, and I swear I'll be home by Labor Day. Off to make the donuts!—er, build the houses, I suppose.

The reminder of the old commercial made me smile. It also reminded me of the fun, witty guy I fell in love with. When Eric returned, everything would be like he'd never left.

Chapter 3

More hours of daylight and the end of our fiscal year meant things slowed significantly at work over the summer. Or at least, they slowed enough that twelve-hour days became a waste of time instead of a necessity. Designers worked hard on the winter line, making them less available for meetings. Several members of the board traveled, leaving me to helm a half-empty ship. Instead of eighty-hour weeks helping me pretend I wouldn't be going home to an empty apartment, I found myself looking for reasons to stay past five o'clock.

The summer dragged at first, but by the beginning of July, Tara made a list of ridiculous things to do in New York City and we attacked it with a vengeance. On the weekends, we ate at overpriced tourist traps, explored every inch of Central Park, and learned the ins and outs of every museum in the city. We watched movies Eric would've hated while speaking only Spanish.

At the end of August, Tara's boss scored an executive suite at a Mets game. She insisted I go to the game, joking that the trip would "prove the existence of the elusive Mets fan."

Whatever I was expecting from a place called the "Sterling Level" at a ballpark this wasn't it. When we entered the room, my jaw dropped. For one thing, you couldn't even see the field from half the room. Big screen televisions around the room displayed the game in case anyone in the suite turned out to be a baseball fan. No idea why real fans wouldn't want to sit in the actual stadium.

"Hey, look! It's just like being at home," I said. "Why would anyone pay thousands of dollars to come to the ballpark if they can't even see the game?"

"This is nothing like watching the game at home," Tara said, "unless you're planning to hire a private chef and bring me champagne on trays between innings."

A waiter appeared at her elbow as if her words summoned him. I accepted a glass and wandered around the room, thinking about how much Eric loved the Mets. He would've adored being here with me.

When I passed the wall separating the bar from the rest of the suit and found the windows, I gasped. *This* was why people paid for the box; I practically stood on the diamond.

"It's beautiful, isn't it?"

A guy about my age gazed out at the field where the players warmed up. He wore an expensive suit and a battered old Mets cap. The hat had seen a *lot* of better days.

"This entire suite is fantastic. I'm so glad I came."

He turned and flashed a dimple at me. "Don't tell me you thought about passing up this opportunity. Because I might have to stop talking to you, and you're already more interesting than my dad's friend who dragged me here."

I took in his curly dark hair, manicured nails, and silk tie. "You're here on business?"

"Sort of. I'm Jason Epstein. Jay." His grip was warm, smooth. "My accountant invited me here. I work for Li'l Tots Corp."

I raised an eyebrow. "Oh really? I'm Anna Guerra. I work for——"

"Toddler Cloths, Inc.," we said in unison.

He laughed, and I sipped my champagne. "You've heard of me?"

"Everyone knows who you are. You're one of

the fastest-rising executives in history. I can't believe you're here, in front of me. What are you doing with an accounting firm?"

A glance at his ring finger told me Jay was single. I nodded across the room, where Tara stood talking to a pretty redhead wearing a camera around her neck. This wasn't the first time she'd thrown me in the path of a good-looking, eligible man since Eric left. She hated him. Even more, she hated the idea of me sitting around, waiting for his return.

I raised my glass to my best friend, who at least had the good grace to blush before turning back to her companion. "My roommate brought me. Tara's going to law school at night, but she's an accountant, too."

"Remind me to send her a thank-you letter. I'd love to pick your brain sometime."

The way Jay looked at me sent a little thrill through me, but I shook the feeling away. I had a boyfriend, who I loved with all my heart. Who would be returning from Argentina any day.

Or so I kept telling myself.

FINALLY, finally, finally, the tourists started to leave, students went back to school, and the calendar changed from August to September. Eric's return was so soon, I could taste it.

Until I got the email.

To: Anna

From: Eric

Date: September 9, 2017, 11:39 p.m.

Anna,

I'm having the most amazing time in Argentina: the people, the history, the culture! Some complications arose with the build, but things are finally starting to flow more smoothly. Sorry for the delays. A bunch of us are going to Easter Island when things wrap up here. Thinking about cruising down to Antarctica after that. This has been the most amazing year for me! The one thing missing is you.

Love,

Eric

For several long minutes, I stared at the screen, blinking rapidly. My boyfriend apparently moved to South America and didn't mention it. I was starting to wonder if his newfound humanitarianism was the basis of an expensive and elaborate break-up: He'd stay away until I moved out of his loft, then return and go about his usual life.

He'd been gone so long, the thought of re-entering the dating world upset me more than a future without Eric. The saddest thing about breaking up was having to pack and move all my stuff. How depressing.

What happened to our relationship? We were so happy in the beginning.

I sighed and clicked the reply button.

To: Eric
From: Anna
Date: September 9, 2017, 11:48 p.m.
Eric,
What the hell, man?

SIGH. Delete, delete, delete. I started over.

Dear Eric,

Are you ever coming back? It's fine, either way, but I'd like to know if I still have a boyfriend. To be honest, more and more, I think this relationship has run its course, and we're both too cowardly to say it. I love you, but I didn't sign up for long-distance. I've been waiting a long time for you to return, but if you're determined to explore the world, perhaps you'd enjoy it more as a single, free man. No hard feelings. Let me know.

Anna

A little better, at least. This was stupid. Emails came sporadically. The village with the Internet cafe was miles from the camp. It might be October before I found out if I still had a boyfriend.

So, I was surprised when my inbox informed

me of a new message almost immediately. Maybe he cared at least enough to wait for my response to finding out my boyfriend may not ever return to America.

To: Anna

From: Eric

Date: September 9, 2017, 11:49 p.m.

Hey baby,

I know I've been gone too long, and I'm so, so sorry. I'm coming home soon. I'm doing good work here. Watching these houses evolve out of nothing, seeing the looks on peoples' faces when we give them a home—don't tell him I said this, but Dad was right. This trip has changed my life. I'm a better man.

I'd never have left if we weren't strong enough to survive the time apart. Please, give me a few more weeks, and I'll make it up to you when I get home.

All my love,

Eric

MY HEART SWELLED at the words, followed immediately by a wave of guilt. Who was I to put my needs ahead of the less fortunate? My parents met while my father was working with Doctors Without Borders; I was the last person in the world to begrudge Eric the chance to help other people. Especially since he came from extreme privilege. He did important work, and he was working to improve himself. I shouldn't give him a hard time. Quickly, I tapped out a reply, hoping he'd read it before signing off for the night.

TO: Eric

From: Anna

Date: September 9, 2017, 11:52 p.m.

I'm so sorry, babe. None of this was your idea. I'm frustrated, and I miss you. It's selfish to think of myself when you're working to make the world a better place. We'll be fine.

I'm putting in long hours but I love the projects and the clients and everything we're working on right now. I even like the thrill of putting out fires when problems crop up. I've been eyeballing another promotion, but I may have an opportunity with another children's clothing company. I met one of the executives—Jason something or other?—last week, and his company may have an open position that's perfect for me. It would be a huge coup. The move to a company with room to advance seems like a logical next step. We're going to set up a meeting soon to talk more.

Glad things are going so well for you below the equator. I'll make an effort to get out more when I'm not working, and you'll be back before I know it. (This is me, putting on a brave face. Do you like it?)

By the way, some girl named Tina called for you twice. Keeps demanding money—Is this the same chick who swears you wrecked her car? She apparently doesn't know you're gone, so I didn't want to tell her. You should email her.

Amor y besos,
Me

I WAITED a couple of minutes to see if he was still online before going to bed. The message arrived before I'd decided what show to stream until I fell asleep.

To: Anna
From: Eric
Date: September 9, 2017, 11:55 p.m.
Anna,
Your brave face is beautiful. The trust is still paying for everything, right? No problems there?

Never heard of Jay "SomethingOrOther." It's not quite as distinguished a last name as "Rutherford." Either way, I bet your resume will sweep him off his feet. He'll be throwing money at you by the end of the week. Knock 'em dead.

Don't worry about Tina. She's nuts. You're

free to tell her I left the country, and I'm not coming back (but I am, I swear it).

THE LAST LINE made me chuckle. If nothing else, Eric always said the right things. How much longer would I able to put up with pretty words instead of a flesh and blood boyfriend and some human contact?

To: Eric
From: Anna
Date: September 9, 2017, 11:57 p.m.
Thanks. :-)
It feels weird living here while your trust pays for everything. Can you talk to the trustee about at least depositing the checks I've been writing for utilities and cable? Taking your dad's money so I can watch the Devils games in HD doesn't make any sense.

Amor y besos,
Me

THE NEXT DAY, I received his reply.

To: Anna
From: Eric
Date: September 10, 2017, 1:58 p.m.
Ahn,
Take the money. Give what you would've

spent to any charity you like. It's my loft, and I'm the one who stuck you there, then vanished. (Plus, my dad hates me paying for a Manhattan loft I'm not living in instead of selling it.) Take Tara to see the Devils - I hear they need your money.

- E

Ugh. The only thing I disliked more than accepting charity was Eric's father, who still thought I was nothing but a gold digger. The email hit on the one way to guarantee I'd accept his gift with a smile.

To: Eric

From: Anna

Date: September 10, 2017, 2:00 p.m.

:-) The Equus Foundation thanks you for your generosity.

I STARED at my inbox for a few minutes after hitting send, willing his name to appear one more time. No reply. He must've signed off. As much as I loved our exchanges, they were no substitute for the real Eric, here, in person, talking to me, holding me, kissing me. I tried to remember the last time we'd spoken on the phone. Spring, probably but I wouldn't let myself scroll through the call history on my phone to verify the date. Communication had been scarce since he left for Argentina.

"One more time," I said aloud to no one. I clicked the "check mail" button. Once, twice, seventeen times for good measure. Nothing, nothing, nothing.

As I reached out to alt-tab to another program, the (1) appeared next to my inbox, and my heart skipped a beat.

It wasn't him.

TO: Anna Guerra

From: Jason Epstein

Date: September 9, 2017, 3:23 p.m.

Dear Ms. Guerra,

It was a pleasure to meet you at the Mets game last week. I especially enjoyed hearing about your plans to expand your company. Our Chief Financial Officer is retiring soon. One of the junior executives is being promoted, but that still leaves an opening. I'd love to get someone with your big ideas and zest for life into his spot, with an eye toward moving up in the next five years or so.

If you're not opposed, I would be honored to take you out to dinner to discuss the possibilities. Are you free tomorrow night at seven? My secretary made reservations at La Chèvre last spring, but my appointment canceled at the last minute, and I'd hate to have to go to the hottest new restaurant in Manhattan all by myself.

Sincerely Yours,

Jay

My eyes skittered across the email before I went back and forced myself to read slowly. My zest for life? What he'd seen was a combination of the free champagne and talking to a man who spent more time picking my brain than looking at my breasts. While we chatted, I'd gotten a much-needed break from thinking about my absentee boyfriend.

On the other hand, another night out could be what I needed to take my mind off things. Tara's fall course schedule didn't give her nearly as much time to hang out with me as over the summer. Most of my other friends were really Eric's friends; seeing them without him made me sad. I'd avoided most of them for the past few months, and they weren't calling much anymore. No big loss, because to be honest, they weren't people I'd have ever chosen to hang out with on my own.

A business dinner at La Chèvre? The place had a six-month waiting list for reservations. The tone of the message seemed friendly. Too friendly? This didn't sound like a business dinner. But maybe I was reading too much into it.

You love fried goat cheese, Anna, and there's a six-

month wait for a table. This is a no brainer. Besides, it's a job interview, not a date.

Was it? I remembered the glint in Jay's brown eyes when we met, the flash of dimple. The heat sweeping through my body when he "accidentally" brushed my fingertips while handing me a glass of champagne. Eric had been gone so long, and he might not be coming back.

Finally, I shook myself out of my indecision: the job opportunity intrigued me. This guy was friendly, and I could use a friend at the moment. No reason to make it more than it was.

TO: Jay
From: Anna
Date: September 10, 2017, 3:28 p.m.
Dear Jay,
Meeting you last week was a breath of fresh air. I'd be delighted to have dinner with you tomorrow night. I have some ideas, and I think you'll be impressed with what I bring to the table. From what I've seen so far, I would very much enjoy working under you.
Best,
Anna

Too friendly? Too forward? Eric's face swam before my eyes. With a frown, I shoved the image aside. Eric was off in South America, doing God knows what with God knows who. Surely, there was no harm in engaging in a little harmless banter, as long as I didn't cross the line. My brow furrowed. After a moment, I deleted the last sentence. Better to keep the tone friendly, without the sexual undertones. Then I took a deep breath and hit "send."

Part III

Life seems sometimes like nothing more than a series of losses, from beginning to end. That's the given. How you respond to those losses, what you make of what's left, that's the part you have to make up as you go.

- Katherine Weber, *The Music Lesson*

Chapter 9

December 2018

White light. Scratchy linens against the backs of my legs. The unmistakable scent of disinfectant filling my nose and mouth. No, something else in my mouth. Rubber. A steady beeping filled my ears. My throat burned. My stomach felt like a thousand elephants tap-danced on it.

Hospital.

Why? How?

The previous days came rushing back. The sex, the drugs, the drinking. Jay, visiting me at the hotel. Washing painkillers down with alcohol. What happened? I couldn't even kill myself properly. This misery would never end. A moan escaped me, muffled by whatever they'd put in my mouth and throat.

Movement in the doorway caught my eye. A flash of white fabric, then a nurse stood in the doorway.

"Oh, you poor thing."

I went to wipe my eyes, but something pulled my hand back. Tubes, tape. Right. Hospital bed. With all these wires and crap, they'd essentially tied me to the damn thing.

The nurse tsked. A tissue touched my nose, and I blew. "Good girl."

Something cool and soft touched my forehead. It felt amazing. I wanted to sink into that cloth, close my eyes, and never wake up.

"Anna?" Her voice was soft, soothing.

My eyes flew open. She pronounced it wrong, but I couldn't correct her in my current state. First things first. Wordlessly, I nodded.

"Anna, sweetheart, you were brought in unconscious. Do you remember what happened?" With each word out of her mouth, I missed my mother more.

I did remember what happened, though. Oh, God. I did. I wished I didn't. I nodded.

"I'm going to remove your ventilator so you can speak. Give me just a second." A moment later, she handed me a glass of water, which I sipped before she took it back.

"How…? What am I doing here?" Pain seared my throat with every word, like swallowing glass.

"One of the employees at your hotel found you. They arrived with your room service tray, and no one answered the door. For some reason, they went inside instead of leaving the tray."

"They're not supposed to leave it…my foot… can't carry while using my canes. I tip them to put on the desk. Door not bolted."

"Well, you're lucky it wasn't. They opened the door, found shattered glass everywhere, and spotted you lying on the carpet in the living room. One of them called 911. You're lucky the young woman who found you knew CPR."

Lucky. Some people would call it that. The word sounded completely alien to me. If I were lucky, I wouldn't be in this mess in the first place.

When I didn't say anything, she continued. With her voice, she should record audiobooks of nursery rhymes. "We found bruising to your upper thighs. Semen on your clothes and legs. Lacerations on labia. Anna, were you raped?"

"No. I've been violated, but only in the metaphoric sense."

Her brow furrowed. "What do you mean?"

"My ex posted nude pictures of me online. He said I have rape fantasies. A total violation. My entire life is ruined. Every day it gets worse. But no rape."

Why was I talking like this? What drugs had they given me? Blarg. Side effect: Oversharing in the extreme. Words bubbled forth, punctuated with humorless laughs. The nurse listened, head tilted to one side. She allowed me to sip the water again.

"Thank you," I said. "But the actual sex? Was consensual. Sex was supposed to make me feel something. And it did: it made me feel like trash."

When I finally halted my motor mouth, the nurse squeezed my hand. "That's awful, dear."

I dissolved into sobs. The nurse wrapped her arms around me. I sank into her baby powder scent and generous bosom, wishing I could get lost forever. She held me, and I cried.

When I stopped, she handed me a tissue and stepped back. "This isn't the first time something like this happened, is it?"

"The revenge porn?"

"No. What I mean is, you have a history of depression?"

My first instinct kicked in: denial. "No, not really. I don't even think I'm depressed now—I'm just going through a horrible time. Everything completely sucks. It's normal to be upset when someone ruins your life."

She frowned. "Depression is nothing to be ashamed of. The first step to recovery is—"

"I know," I said, "but, I mean…My ex posted nude pictures of me online the same day a hurricane left me homeless. My boyfriend broke up with me. I got fired. Anyone would be down in my shoes."

"You're right," she said. "But not everyone would try to kill themselves. I've seen your medical records—not everyone tried to kill themselves when they were thirteen, either."

I swallowed, avoiding her eyes. "It was an accident."

"Both times?"

My fingers twisted in my lap. There was nothing to say to that. My mother hadn't believed my hand slipped while shaving my legs. Mamá sat on the toilet while I bathed for three months after I was released from the hospital. This nurse didn't believe I accidentally used a bottle of whiskey to wash down a bottle of pain pills. I wondered how long they'd keep me locked up this time.

All I wanted was for my life to go back to normal, but I had no normal life to return to. A couple of weeks in "recovery" might do me some good. Maybe I could ask them to lock the door, throw away the key, and let me stay forever.

"Your record shows you've been prescribed anti-depressants in the past. Have you been taking them?"

"Not since I was a kid. I took them for a while after…the incident. Then I felt better, so I stopped. That's it."

"It doesn't always work that way. While you're here, you should talk to—"

"Go away. Leave me alone." I leaned back and shut my eyes. "I didn't try to kill myself. I had a headache. Everything in life sucks, and I just wanted to make the pain go away. But it never does. All it does is keep getting worse. Anti-depressants won't fix my life."

"Medication may not be able to stop bad things from happening, dear," she said. "But it may help you feel less overwhelmed. You may see some options you're missing right now."

I ignored her.

A shuffling and a couple of squeaks told me someone else—or possibly multiple someones— entered the room. Fingers grasped my elbow. Something cool touched my forearm. A pinch shook me out of my despair for a heartbeat. Then coolness filled my veins. Beautiful, white light shone inside me. Peace.

As I sank into blissful unconsciousness, one clear thought rose to the jumbled service of my mind. *Quiero a mi mami.* If only Mamá were alive to help me. If only I could go to see her.

EVENTUALLY I BLINKED AWAKE, with no idea

how much time had passed. It took a moment for things to come into focus enough to remember I lay in a hospital bed. Blinds prevented light from coming through the single window, so I might've been out a couple of hours or several days. It didn't matter. I had nowhere to go when I left the hospital, nothing to do.

No one to call.

No boyfriend, no job, no family or friends in town, no hope.

A voice jolted me out of my ongoing downward spiral. "ANNA! You're awake!"

The black and burgundy hair and patchouli scent belonging to Tara engulfed me. For a long moment, I breathed in her closeness. Something in my heart shifted. My best friend was a beacon, forcing back the sadness, chasing away the dark cloud threatening to overwhelm me. For the first time, I felt deeply how badly I'd missed her.

She straightened, and a palm collided with the side of my head.

"Ow! What was that for?"

"'What was that for?' she asks," Tara said, as if narrating to a third-party. "Like it's totally normal for my best friend to try to kill herself while I'm out of town. Like it's cool that she failed to mention everything she was going through. Anna, you didn't even tell me what Eric did! Here am I, thinking things are more or less fine, and you're slowly sinking into a pit of despair. I can't believe you didn't call or text me."

"I didn't want you to worry about me when you're supposed to be taking care of your mom. You didn't take a year off from law school to deal with my problems."

"Oh, of course! She didn't want to worry me, so she just lands herself in the hospital again." When she looked up at the ceiling, I wondered if these comments were directed at Mamá. "You scared me to death, you idiot. What the hell were you thinking?"

"I wasn't trying to kill myself, not consciously. I just wanted it all to go away."

"I'm so sorry I wasn't here for you." Tara's face softened for a moment. When mine crumpled, she glared at me and whacked the side of my head a second time. This time it smarted a little. "What total bullshit. You forget, I've heard that line before. When you want to get away from it all, you book a cruise to the Bahamas. You don't swallow a cocktail made with painkillers or slit your wrists. Do you ever stop to think about anyone other than yourself?"

Her lips trembled. Tara used sarcasm and biting commentary to hide her emotions. If she started to cry in front of me, I wouldn't be able to bear it. To distract myself, and her, I pressed the button to raise my bed into a seated position.

A nurse entered to take my blood pressure and drop off a cup of water. I sat in silence through her ministrations, grateful for a moment with my thoughts. Tara pulled out her phone, waiting. The moment the nurse left with a promise to bring dinner soon, she launched into another tirade.

"You don't call, you don't write, you don't answer your phone or texts. You just vanish off the face of the earth. Your Facebook and Twitter are gone—"

"I told you I changed my number." I broke in.

"Oh, she changed her number, did she?" Tara threw her hands up the air, directing her words at the wall over my head. Then she started pacing. "Great! That totally makes up for the fact that your phone was off every time I tried the new number. Especially since the house is destroyed, and we can't actually live there anymore."

To the average observer, my best friend sounded horribly selfish, but I knew she used anger and sarcasm to mask how scared she must've been when she found out what happened to me. "You were in Oklah—"

"Right. It's impossible to communicate with someone across the country here in 1846. I guess the Pony Express message you sent me crossed paths with my carriage somewhere on the Oregon Trail. Also, Mom's in Indiana."

The corners of my mouth tilted upward a fraction. "I'm sorry. I didn't want to worry you. I couldn't talk to anyone. I thought it would be better to just fade away."

"You're an idiot." Tara finally met my eyes. "You scared the crap out of me. I would be utterly lost without you." She perched on the side of the bed and squeezed my hand. "If you ever try that bullshit again, I'll kill you myself."

"I know. I'm sorry."

"When I think I could've done something if I'd been here for you—"

"Don't ever think that," I told her. "None of this is your fault. It's Eric's fault, every bit of it."

"Fucker. I always hated that guy. Glad he finally gave me a reason." I chuckled for the first time in weeks. My heart finally lifted, a tiny bit. "Are you ready to talk about what happened?"

The entire story tumbled out. Not just the pictures, but the billboards, the police response, the guy at the club. Halfway through, Tara started pacing the tiny room again. She punctuated my story with the occasional growl or curse muttered under her breath, but didn't interrupt until I finished.

"And then you got here," I said. "How did you get here? Who called you?"

"I'm still your emergency contact, doofus. The hospital has a magical telephone. It apparently reaches all the way from New York to Indiana, unlike yours. They called me when you were brought in."

"Did I mention how sorry I am? *Lo siento, mi cielo? Te necesito?*"

"Don't talk to me like that. It's impossible to be mad at you when you Spanish me, and I intend to stay mad forever." She tugged a lock of hair, twisting the burgundy tip between her fingers. "Hey, where's Jay?"

Dual pangs of sadness and irritation hit me. "We broke up. His father said that, as head legal counsel for a children's clothing company, he couldn't date someone with my 'tarnished reputation.' Not now, when we're trying to break into the Asian market. Well, they are. I've been given a very generous severance package to finance my time away."

"That bastard! Want me to kick him in the balls for you?"

"No, it's fine. I understand." Tara opened her mouth, and I raised one hand. "No, I'm not excusing his behavior. I don't understand how he could be such a weasely prick. What I understand is that, clearly, Jay's not the one for me. At least I know now and not in ten years when we've got three kids and a five-bedroom house in Connecticut to divide."

She nodded. "So you two can't come back from this?"

I held her gaze. Tara got nearly a perfect score on the LSATs. She didn't need me to tell her she was asking a stupid question.

"Sorry," she said.

"Besides, he's already seeing someone else," I mumbled.

"UGH! That bast—"

A discrete cough drew my attention to the doorway. The male police officer from Jay's apartment, whose name I'd never learned, stood in the doorway, hands in his pockets. I blinked repeatedly, wondering if the hospital accidentally gave me something to induce hallucinations. I couldn't think what on earth he'd be doing in my hospital room.

"Excuse me, ma'am," he said. "Is it all right if I come in?"

"Depends. Are you here to arrest me for the attempted murder of myself?"

Tara's eyes widened, and she poked me. "You can't talk to the police like that," she hissed.

The officer grinned and stepped into the room. "It's okay. Detective Stern isn't here. She's busy having something adjusted."

I smiled, and Tara's eyes swiveled back and forth between us. "I'm Tara, Anna's roommate. Also her lawyer, or I will be as soon as I pass the bar. Who are you?"

"Detective Sayid Egan. My partner and I got the call a few weeks ago when those billboards went up. My partner…uh…didn't make a good first impression on your friend here." I snorted, but he ignored me. "I promise, Anna's not in any trouble. The NYPD closed the book on the vandalism and prostitution charges, because there's no way to prove who put up the billboards."

Tara glanced between the two of us, and I nodded at her. "I don't mind talking to him for a few minutes. Besides, I know my rights."

"Interesting," she said. "Okay, I could really use a cup of coffee, so I'm headed to the cafeteria. Don't be afraid to refuse to answer any questions until I get back." Her raised eyebrows and the puckered lips she aimed at me over Detective Egan's shoulder left no question what she thought I should be doing while she was gone. My return expression tried to convey equal parts, "Are you crazy?" and "I'm in a hospital bed." Sure, the guy was hot, but this was neither the time nor the place to dwell on that.

As soon as the door closed behind her, I spoke. "Sorry for the rudeness. I've had a bad day."

"I can see that. Are you okay?"

A snort turned to a giggle turned to a sob. He handed me a tissue and waited while I got my breathing under control. I blotted my eyes. "I'm sorry. I don't even know how to answer that."

"I guess it was a pretty stupid question."

That was such an understatement, it didn't require a response. "What are you doing here?"

"The call came through on the radio: a woman in her early thirties, dark hair, brown skin, found unconscious in a hotel, possible suicide, prosthetic limb at the scene. I did the math and stopped by on a hunch."

So he was smart, too. Too bad he'd yet to see me at anything other than my lowest moments. In some other life, we could've been friends.

He continued, "When we met, you seemed so lost. Did I tell you I have a sister?"

I shook my head.

"Yeah, I do. A couple of years older than you. If something like this happened to her, I'd want her to know someone was looking out for her. I thought, all things considered, you could use someone on your side." He gestured toward the door. "Your roommate's taking good care of you, but if you need anything…And if that guy contacts you directly, the ex who posted the pictures, for any reason, I'll bring him in on stalking charges faster than he can say 'revenge porn.' I promise."

A ghost of a smile crossed my lips. "I appreciate the effort. You didn't have to come all the way down here."

"I wanted to. No matter how bad things seem, you're not alone. Nothing's worth taking your own life."

"Thanks, Detective."

"Please, call me Sayid."

He handed me his card for the second time since I'd met him, reminded me again to call if Eric bothered me, and vanished. This time, I didn't crumple the card up.

Three seconds after he left, Tara appeared in the door, sans coffee. She must've been waiting outside the whole time. "Are you going to tell me what that was all about?"

I filled her in on our original meeting. "He just feels bad because his partner was such a bitch. And he's got a sister."

"Ah, well. He's easy on the eyes. Glad he wasn't here to give you a hard time. So, what are you going to do next?"

"About the police?"

"About life."

"Oh, right." Duh. An obvious question, but one I couldn't answer. "What do you mean, 'do'? Two months ago, I was a high-powered career woman with a high six-figure income living in a beautiful three-bedroom house in Red Bank. I was one-half of Number Thirteen on Manhattan's Top Twenty Power Couples. Today, I'm single, alone, believed by many to be a prostitute and/or a porn star, unemployed, homeless, and lying in a hospital bed on suicide watch."

"Hey, it could be worse. You could be sharing a room with a Nickelback fan or some sixteen-year-old on starvation watch after she refused to eat for a week because Daddy bought her a red Maserati, but she wanted the black one. Possibly both."

I shuddered, giggling. "You may have a point."

"So, again, I ask: What are you going to do? There's nowhere to go but up. I need to go back to Indiana in a few days, but Mom's on the road to recovery. And you *will* keep in touch and I *will* figure out how to get a cell signal to text you at least once a day."

"They're going to keep me here for probably at least a week." I paused and took a deep breath, not really sure I'd made the decision until she asked about my plans. But there was something I needed to do. "After that, I was thinking about going away, actually—heading south."

Tara raised her eyebrows. "Oh, yeah? You think you're ready for that? You think ole Benito's ready for that?"

My heart pounded, reminding me that Tara knew me better than I knew myself. I hadn't seen my father since Mamá's funeral.

"I don't know, but it's time. He called me when this first happened and invited me to visit. I need to go home for Christmas."

Chapter 10

A few days after I woke up in the hospital, I voluntarily signed the documents to be transferred to an inpatient mental facility. Oddly enough, living in a place cut off from the world was incredibly peaceful: We had no internet, no cell phones, prescreened television, no porn. None of the patients had any idea who I was. If the doctors and nurses recognized me, no one let on.

There were beds too narrow to feel empty, blank walls, lots of time to think. I did what I was told. During meal times, I sat in the cafeteria and ate bland foods from a plastic tray. During rest times, I slept. I watched television with the other patients, played checkers during free time, and took medication when it was handed to me. They told me to report to therapy; I went. Not a single decision belonged to me. Although the old me would have been climbing the walls, furious to be so powerless, now I found the break from reality blissful. Part of me never wanted to return to the "real world" beyond the doors of the hospital.

Only my psychologist, Dr. Bracken, brought up the photographs in our sessions. Unfortunately, she didn't agree with my assessment that the best-case scenario was to stay in the facility until the internet ceased to exist. But I took the anti-depressants, went to therapy, and eventually started to remember the good things in my life. After a couple of weeks, when my progress led her to believe I wouldn't try to kill myself again, Dr. Bracken recommended I check out and go home.

After twenty-one days in the quiet of the hospitals, the bustle and noise of New York City's Christmas season nearly sent me tearing back inside to beg Dr. Bracken to reconsider. Or at least see if she'd double my prescriptions. I stood for a moment, breathing in and out, struggling to avoid a panic attack.

Finally, I hailed a cab and gave an address. The driver made a brief stop at the hotel where Tara was staying in my room to grab the stuff she'd packed for me. After all we'd been through in the past few weeks, I wanted to bring

Hermione, but she was very happy to see Tara again. I couldn't separate them.

After I snuggled the cat good-bye, Tara and I went straight to Penn Station. The thought of staying in the city another second made my skin crawl, but I couldn't stand the thought of flying, especially less than a week before Christmas.

Too many people filled the airports. Lots of web surfing, and too many tabloids, newspapers, or magazines had gleefully witnessed my downfall. Even though a couple of months had passed, and even with my new hair and sporting my glasses full-time, I wasn't up for sitting in an enclosed space where people could stare at me for several hours wondering why I looked familiar. I couldn't drive because I'd never replaced my car after the storm, and while I could rent one, I preferred not to be behind the wheel right now. Instead, I read the boards and booked a sleeper car on the first train headed south.

Miles melted away as the train chugged down the tracks. I should've called to tell my father I was coming. I knew he'd be happy to see me. But calling would cement my decision, which meant I had to go. Even once I bought the ticket, I still could change my mind, get right back on the next train home. Or maybe keep going—buy a ticket to Tallahassee after we pulled into Charlotte, or head west. A train ride across the Southern half of the country could be exactly what I needed to clear my head. I'd heard Christmas in Florida was a delightful way to chase away the winter blues.

In the end, I disembarked on the platform when the conductor called my stop. My feet carried me to the taxi stand, and my mouth gave the address before I could stop to think. My mind might not be sure about this, but my heart wanted to go home.

Mamá died when I was twenty-two, more than ten years ago. Everything happened so fast. One day, I boarded a plane to spend six months backpacking around Europe after graduating college before starting a job lined up in Charlotte. I didn't have a smartphone then, and I rarely took time out of my trip to check in, blaming the time change instead of my own selfishness. Next thing I knew, I arrived home to my solemn-faced father, an empty home, and the horrible knowledge that if I'd been here, I could've prevented her death.

This wasn't the usual survivor's guilt. My mother died of renal failure. I would've happily given her one of my kidneys in an instant if anyone had told me she needed it. They chose not to. The doctor made the diagnosis before I left, but my parents didn't want to ruin my trip. They kissed me good-bye at my graduation, Mamá hugged me tight, and I never saw her again.

Maybe they would've said something if I

called more. Or if I'd been in town, they might have eventually told me the truth. I could have seen her decline and forced them to let me help.

But I would never know what might have been. The power to save my mother's life had been taken out of my hands. Too upset to remain in the house where we'd all lived together, I packed a bag after the funeral, headed to Tara's apartment in New York City, and never looked back. Papá and I still talked, and he'd been to New York to see me, but I hadn't been able to bring myself to return to the house where Mamá lived at the end.

The time away made the trip home doubly terrifying, especially given the reason for my return.

When the taxi arrived at the address, the driver had to ask me twice if I planned to get out before the words registered. I trudged up the front walk, eyes glued to the pebbles leading up to the bright red door. My fingers gripped the railing for strength. The other hand hovered near the metal exterior door, as I debated whether to ring the bell or go on in. An instant later, the decision was made for me when the door swung open.

"Finally, you've come to your senses." Papá swept me up in a bear hug, obliterating my emotional barriers. "It's good to see you, Muñeca."

I wrapped my arms around him, buried my face in his blue cashmere sweater, and burst into tears.

A FEW HOURS LATER, I sat, still in my pajamas, watching some reality show marathon on television. My eyes focused on the show, but my brain ignored it, wondering instead how my life had gone from picture-perfect to an utter nightmare. I didn't have the first idea how to begin moving on. Running away didn't seem like the answer, but I couldn't see any other options.

When my father wandered into the room, I sat up to make space for him on the couch. He settled into the corner and stretched his arm around the back. I snuggled into him, like when I was a kid. The silence spoke volumes, covering years of apologies and platitudes and catching up and covering long-buried events. A catharsis fell over me.

The grandfather clock in the hallway ticked off several minutes before either of us made a sound.

"Did I ever tell you about the time your mother and I broke up for a while?"

That news brought me sitting up to look at him. "What are you talking about? You guys had a hard time after the accident." I swallowed, not wanting to directly bring up my first attempt to take my own life. "But you made it through."

"Not then. This was before you were born."

"That's impossible. You two had the perfect fairy tale romance, complete with Evil Queen." As a child, I must've heard the stories a zillion times, until I could recite my parents' history like I lived it myself.

He chuckled. "A lot of relationships seem perfect from the outside, but that's not always how it works, Muñeca. It was a long time ago, in 1974. My medical project in Peru was coming to an end, and Doctors Without Borders was sending me to Colombia. Your grandmother worked long hours, so your mother was raising her brothers and sisters. She couldn't go with me, and we were both so young…" He trailed off, lost for a moment in the memory.

I followed the direction of his gaze to the wedding picture on the mantel. *Benito y Soledad*, read the inscription on the frame. My father with the thick black 1970s mustache he'd been so proud of, long after the styles changed, his eyes caressing my mother. She wore the same love-struck expression in her dark eyes and full lips. As a child, I turned their features into a jigsaw puzzle, putting his rounded chin with her snub nose and adding his high cheekbones until my own face emerged.

Love radiated from the photograph. They'd both been so young. My father was still young.

"Do you ever think you'll remarry?" I asked.

His eyes glistened. "No. We all get one great love in this life, and mine is gone."

As much as I appreciated his devotion to my mother, part of what he said disturbed me. What if one love was all a person ever got, and I wasted my chances on men who didn't appreciate me?

"This isn't about me. I moved away; we exchanged letters for a few months. Mail came sporadically. I might wait weeks for a letter, then get three in one day, all sent separately.

"Life was hard. You wanted someone to share it with. I developed a friendship with another American volunteer. At the same time, your abuela was pushing Soledad to date a local man in the village. She wanted your mother to stay there, have babies, and take care of her family."

"No job? Mamá would've hated that life."

"So she did. But for her mamá, she tried. Soledad sent me a letter, breaking things off. She wanted to make peace with her family, to force herself to love the other man and stay in their village." He leaned forward, completely lost in the memory, and I shifted to the other end of the couch. "When I got her letter, I was so furious. My friends told me the best way to get even was to show everyone else in our area the pictures I had of her, tell everyone she cheated on me."

"No!" My eyes widened, and I scooted further down the couch. I couldn't believe my father would do something so heinous.

"I didn't do it." He reached for me, but I stayed put. "The point is, we were all so lucky back then and we didn't realize it. What if we'd had the internet when your mother broke up with me? If it had been so easy for her to text me naked pictures on a smartphone when we dated? What if I'd gotten a Dear John letter via email?

"Would I have let a friend talk me into it? Or would it have been easier to video chat with your mother, see her beautiful face every night before bed?" Papá shook his head. "I don't know. But I'm so sorry for what you're going through. At the end of the day, I never could allow myself to do something like that to someone I loved so much, even though she probably never would've known."

The words soothed me, and I eased back next to him. I still wasn't sure what the point of this story was, unless to tell me he understood why Eric did what he did. Personally, I didn't have a lot of empathy for that jackass.

"Things are so easy for your generation, with the internet. It also makes some things harder."

"I know. I always wondered how things

would've been after the accident if social media had existed. Maybe I'd have connected with other people in the same situation. Things might have been better. Or maybe online bullies would've made it all worse."

Papá smoothed my hair back and kissed my forehead. "I'm glad things weren't worse. You've always been strong. You've had to be. Life's thrown a lot of curveballs at you."

"Giving up when things get rough isn't strong." Neither was popping anti-depressants like candy, but Dr. Bracken had given me a three-month prescription. When I was thirteen, those pills had been the lifeline I needed to get me out of bed. At thirty-four, they gave me the strength to reach out to my father and ask for help. I wasn't nearly as strong as he thought.

"No, but slogging through it is. You've got a bit of sadness in you, always have. When things go bad, your brain tells you it's your fault. Always tries to make you think you deserve bad things. But you fight back. You fight and struggle every day to push the sadness back so it doesn't control you. When this is over, you'll be stronger than ever. Sometimes, you're so strong, you think you don't need your old man." He blinked away a tear at the corner of his eye, cleared his throat. "I'm so glad to see you, Muñeca. Sometimes the strongest thing you can do is let someone else take care of you."

Tears welled in my own eyes. "I missed you, Papá. I should have called more. But ever since Mamá, it's too hard."

"I understand. But Soledad had the sadness, too. I'd see it sometimes, a hint of a shadow, even when things were good. When she got sick, she didn't have the strength to fight both the illness and her depression. She struggled so much to be happy when she was younger, to stop people from seeing how she really felt. I was weak. I didn't want to see her suffer. So I let her end her pain." He pulled me closer for a moment. "I'm not weak anymore. I'm not about to let you go, too. We will fight this thing together, whatever it takes. I love you."

"I love you, too."

THE DAY after I arrived in North Carolina, Tara called. She started talking as soon as I answered the phone. "Have you been taking your medication?"

"Merry Christmas to you, too."

"Whatever. Happy Festivus. Are you taking your medication?"

"What are you, my mother?"

"I'm the person who's watching out for you because you're not taking care of yourself," she said.

"I don't need—"

"Yes, you do." The tone of her voice told me not to argue.

"Yes, *Mamá*," I teased, "I've been taking my pills. Every day. Papá is taking good care of me."

"Good girl," she said.

"Is that why you called? To nag me?"

"Of course not. The nagging is a bonus. Anyway, I've been doing some research."

"Yeah? You're spending your break working on exciting stuff like how to probate wills or when to get a prenuptial agreement?"

"Even more exciting stuff: When to file a police report after some entitled rich boy posts nudie pictures of you on the internet."

My pulse sped up. "Are you serious? I talked to the police, and Detective Bitch Face was unhelpful at best."

"You seem to be forgetting how extremely helpful Detective Hottie was when he appeared at your bedside to offer his services." I chuckled and shook my head at the nickname she'd given the officer.

"You're impossible. I can't even begin to think like that right now. He's all yours, Tara. Really."

"Nah. I like my men a little more androgynous. Anyway, you're right: New York's finest aren't likely to help you. Neither you nor Eric lived in New York when the pictures went up, and your permanent residence is still New Jersey. The billboards are vandalism, but that's not something the NYPD spends a lot of money investigating."

"Also, Detective Egan said the case was closed."

"You mean Detective Hottie?" she asked. "Anyway, I'm looking into whether you can file a civil action."

"Hold on a second. Is revenge porn illegal in New Jersey?"

"Yeah. It's actually a felony to make sex videos or take nude pictures of someone without their consent or secretly, where a person wouldn't expect to be videoed or photographed."

"Does it only apply if he used a hidden camera?"

"Nope. It's also a felony to distribute intimate pictures without the subject's consent, no matter who took them. He could be fined up to $30,000 per picture."

My hopes fell. "That's it? Thirty grand is chump change to Eric. It's not even two months of his salary. There are only a couple of pictures. That's not something to get excited about."

"It's a crime of the third degree—He could actually go to jail for three to five years."

"You think so? Come on, he's a rich white guy from a good family. He's more likely to get appointed to the Supreme Court than serve any time in jail."

"That's not why I'm excited," Tara's voice still carried a smile. "He intentionally interfered with your job. You can seek lost wages, past and future. You can also ask for punitive damages of up to $350,000. Then there's intentional infliction of emotional distress, which carries pain and suffering on top of your medical bills. New Jersey doesn't put a cap on that, so you can ask for whatever you want."

Five thousand pounds lifted off my shoulders. Eric had more money than God, he wouldn't care about being told to pay me. But the idea of a judge having the authority to punish him would stick in his craw. "That's amazing! Tara, you're a genius! I love you!"

"Yeah, I know. I love you, too. Merry Christmas."

Hope surged within me for the first time in weeks. I leaned back in my chair and put my feet up on the desk. Papá would flip if he walked in, but it didn't matter. "So what do we do?"

ON JANUARY 2, I started making calls. The first

lawyer told me I should be ashamed of myself for allowing nude pictures of myself into the world. As if the act of creating the pictures and sending them to my boyfriend mean I deserved to have them blasted on the internet. I called him a "close-minded, Puritan asshole" and hung up. When the second lawyer asked if I'd voluntarily posed for the pictures, I hung up on her, too. The third lawyer on my list was too busy to take on new clients; a fourth wanted a hundred-thousand-dollar retainer upfront. On and on it went. Call after call, no one would take my case.

I dialed an unfamiliar number for the twenty-third time, wondering if I should expect derision, amusement, or flat out disinterest.

"Meili Chang's Office. Meili speaking."

"Hi, Meili. My name is Anna. My ex posted nude pictures of me on the internet."

"Oh, my goodness! That's awful." Wonder mingled with horror in her voice. Not derision, not amusement, no hint of laughter.

Her response encouraged me. The entire story spilled out: the hurricane, the pictures, getting fired, and breaking up with Jay. Taking "happy" pills that made me do horribly uncharacteristic things. My suicide attempt. She didn't utter a word of judgment. Nothing but a few sounds of sympathy and "go on"s.

When I finished, she didn't speak for so long, I wondered if she'd hung up. Maybe I'd poured my soul out to an empty void. Fitting. I cursed myself for telling her too much, too soon.

Then Meili spoke, her voice hardened. "I've got two words for you, Anna: Punitive. Damages. We're going to make him pay. How did this happen? Tell me everything."

I went back to the beginning of our relationship. When I got to the part about how the pictures came into existence, I stumbled a bit. She didn't interrupt or cluck her tongue or blame me, so my voice grew stronger as I continued.

When I finished describing my first date with Jay, Meili remained silent on the other end of the phone for so long, I wondered if my phone had dropped the call.

"Oh, Anna," she said finally. "Is Eric aware of when you and Jay started dating?"

"I'm not sure. We exchanged some awkward emails about whether he was ever coming back and if we should continue our relationship. Eric said all the right things, but he wouldn't follow through on any of them. I got tired of feeling like the whole relationship was an illusion, and I was the only person dumb enough to think he was coming back."

"I can understand that. What did you do?"

"Our emails tapered off. I stopped initiating them, which made me realize that I'd been the first to send for several months. Then I met Jay, who seemed so sincere, funny—and present. I didn't want an online boyfriend anymore. A week later, I emailed Eric to tell him I moved out of our apartment. I said trying to maintain a relationship while he was thousands of miles away, with no phone and limited internet access, wasn't working. My feelings changed. He never replied."

"When was that?"

"About a year and a half ago. We'd been dating for two years, and we'd been apart for half that time. It wasn't working. He must've seen the email eventually, because he blocked me on Facebook sometime around last Christmas."

On the other end of the phone, clacking keys filled the silence. "Well, Facebook disabled your account after Eric hacked it, so I can't see your profile. Did you post a lot of pictures of you and Jay together? Did you update your relationship status?"

"No, I'm pretty careful about what I show the public. The executives of companies that make children's products have to be careful about our images. Junior executives even more than the seniors, if we want to get promoted. Parents won't buy sneakers or toys from a company with a bad reputation. My profile has always been locked down. Same with Jay. Eric must've seen the *Forbes* article. We didn't know about 'Manhattan's Top Twenty Power Couples' until the night before the magazine hit the newsstands."

More clacking suggesting Meili was searching for the article, too. "When was that?"

I thought for a minute. So much had happened, reviewing my past life seemed like watching a movie about alien invaders taking over the earth. "August. My copies of the magazine were in my apartment when the hurricane hit, but I can probably find the article online."

"No need. I've got it. Do you know when Eric returned to the States?"

"Not a clue. He didn't exactly ask me to pick him up at the airport. I'm just assuming, because he found the article. He might be back, but someone could've emailed it to him."

"I'll do some digging." Meili cleared her throat. "We've certainly got our work cut out for us. For one thing, it's going to be tough to prove Eric posted the pictures. I know you didn't send them to anyone else, but he hacked all of your accounts, so he can easily say the culprit must've stolen them from your sent mail folder or hacked your cloud."

"How can we prove he's lying? I can't swear it wasn't a hacker. But I highly doubt it. A run of the mill hacker has no reason to make everything so vicious."

"We'll work on getting proof. Meanwhile, keep a low profile. If Eric reaches out, don't talk to him without contacting me first. When can we meet?"

Chapter 11

Another week passed before I felt strong enough to meet Meili in person. She was visiting friends nearby for the weekend, and she agreed to detour to Charlotte so we could talk and sign the papers.

Papá drove me into the city to meet her at a popular restaurant. The suburbs were too small. I couldn't draw a breath without running into six people from high school. Since arriving in town, I hadn't ventured beyond the sanctuary of the backyard. As far as I was aware, none of the neighbors even knew Papá had a guest.

After I arrived, I paced the foyer, peeking out the windows from beneath a pink sparkly wig and over the top of giant sunglasses.

"You're trying too hard to hide," a voice behind me said. "'In places like this, a disguise makes you stand out. People will scrutinize you more than if you'd shown up as yourself."

My face flamed. "What do I do?"

"Take off the wig, wear normal sunglasses, and we'll head somewhere else. We'll put your back to the room, and no one will bother looking at little old me." She shook my hand in a warm, firm grip. "I'm Meili, by the way, and don't feel bad. That stunt would've worked in New York, London, or Paris. But here, you stick out like a sore thumb. Besides, a lot of people won't want to admit recognizing you from porn, so they won't say anything to you."

At five-feet-eight inches tall, with long, silky black hair, an expensive, tailored black suit, and an authoritative air, it seemed like a stretch to say "no one" would pay any attention to Meili. Although her website claimed she'd been admitted to the New York bar for twenty-five years, I spotted not a single wrinkle nor a trace of gray hair on her head. Somehow, I suspected the signs of aging were terrified to appear anywhere near this woman. No matter how old she was, Meili was a knockout. She could stop traffic without half trying. But if people looked at her, no one would pay attention to me, which was what I wanted.

As soon as I settled into the cracked vinyl booth at a coffee shop around the corner, Meili pulled a sheaf of papers from her briefcase and set it on the table. I had to lean forward to hear her over the clattering of dishes and hum of conversation filling the room.

"Let's start with the unpleasant stuff first," she said.

Inwardly, I chuckled. The legal terms of our agreement were hardly the 'unpleasant stuff' compared to everything else.

If Meili noticed my amusement, she ignored it. "I am your lawyer. It is my job to protect your legal interests at all times. You are in large part agreeing to trust my judgment on how to do that, but you do get a say in any tactical discussions, settlement negotiations, and exactly how much blood we want to draw."

Her brisk manner put me at ease. It had been a long time since I met someone who didn't treat me either like someone "tainted" or a victim.

She pointed at a spot on the contract. "This part says I have to keep anything you tell me in the strictest confidence. I'm not allowed to share your secrets with anyone else. That's going to include everything we talked about on the phone last week. Attorney-client privilege transcends death. I would go to jail before betraying you. Your secrets are safe with me."

I smiled wryly. "I think the whole world knows my 'secrets' at this point. But thank you."

"Secrets aren't just about your body. Privilege covers all of our conversations, which includes things like trial strategy. We'll get to that later." Meili flipped the page and pointed to a spot halfway down the page. "Here is where we talk money. Usually, I'd front the expenses, but this case is fairly risky, and trying to prove your ex posted the pictures could get expensive. So, in this case, you'll pay my expenses upfront. Things like filing fees, paying a private investigator, courier fees. I take my legal fee from the recovery—one-third if we settle, half if we go to trial."

I blanched. Half my money? After everything I'd suffered, she'd swoop in and walk away with half of it?

She paused for a minute, studying my expression. "It sounds like a ton of money—and with your damages, it is. But if we don't win, you pay me nothing except my expenses. I don't get a single penny for all the hours I put in on your behalf. This is a risk for me, too. That gives me an incentive to fight for you."

That sounded much better.

"Okay?" I nodded, and she said, "Great. If we end up having to appeal, I'll take sixty percent of the total award after costs. Oh, and you're paying for lunch."

"Not a problem." Working a hundred hours a week for more than ten years didn't lend itself to a lot of spending, so even living near New York City, I had plenty of money saved. "Do you need a retainer?"

"In this case, yes." She pulled a white square device out of her bag and plugged it into her phone. "I take all major credit cards. Five thousand upfront, due when you sign. I'll let you know if I need more. You get an accounting every month showing what I spent, and if we get lucky enough that I don't use some of it, you get it back at the end."

I took the pen she offered and handed over my credit card in one fluid motion, scribbling my name so fast, the illegible scrawl could've said anything.

Meili leaned forward and pressed her fingers together, her voice low. "Anna, I have to tell you: We might get ridiculously lucky."

Hope fluttered, but I pressed it down. "What do you mean?"

"Where does your ex live?"

"We met in New York, but Tara says his Facebook shows him living in Silicon Valley. I don't know when he got back to the U.S. or where he is now. Our last conversation was ages ago and essentially amounted to 'I'm moving out.'"

"Okay, thanks. That's good news: A couple of years ago, California passed a law making it a crime to post private pictures of another person online. If we can prove he did it from California, that might help."

"Yeah, Tara told me that, but I don't get money in a criminal case, do I?"

"You don't." She paused for effect. "But if he's found guilty in the criminal case, or if he takes a plea bargain, we can use the conviction against him in civil court. The biggest problem we're going to have is proving he posted the pictures. It will require a lot of legwork. We might need a private investigator, and we'll have to subpoena documents from the websites. They'll stall us. Some of the bigger sites are notorious for resisting providing any personal information about their users."

My heart plummeted. The tiny flutter of hope in my chest stopped. Meili squeezed my hand.

"Hey, I'm not saying this to discourage you. We'll work with what we have. The burden of proof in a civil case is much lower. It may be enough to show he had motive, opportunity, and access to the pictures."

"I can testify to that."

"I'd prefer not to have you testify about taking the pictures if we can avoid it. The jury still might look down on you. That's why a criminal conviction would help. We won't need any other evidence—the criminal records are conclusive, indisputable evidence that he knowingly and intentionally posted the pictures online. That makes the trial cheaper and easier, because we only need to prove your damages. Those should be obvious to any rational juror. You lost your job?"

I nodded. "I was making almost a quarter of a million dollars a year before bonuses. And I loved my job. I loved the meetings, choosing new products, seeing children out there wearing our clothes, everything. I helped start a program where a portion of the company's profits goes to fund scholarships for children from low-income families. There are so few women in management positions, especially women of color, that I felt like I gave young girls something to aspire to when they grow up. Ironic, huh?"

She nodded. "You'll be a role model again. Multiply two hundred fifty thousand dollars times the number of years it'll take this mess to blow over. Now triple it, because we want pain and suffering." Meili pulled out a calculator, tapped some buttons, and turned the display toward me.

80087355. Boobless.

I giggled.

"Sorry, you looked like you were going to cry." She tapped again, then showed me the display. My jaw dropped.

A smile nearly split her face in two. "That's the reaction I like to see from my clients. I'll type up a statement for you to give to the police and email it over to you by tomorrow afternoon. Meanwhile, keep a low profile for a few days."

"No problem. This is the first time I've left my father's house since I got home."

Listening to Meili rattle off ideas about strategy, tactics, and punitive damages lifted my spirits for the first time since I got the first message calling me a slut. The knot in my chest began to loosen. Maybe we wouldn't find what we needed to prove Eric posted the pictures, but at least we could call him into court. Someone needed to hold my ex-boyfriend accountable for his actions, and no one deserved the privilege more than I.

KEEPING a low profile was excruciatingly dull when I didn't feel safe even going online. The temptation to seek out things people said about me was too strong, and that road led to bad places. Better to leave the computer turned off and pass the time in other ways. Thankfully, I had a subscription to eBooks through the public library and Tara calling me a couple of times of day to check in. I'd have been climbing the walls without her.

When my phone rang, I sat on the couch watching reruns of *Beverly Hills, 90210* on the soap opera channel. American soap operas were no

Telemundo, but something about that garbage was so riveting, I almost didn't hear the call. I ran down the hall to grab the phone from the kitchen counter where I'd plugged it in earlier.

"Hey, Tara."

"Hey. I have a question for you."

"Shoot."

"Have you been on Facebook since all this happened?"

I shook my head, then shook it mentally at my folly. "Nope. I tried to log in the morning everything hit the fan, but my password had been changed. I reported it as hacked, but honestly, I don't know what happened."

"You should log in."

"Why don't you tell me what's going on? I don't want to see thousands of people calling me a whore." Although part of me wanted to wait for Tara to get around to telling me whatever she was getting to, I walked down the hall toward the computer. It took ages for the thing to boot, so if I started right away, it should be done by next Tuesday. I might have some information from Tara by then.

"No, it's not that." She cleared her throat. "Did you know Eric and I were Facebook friends?"

I chuckled. "You hated him. Why on earth would you be Facebook friends?"

"Years ago, when you first started dating, I sent him a friend request so I could invite him to your birthday party, remember?"

"Yeah, I remember he was there but didn't know you friended him." My dad had the oldest computer in the world. At this rate, I'd be forty before it finished booting. "I figured you grabbed his number out of my phone or something. Honestly, it's not something I spent a lot of time thinking about."

She laughed. "No, I used the power of social media. And I never un-friended him. He left the country, and I never log in, so I guess he forgot we're still 'friends,' just like I did. Until I went to visit his page."

My fingers clacked across the keys. A moment later, the log-in page appeared on the screen. "Okay, yeah, I'm logging in. Keep talking."

"I think you should see these posts with your own eyes."

"I really think if you don't tell me, I'm gonna put the phone down, drive to New Jersey, and strangle you."

"Anna, he admitted everything."

My jaw dropped so fast, I nearly dropped the phone. My pulse raced. "No! Are you serious? He can't be that stupid."

"Well, he's not. Not entirely. Members of the

general public can't see his page. But I can. Can you see it?"

"Hold on." The keys clicked together, and a moment later, the page finished loading. "That user does not exist. Let me try again."

"Don't bother. I'm sure he blocked you. I'm emailing you screenshots."

My right foot tapped impatiently on the floor while I waited. When the email arrived, I zoomed the mouse to open it so fast, I sent it shooting off the mousepad and across the desk. I cursed under my breath when it clattered onto the floor. Stupid computer. Who still had a desktop computer? A deep breath steadied my nerves, and I retrieved the device.

Eric Rutherford

Nov. 9, 2018 * Mountain View, CA

"Revenge is a dish best served cold." - William Shakespeare

"Tara, that's nothing. He could've been talking about anything. Or, hell, he could've actually been quoting Shakespeare."

"Let his lawyer make that argument, sweetie. I've got more screenshots. Made copies in case he realizes we're still connected and deletes the posts or blocks me. Check out the next one."

Eric Rutherford

Nov. 10, 2018 * Mountain View, CA

It's been a long time. Spending the evening

thinking about a certain someone on the east coast.

"He lived in New York for years. That post could be about anyone. I'm sure I'm not the certain someone he's thinking about."

"I'm sure you are," she said. "All you have to do is convince the jury that, read together, these posts suggest he was planning to do something to you right before the pictures went up. It can't be a coincidence. The jury's allowed to draw logical conclusions from the evidence presented to them."

That made sense. "Okay. But how do we prove he was talking about me? He's got thousands of friends and colleagues in New York City alone, not to mention the rest of the northeast."

"Keep reading."

Most of my hope had evaporated before Tara called, but a positive emotion started to rise in my gut. I nestled the phone between my ear and shoulder and scrolled down to the next image.

Eric Rutherford

Nov. 10, 2018 * Mountain View, CA

I hear there's quite a storm up in the northeast. Putting a lot of lights out. Someone's going to get a big surprise when she gets back on her feet...er... foot.

"Holy shit," I breathed. My pulse raced. "Are these real?"

Eric Rutherford

Nov. 10, 2018 * Mountain View, CA

Hehehehehehehehe. Pretty icy in some parts of New Jersey, huh?

I blinked furiously, in case it was all a dream. Then I pinched myself. The images remained. At the bottom of the messages, I noted the numbers next to the thumbs up and comment icons.

"Anna? Are you still there?"

"I'm here." A weight lifted from my shoulders. My back straightened, and something so foreign pulled on my face, it took a moment to recognize the smile. "Are there any replies to any of these messages? Any context?"

"A few friends posted asking what he's talking about," Tara said. "You can see he got a bunch of likes, probably half of them from people who just scroll through their phones and like whatever they see."

"He didn't give any explanations?"

"Nope. No response to the questions."

"It's not exactly a confession," I said. "But I need to call my lawyer. This could be exactly what we needed. I can't believe it, Tara, but we're going to win."

Chapter 12

After spending more than a decade in New York City, life in North Carolina moved at a slower pace than I remembered. I reveled in long, luxurious days reading and sipping sweet tea. Before long, I settled into a routine: walk in the morning with Papá, lunch somewhere quiet out of the way, read for a couple of hours, check in with Meili, stay offline, keep my head down until I needed to head back to New York for the trial. Severance pay appeared in my bank account every two weeks. I dreamed of another life where I might one day work again.

In June, Tara returned to the Tri-State Area permanently. I told the contractor to call her with any and all questions about the house. Her word was law. Anything went, as long as we didn't spend more than the insurance company gave me, and Tara didn't have extravagant tastes. I might wind up with a fitness pole in the living room, but I didn't have to worry she'd install marble floors throughout the house or get solid gold bathroom fixtures or anything like that.

One day near the end of summer, my phone rang while I was getting a pedicure. People thought it was weird, but I still wanted to make my five remaining toes pretty. Nothing beat a calf massage and twenty minutes in those chairs. Besides, trying to fill twenty-four hours a day when you couldn't go to work was boring. With an apology to the aesthetician, I reached to shut off my phone—but then Meili's name and number appeared in the display.

"Hi."

"Hey, Anna. I've got some bad news and some borderline hilarious news. Which do you want first?"

"Well, I could use a laugh these days, but it's better to rip off the Band-Aid. Give me the bad news first."

"Eric's lawyer filed a Motion to Dismiss the criminal charges pending in California, and the judge allowed it."

My chest heaved at this blow. The phone dropped into my lap. I leaned forward, biting back tears of frustration. The woman kneeling at my feet paused, foot file raised in a questioning gesture. I motioned with one hand for her to continue. "I'm fine. Sorry."

She motioned, asking if I wanted a glass of water, and I nodded. She vanished, and I forced myself to pick up the phone, where Meili was still talking.

"—as bad as it sounds, Anna."

"Wait. I'm sorry—hysterical deafness. What are you saying?"

"This sounds bad, but it doesn't totally kill our case. Yes, a criminal conviction would've been a slam dunk in a civil case. But the opposite isn't true, because the burden of proof is so much higher in criminal court. Remember O.J.?"

I'd been nine years old the day the world dropped everything to gape at a white SUV driving about four miles an hour around Los Angeles. In my youthful naivety, I'd been angry the chase pre-empted that night's episode of *Full House*, which would've been a re-run. "Yeah, I remember."

"Same idea. After the criminal jury acquitted him, a civil jury awarded the families of Nicole Brown and Ron Goldman thirty-three million dollars."

"You don't think—"

"Thirty-three million?" She snorted. "It would be nice, but no. We'll get to that in a minute. The dismissal is no big surprise. We don't have proof beyond a reasonable doubt that he posted the pictures while in California, which is what we'd need. The fact that he lives in New York makes that tough. So, this is bad news, but it's not shocking, and it's not a total setback. I wanted you to hear it from me."

I exhaled loudly, a sound of equal parts frustration and pain. The aesthetician looked up from massaging my left calf, but I shook my head at her and pointed at the phone. She continued.

"We could report him to the police in New York," Meili said, "but we have the same issue. He's got witnesses who would swear up and down that he was in Palo Alto the night of the hurricane, which is when the pictures went up."

"Can he really claim in one case that he was in California and another that he was in New York?"

"Not if he had taken the stand and testified, no. But he didn't—he got a dismissal. The judge didn't make any specific finding about where he lived on that date. Anyway, it's water under the bridge. I don't think filing criminal charges in another state would help our case, and you run the risk of him countersuing for malicious prosecution."

"Thanks."

"Eric is going to consider this a win, so stay off the internet for a few days."

"Ugh. Seriously?"

"Well, you never know. He might think this is a good time to re-post the photos. I'll be collecting them for evidence if he does."

I slumped in the chair, bringing one knee to my chest and willing myself not to start crying in the middle of a pedicure. Would this never end?

"The good news is, Eric doesn't have your new email address and phone number, right? Or your address?"

"No. Only you, my dad, and Tara. None of you are sharing. No one else even knows I'm in North Carolina."

"Excellent. That brings me to the hilarious news."

I'd forgotten she said funny news even existed. I pulled myself upright in the massage chair, sipped my water, and took a deep breath. "Hit me."

"We've got a settlement offer."

"That's not funny, that's good! It means we've got them scared, right?"

"Usually, yes. But the offer itself is ridiculous. So low, it's insulting. The only reason it's even re-motely good news is that Eric probably won't fire off another barrage of photos before we respond, and I can get an injunction against him first."

"Thanks. I don't think he knows where I am, but I'd also rather get an injunction before he finds out. The last thing I need is the storm to follow me here." For a second, I glanced at the woman filing my toenails. She was unquestionably listening, but I didn't see her calling the *New York Post* when I left the salon.

"I agree. The motion's ready to go; we just need a hearing date. If he posts again once there's a court order telling him to take the photos down, the judge'll throw a fit. That's good for us."

"You're stalling, Meili. What's the offer?"

"Twenty-five thousand dollars."

A bark of laughter exploded from my stomach. The aesthetician scrambled backward as I involuntarily kicked my right foot outward. My shoulders shook, and for a moment, I wasn't sure if I was laughing or crying.

The offer was so ridiculous, for a moment all the words I could think of to reply were Spanish. "Are you serious?"

"Unfortunately, yes, I am. Worse, they're serious. I'll spare you the letter attached to the offer, basically calling me a criminal for using a delusional woman of color to take advantage of the #MeToo movement to extort money from a poor, helpless, trust fund baby."

"Ugh." I leaned back into my chair, for the rest of what was becoming the least relaxing pedicure in history. "That's ridiculous. Not only is that less than I'm already out from getting fired, but it's literally pocket change to them. The lawyer's probably already been paid five times that. Come on, Eric spent fifty thousand dollars on a dining room table that expands when his poker buddies come over! Twenty-five thousand is nothing."

At my comment, the woman at my feet shook her head, mumbling under her breath that sounded suspiciously like "idiot." I made a mental note to leave her a big tip when I left.

"So that's a no, then?"

"Honestly, I'm surprised you haven't already sent them back a Howler."

"Well, I am required to relay all settlement of-fers to you, even the ludicrous ones, unless you tell me otherwise. But also, like I said—I'm stalling. Hoping to buy some time. Plus, I wanted to talk to you about a counteroffer."

"You think we should counter?"

"It's up to you. I did some digging. Eric's trust fund is a revocable trust. Whoever set it up failed to include a spendthrift clause."

"What does that mean?"

"For one thing, it means they used a bad lawyer. Let's hope their personal injury lawyer is equally lazy. A spendthrift clause is usually part of the boilerplate language included in every trust. It says that the trust principal can only be used to pay the beneficiary. The purpose is to stop a person's creditors from taking the money held in trust for him. I don't know if Eric's father thought his son was infallible or wanted to help instill a teeny bit of responsibility in him or what, but his folly could be our gain."

I considered her comment for a moment, stretching out my right toes for a coat of red polish. "Eric's father always wanted him to be his own man, stand on his own two feet. He probably thought if Eric got sued and lost everything, it was his own fault."

"Well, good. Stupid for him, but good for us. Also, I filed a *lis pendens* on Eric's loft. As soon as he moved out, he gave up the protection of homestead laws."

"What does that mean?"

"It means if you get a judgment, we can force him to sell it to collect your money. There's no mortgage, and it's in SoHo, so we should be able to get at least four or five million for it."

I gasped. "Do you think a judge will give us that much?"

"I'm not sure, but we're preparing for a fight. If you want to go to court on this, I will, and I can ask for any amount you want. Part of trial is going to be sitting there, in front of twelve strangers in the jury box and however many onlookers, reading all of those texts out loud. The emails, the death threats. Answering questions about your personal life. I'll do my best to keep your sexual history out, but you never know what the judge will find relevant.

"If we win a judgment, Eric could appeal. Appeal, appeal, appeal. He and his lawyer, Jeb Carter, may try to eat up all of your winnings with my legal fees and costs. They'll delay, drag their feet, and do everything in their power to prevent you from getting a penny. But if we settle, they hand over a check, we dismiss the case, and you're home in time for lunch."

Her words made a lot of sense. Avoiding a court battle that thrust me back in the public eye certainly sounded appealing—but I was already in the public eye.

"If we do that, Eric gets away with everything?" My chest tightened at the thought. He couldn't just buy his way out of ruining my life.

"Well, he has to pay, but usually these agreements contain a confidentiality clause, yes."

"No deal. I want the world to know what he did. We're going to trial."

"So you won't consider settling for any amount? Not even if they offered, say, three million dollars?"

"No deal. This isn't about the money. It's about stripping him naked and letting the world see his true colors. I want to make him pay."

The aesthetician grinned and flashed me two thumbs up. "You show him!"

THE DAY after Meili formally rejected Eric's settlement offer, Tara called me. "The bastard is back at it."

"What do you mean?"

"He emailed me the pictures again this morning, with links to the websites where they're posted. From a dummy account, but I know it's him."

Her words should've surprised me, but naturally, the first thing Eric would do after finding out we rejected his insulting settlement offer was show me I couldn't stop him from doing whatever the hell he wanted, especially since the criminal case against him had been dismissed. A wave of familiar despair hit, but it was quickly replaced with determination.

"This nightmare is never-ending. I can't believe him." I brought her up-to-date on their offer, our response, and my decision not to settle for any amount of money.

"So what's the next step?" Tara asked.

"We're going to file an injunction prohibiting him from posting these pictures anywhere else. Of course, it'll be nearly impossible to prove he was the one who did it if the same picture shows up on other sites. He may not be stupid enough to brag about it on Facebook a second time."

"I'm sure he's not. I went to his page as soon as the email arrived, but I've been blocked. He's smarter than I thought, after all. I'm going to ask my brother to see what information Eric makes available to the public."

"Don't bother. If he's caught on to me using my friends to keep an eye on him, it's probably too late. I bet he made his profile private."

"I'm sorry, Anna," Tara said. "What happens after you get the injunction?"

"Mostly, we wait. The trial's not scheduled for another two months. We don't need any more discovery, at least not things we're likely to get from them. Meili's still trying to get records from some of the websites, but most of them are held offshore, and they're stalling us. We're not going to bother trying to settle. After everything he's put me through, I want a public trial. In fact, I'm thinking about inviting the media to record the expression on Eric's face when Meili asks the jury to award me more than five million dollars."

Tara whistled. Her reply was hushed, almost reverent. "You're asking for a cool five mill? Meili is my hero."

"That's nothing compared to what he'll eventually inherit, and he's got a good salary. He'll be pissed off if he has to pay, but it will barely cramp his style."

"Still, I think I want to be Meili when I grow up."

"Then I should probably stop distracting you from studying." Tara had an MBA, too, but one advanced degree hadn't been enough for someone with her giant brain.

"Yeah, I gotta go in a sec, but seriously—how are you doing?"

I considered for a minute before answering. "I don't know. I'm sorry."

"But, you're okay? I mean, you're not—?"

"I'm not going to try to kill myself again, Tara."

"Good." The relief in her voice was palpable. "Because if you did, I would kick your dead ass, stalk your ghost, and make your afterlife miserable."

Her words brought a smile to my face. "*Te quiero.*"

"I love you, too."

We said good-bye and hung up.

Immediately, I called my lawyer. It didn't take long to fill Meili in on what happened. She recommended keeping a low profile.

"I'm going crazy, Meili. I can't let Eric imprison me in my own home forever. Or worse, in my father's own home forever. I think I've watched every single Spanish soap opera ever created. My accent now rivals my mother's."

"Okay. I'm not saying you can't leave the house. Just, whatever you do, don't contact Eric. Don't reach out to him. Let him wonder where you are, if you even know or care what he did."

Half an hour later, I stepped off the city bus and entered the public library. There was no better place to entertain myself for a few hours. Twice while I browsed, movement caught my eye at the end of the rows. Suddenly, the quiet of the library seemed less peaceful, more menacing. I grabbed a bunch of books without looking at them, checked out, and went to the mall where I could get lost in the bustling Saturday crowd.

Shopping used to make me happy. Now, I walked past the stores, barely glancing at the contents. I forced myself to enter the Louis Vuitton store, check out the type of handbags that once made me drool. My heart rate remained the same. The creamy leather did nothing for me. Another casualty of my relationship with Eric.

"Anna?"

A woman about my age stood behind me, with short blond hair and a friendly smile. The lines around her eyes were deeper than the last time I saw her, she wore khaki pants instead of a uniform, and had developed a lot more muscle. It took me a minute to recognize my high school lab partner.

"I thought that was you!" Caitlyn said.

"Hey!" I paused, but there was no non-awkward way to ask this question. "Were you following me?"

"Not following, exactly. I thought I spotted you in the library, but I felt weird saying anything without being sure. Then when I ran into you again here, I thought, 'hey, it's fate.' Right? How have you been? I heard you moved to the city and became some big shot."

Warily, I studied her. Everyone in New York was aware of what happened to me. People from Papá's church talked about it. What were the odds I'd managed to stumble across the only person from my past who hadn't seen the pictures? Zero.

"Things are going well, thanks," I said, turning away from her. "I'm really busy, though, so I have to—"

Caitlyn's arm shot out, making me halt. "Please don't run away. I've been overseas for the past year, getting shot at in the Middle East. Came home to find my husband divorced me, married my sister, and stole all my money. It's nice to see a friendly face."

"You joined the military?" At least that explained why she didn't know what happened.

"Yeah." She ran one hand through her short,

once-curly locks and smiled sheepishly. "Thought the hair gave me away."

I relaxed enough to exchange pleasantries, give an update on my Papá, express sympathy for her divorce. "It was nice to see you, Caitlyn, but I've got to get back."

"Sure thing. I'm glad I ran into you."

Our chat left my spirits raised enough to give shopping another try. I wandered through a clothing store, piling casual non-work clothes into my arms. No need for power suits these days. When I could carry no more, I headed into the fitting room.

Doing a normal activity felt good. I pulled clothes over my head, twisted, admired my reflection, and tossed them into piles. I looked pretty good for someone who'd lost everything.

A scratching on the door tore my attention away from those thoughts.

"There's someone in here," I called.

No response, but the door to the next room creaked open. After another look at the green cashmere sweater, I pulled it off and threw it into the growing "maybe" pile. At this rate, I'd need to pick up another suitcase before heading back to Papá's house.

As I was shimmying out of the four-hundred-dollar pair of jeans I'd found, something thudded in the stall next to me.

"Are you okay?"

Still no response. Something wasn't right. I tapped on the wall. "Hello?"

The back of my neck tingled. Shopping wasn't fun anymore. Time to get out of there. I started digging through the pile of clothes around me to find my own t-shirt and leggings.

"Anna?"

Startled, I looked up. Flashes of light exploded in my face. I screamed, raising my hands instinctively to cover myself. It wasn't enough. Nothing I did was ever enough. With shaking fingers, I fumbled at the lock, still screaming for help.

Outside the fitting rooms, feet thudded onto the carpet. "Is everything—What the hell? Security! Someone call security!"

I bolted past two very startled shop girls dressed in only my bra and panties. A security guard raced past me, and something thudded against the fitting room door. Voices blurred together, and a moment later, the security guard emerged, dragging Caitlyn behind him.

"What is going on here?"

"Sorry, Anna," Caitlyn said, not exhibiting a drop of remorse. "There's a website, wheresanna.com, offering good money for tips on your whereabouts. I didn't know if it was legit, but it said they'd pay more for photographic evidence. My ex left me in a real bad position, and I need the cash."

My fist connected with her jaw so hard her head snapped backward.

"You bitch!" Caitlyn lunged toward me, but the security guard had her in an iron grip.

He winked at me. "I'm going to pretend I didn't see that. And I'll be back to get your statement."

After they walked away, I returned to the dressing room for my clothes. When I emerged, a tall, older salesclerk handed me a smartphone. "Found this on the floor between the stalls. I'm going to assume it's yours?"

The look on her face told me she wasn't that stupid. Still, I accepted the device gratefully, hoping Caitlyn didn't send pictures to a cloud as they were taken.

With all my strength, I slammed the phone against the wall. I let it fall and stomped until bits of plastic littered the ground beneath my feet. Then I found the SIM card and snapped it in half with a surge of grim satisfaction.

Chapter 13

Two hours sounds like a pretty insignificant amount of time in the grand scheme of things, right? That's how long it took me to wait for the cops to arrive, give a statement, beg them not to release my name, and for two officers to drive me from the mall to my father's home. Somewhere in those two hours, all hell broke loose. Again.

When I arrived home, the front door stood open. Pieces of plastic littered the front walkway. When I tripped over a curlicue phone cord, I realized what the yellow fragments represented: The telephone formerly hanging on the kitchen wall. I'd spent hours as a teenager twirling the yellow cord around my fingers while I talked to a cute boy or Tara, miles away in Jersey.

Before I reached the door, my father appeared

in the opening, muttering to himself. Another plastic missile whizzed past my ear. I ducked, nearly toppling to the cement walkway.

"Papá!"

He blinked a few times. "Anna? Where were you?"

"I was at the mall. You won't believe what happened."

"Someone found out you were staying with me?"

"Yeah. Remember Caitlyn? Wait a minute. How did you know?"

"The phone's been ringing off the hook. A couple of reporters asking for a comment on what happened with Eric, but mostly just jerks with nothing better to do than make obscene calls. A couple of mouth breathers."

Caitlyn. Freaking Caitlyn. To think I let her copy my homework after she snuck out to make out with the football team's mascot instead of doing it herself.

"Had to rip both phones out of the wall."

That probably felt far more satisfying than turning off a cell phone. There wasn't even a word for the feelings overwhelming me. I shut my eyes and counted to ten, as if my life would flip back to normal by the time I opened them. Instead, before I hit "four," my frustration was so overwhelming, I couldn't think what number came next.

"I'm sorry, Papá. I'll pack up my stuff and go." My voice was wooden.

"Don't be ridiculous. The phones are gone. I'll rig a couple of surprises for anyone fool enough to set foot on the front lawn. We'll go inside and hunker down, weather the storm together. You don't have to deal with this alone."

Hope blossomed in my chest, but I stomped on it with all my might. "You mean it? When this happened the first time, Jay—"

"That lunkhead never deserved my daughter. Forget Jay. Come in. I'll make your great-grandma's *champurrado*, and we'll stream movies with that Chris you like."

Not even the bitter anguish of the past few months could quell the emotions welling up inside me. Tears in my eyes, I wrapped my father in a hug. "Thank you so much, Papá. I'm so sorry to have brought this to your front door."

"Don't be sorry. You did nothing wrong."

"Still, I feel bad. You shouldn't have to deal with this."

"Hush. Sorry and five dollars will buy me a cup of overpriced coffee. You get even with Eric, and then you can thank me. But never be sorry for asking your father for help. We are family, Anna.

Family sticks together. We will get through this. *No hay mal que por bien no venga.*"

Rough translation: Every cloud has a silver lining. If nothing else, Eric's actions brought me back to my father.

I wrapped my arms around his waist and rested my head against his shoulder, sniffling. It took a moment to compose myself enough to continue inside. Papá went into the kitchen to make some comfort food, while I cursed myself for not checking into another hotel, far away, under an assumed name, crawling beneath the blankets, and never leaving. Bringing all of this to his front porch had been selfish of me.

Watching Papá move around the kitchen chased the numbness from my veins, replacing it with a sense of familiarity and security. It surprised me that it took someone this long to realize my father lived in North Carolina and dig up his address and listed telephone number. After all, I sat in the same house where I'd gotten dressed for junior prom.

Eric had never met Papá. Apparently, he either hadn't been listening when I told him where my family lived, or his relationship with his own father was so bad, it never occurred to him that I might reach out to mine in a time of need.

As weird as it felt to be grateful to my ex for anything, I thanked Jesus for making Eric so self-involved. He never considered whether other people might want to help each other, because he cared only about helping himself.

AUGUST 2019

Eight months after I arrived in South Carolina, Meili called with the news I'd been waiting for: We were going to trial, so it was time to pack my stuff and head home. Jury selection started in the middle of September. I'd need to be home before the first day of court, whether I liked it or not. Reconstruction of the house had been completed; Tara had already moved back in. There was no reason for me to hide out in North Carolina, especially now that Eric had found me.

If I left, people would get bored and leave Papá alone soon enough. At this point, it seemed easier to let the paparazzi find me than to keep trying to hide. They had to get bored eventually. Plenty of real celebrities for them to bother. Even in the twenty-four hours news cycle, they couldn't need to fill up airtime badly enough to focus on me forever.

Meili would file another request for an injunction, and she'd go to court immediately so the judge could issue an order before Eric knew the motion existed. The house in New Jersey no longer belonged to me—at Meili's direction, I'd sold it to "The Jesse K. Family Trust" back in April for one dollar. During my relationship with Eric, my childhood crush on the *Full House* character had, oddly enough, never come up. The injunction should stop him from reposting the address, even if he figured out I still lived there. Either way, I wanted to go home. If necessary, I'd hire a security guard and install a fence to keep people away. It worked for former presidents.

"I'm going to court first thing in the morning, but I'll email you the papers tonight. I'll call you tomorrow either way to let you know what happens," Meili said. "Send me your flight information so I know when you'll be back in town. We need to meet again."

"No problem. Thanks for everything."

As soon as we hung up, I booked a plane ticket and texted Tara to let her know I was coming. It was time to stop hiding.

Three days later, Tara met me outside security at JFK. "A wheelchair, huh?"

I shrugged. "It's a big terminal. Have you ever noticed people never make eye contact with a person sitting in a wheelchair? Useful when you're trying to disappear."

"I don't want you to disappear." She leaned down, enveloping me in a warm embrace. "We'll get your life back. When we're done with that bastard, you could buy this airport if you wanted."

I laughed but didn't let go. "I missed you."

Tara wheeled me to the front of the airport to return the chair, then led me through the maze of parking to her car. As soon as we settled into our seats, she pulled a red scarf out of her purse.

"What are you doing?"

"It's a surprise."

"I know you're taking me to the house, Tara. Where else would we possibly go?"

"Shut up and wear the blindfold." She pouted until I relented.

As the car maneuvered through the traffic, Tara kept up a steady stream of chatter about her family, our mutual friends, some horrific first dates, and the upcoming bar exam. I filled her in briefly on the lawsuit, the injunction Meili obtained earlier in the week, and my father. Shortly after I finished, the slowing car told me we left the expressway for surface roads. This route was so familiar, my mind followed the car up and down the turns to our street.

When the car stopped, I reached for the blindfold. "Don't you dare," Tara said.

"Seriously, what did you do? Have mirrors installed on every floor and ceiling? How bad can it be if you don't even want me to look?"

"Hush. Hold on a sec."

The car door slammed. A moment later, a rush of thick air hit my face as the door opened into the New Jersey heat. Tara helped me out of the car. Once I reached the sidewalk, she removed the blindfold. I stood for a long moment, blinking rapidly in the bright sunlight.

The outside looked exactly the way it did before, except for one thing: Tara had strung a "WELCOME HOME" banner across the front. Red and green balloons festooned every available surface.

"Red and green, huh? Interesting choice."

"You didn't have a very Merry Christmas last year. There's a tree inside." She squeezed my hand and stared pointedly toward the house while I sniffled and wiped my eyes.

"Neighbor must be chopping onions," I muttered.

We started at the front entry, where the old red tile floor I'd never liked had been replaced by gleaming hardwood. A fluffy brown tabby cat raced around the corner when we entered. My heart felt a thousand times lighter when I picked her up.

"Hermione! I've missed you, sweetie."

The cat snuggled against me, and I scratched her head while we examined the rest of the house. Things were looking up already.

"The most important thing," Tara said, "is right through here."

"Did you add a disco ball to the living room?"

"Better." She stopped in front of me and waited. I took in the new grey sectional, this one free of claw marks, and the suspiciously large flatscreen before I noticed the mantel.

One hand flew to my mouth. "How did you—?"

"Remember when I did that photography class? To impress Janine?" I nodded, thinking about the redhead from the Mets' executive suite. The relationship had ended even before the six-week course did. "Well, they taught us how to do a photo collage. After sifting through all our destroyed pictures, I called your dad. He gathered up everything he could find, scanned it, and emailed me. Including this one."

My mom's face smiled out at me from the

mantel. My blue cap and gown were once again pristine. Then everything blurred. Tara's arms engulfed me in a hug.

"I can't believe it. I had no idea!" I murmured against her shoulder.

"'Course not. I told him not to tell you."

"You're the best friend ever."

"Don't get all sappy on me yet," Tara said, "or we'll never get through the tour."

I stepped back and blew raspberries at her, but obediently followed down the hall.

In the kitchen, granite countertops and an island with three barstools gave me the storage I'd always craved and made the space feel more inviting. I could see Tara sitting on the stools, chatting with me while I made *huevos rancheros* on the new cooktop.

"Tara, this place looks amazing," I said as we moved into the bathroom.

The old bathtub had been replaced by one twice the size, with jets and handrails. A shower stood beside it.

"I know, right?" Tara said. "But, seriously, the designer did almost everything. All I did was point out you hate those sinks with the bowl sitting on top of the counter, and I never understood why."

I grinned at her. "They're so weird! Anyway, I hate to point out the obvious, but this bathroom is twice the size of the one we had. What happened?"

"We moved my closet to the wall shared with the third bedroom. The room's a little smaller now, but it still works for an office. We weren't going to get a third roommate, right?"

"No, definitely not. I'd never find anyone who compared to you."

"And don't you forget it. Wait until you see your new closet."

As I followed Tara down the hall, for the first time since November, I started to feel like things might one day be all right. It was good to be home.

Part IV

If you prick us, do we not bleed?
If you tickle us, do we not laugh?
If you poison us, do we not die?
And if you wrong us, shall we not revenge?

- William Shakespeare,
The Merchant of Venice

Chapter 14

October 2019

Once I moved back home, time flew. The Saturday before the trial began, I visited Meili's office to prepare. For the first time in almost a year, I replaced my large-rimmed, face-hiding glasses with contacts. I returned to my usual amount of makeup and swept my hair up to make my bangs less obvious. The "disguise" hadn't fooled the reporters, and it certainly wouldn't fool anyone who happened to see me entering or leaving the building where my lawyer kept her office. If I wanted to have the option of hiding behind glasses/makeup/bangs in the future (or a better disguise), I needed to more or less resemble my old self for the trial.

We sat at a gleaming oak table in a conference room. Papers scattered across the entire surface, and boxes of paper sat on all but two of the chairs. Meili's secretary ushered me to one of the seats and left to get me a cup of coffee. We made small talk until he returned, but as soon as the door closed, my lawyer transferred into business mode as smoothly as if she'd flipped a switch.

"Okay, this is going to be a long day, and we've got a lot to cover, but we'll take a break if you need to. Ready?"

I nodded. If I wasn't ready to talk about all this stuff with my lawyer by now, I'd never make it through court.

"Good." She studied me for a moment, then nodded. "Now, you work in fashion, so you know appearance is everything. But we need to talk about the image we're going to create for the jury. You're Anna, ball-busting career woman who rose to the top with a salary comfortably in the six figures and annual bonuses exceeding many people's yearly earnings. You started out with money, sure, but you worked for everything you had. Your parents didn't give you a fancy education, they gave you a work ethic. You made your own way to the top, overcoming depression and physical disability. Before you were even thirty, people watched your career, predicting great things for you. You're one-half of one of

Forbes's 'Manhattan's Top Twenty Power Couples.'"

"Not anymore," I interjected.

"True, but not the point. No one else lived your life, experienced your path. You spent a lot of time cultivating your professional image. But you're also Every Woman. You're a friend and a daughter; you're the woman at the grocery store, at the laundromat, or walking down the street. The message we want to convey to the jury is: this could happen to anyone."

"Anyone stupid enough to email nude photographs to her boyfriend."

"No." Meili's voice took on an edge. "It doesn't have anything to do with your actions or intelligence. You're a smart woman. This isn't about your age, your race, your job, your choices. People hack women's email accounts and clouds to steal pictures never sent to anyone, never intended for distribution. High school boys make videos of themselves raping girls and post them on the internet. The guy who started all the revenge porn sites made pictures using Photoshop. This. could. happen. to. *anyone*. You are the face of all women."

"What does that mean?"

"Well, first, it would've been great if Jay stuck by you so the world could see the power couple in distress—"

"It also would've been nice if someone had held my hand and supported me instead of leaving me to drink myself to death. But I don't want Jay to be part of this. There would be too much focus on the company, and the shareholders are innocent."

"That's fine. Now he's the jerk who ditched you in your time of need. No, what I was going to say is—no dating." Meili leaned forward, her hand tapping the table. "I mean it. No first dates, no coffee dates, no casual hook-ups, nothing. Not until this is over. You're so chaste, Mother Theresa's the whore of Babylon next to you."

"Because there's something wrong with a woman who enjoys sex? The jury won't give me money if I'm a slut?"

"Calm down, Anna," she said. "I'm on your side. The world sucks sometimes. The point is, we're telling a story, and part of the story is to paint a sympathetic picture."

I glared at her, and her tone softened.

"It's not about what you deserved and what you didn't deserve. It's about showing how you've suffered. Like it or not, we live in a prudish world, and the jury is going to think you suffered more if you can't find a halfway decent guy to date now that this has happened. We want them to think you're over thirty, you're single, and this whole thing has ruined your chances for love, on top of everything else."

"That's total bullshit. Women don't come stamped with an expiration date."

"You and I know that. But we want the jury to give you as big an award as possible. We need to generate sympathy. It's how seven-figure verdicts are won."

The idea of a woman over thirty being unable to find love made me see red. But she might be right that not being in a relationship could win me points with the jury. I hated it, but it's not like I wanted to date anyone. Grinding my teeth, I slumped back into the chair without further comment. Meili watched me shred a piece of paper before she continued.

"Now, I know you don't like to call attention to your disability, but—you need juror sympathy."

"I'm not using my fake foot to get money. My parents and I agreed to a settlement twenty years ago. I got enough money. I'm not milking this thing for more."

"I'm not asking you to. All I'm asking is that, when we're in court, you wear skirts. Professional, knee-length, businesswoman skirts. No pants. Let the jury see the leg, wonder what happened. I won't mention it or call attention to it if you don't want me to."

"I'll think about it." She was right, but my

pride still grated at the notion that a woman who allowed nude pictures of her to exist deserved to be humiliated when someone she trusted shared them with the world.

"Great. Now, for a lot of women, when they're in the witness chair, we tell them, keep your voice low, sniffle a lot, dab at your eyes with tissues, long pauses. Essentially, many people who take the stand are encouraged to play the victim." My eyes flashed, and she raised a hand. "I'm not going to recommend you do that. You're a fighter. Let the jury see how you've suffered, how you've fought. We want the jury to root for you and hand you buckets of cash."

That sounded about right. "I'm fine talking low to make them lean in, like we're part of some confidential conversation, as long as they can hear me. But I don't need to play the victim. The facts of this case speak for themselves."

Her eyes held mine for a moment before she nodded. "I agree. With that said, when we start going through the texts and emails, it's going to be an emotional experience. Don't hold back. If a text makes you flinch, flinch. Some of these messages are pretty awful. I got choked up reading through them, and they aren't even directed at me. I don't want crocodile tears, but don't hold back. Let the jury see your pain. We want them to feel as bad as you did."

My fingers dug painfully into the arms of the chair, but she was right. "Okay."

"Also, yesterday the judge granted our motion to exclude evidence that you were the one who emailed the pictures. It's not relevant to whether you gave Eric permission to distribute them."

"That makes sense. Good news, right?" A tiny curl of hope began to form in my belly.

"Absolutely. They didn't fight too hard. After all, if you owned the pictures, it weighs against a jury finding you allowed him to share them with other people. Still, we got lucky. Our judge seems sympathetic. He has two daughters, one teenager and one in her early twenties. I think he's imagining how he would feel if this happened to either of them. He's also from a poor family, worked hard to get where he is. He seems to lack patience for people who were handed the world on a silver platter."

The tiny curl unrolled into a noodle of hope. "That sounds good for us."

"It could be. Mr. Carter filed a motion asking the judge to recuse himself on the grounds that he's biased against the wealthy. They also want a change of venue, claiming Eric is too well-known to get a fair trial this close to the City."

"Where do they want to move it?"

"Ideally, California, I think. But that's ridiculous. A New Jersey judge can't transfer a case to

California, and they know it. The judge already denied their motion to dismiss for lack of jurisdiction, so this is a stall tactic. New Jersey's one of the smallest states in America. If Red Bank is too close to the city for him to get a fair trial, so is pretty much everywhere else in the state. It's not like if we'd filed in New York, and the judge could transfer the case to Buffalo."

"Okay. So why file the motion?"

"I don't think they want to move the trial so much as they want a different judge. They're not likely to get either: Judge Patel seems to want to keep the case. Really, they're laying the framework for appeal."

"Is that something I need to worry about? Giving them grounds to appeal?"

When considering trial strategy and what to do, my concerns always centered on testifying in front of the jury or whether people would believe me. It hadn't occurred to me I also needed to prepare for what happened if we lost the trial. The thought of losing the case, with letting him get away with everything, sent me right back to the edge of despair I spent too much of the year teetering on. I couldn't allow myself to entertain those thoughts.

"Don't worry about appeal; that's my job. We need to win first. Let's talk about cross-examination. They're going to ask you some difficult questions. We need to be prepared to answer them."

"I'll be ready," I said.

"Excellent. Then let's go through everything. I don't want them to get away with any surprises."

DRAWINGS OF EVERYTHING imaginable covered the walls of the shop, some color, some black and white. Cartoon characters, symbols, Chinese characters, superheroes, even that guy from *Twilight*.

"How about that one?" Tara pointed. "I could get the Chinese word for 'soup' tattooed on my ass. Or maybe 'I'm a dumbass American who doesn't know what this means' all the way down one arm."

Behind the counter, a blonde with tattoos covering every available speck of her arms laughed. Her white teeth gleamed. "You want something in a foreign language, you have to sign a waiver and show me you know what it means. We also refuse to permanently ink anyone with misspelled words." She held out a hand. "I'm Beth."

"Tara," she said. "This is my BFF, Anna. We're getting tattoos. Obviously."

They shook hands, eyes meeting for a moment

too long to be purely professional. My best friend might be leaving here with more than a tattoo.

I stepped forward. "I'd like to get a semicolon on the inside of my left wrist."

Beth's eyes flickered to the inside of my wrist before she met my gaze. "Like Project Semicolon?"

"You've heard of it?"

"Yeah. Choosing to put a semicolon at the end of your story instead of a period." She pointed at a black spot on her right wrist, nearly hidden by the surrounding red and gray pattern. "I added this one after we lost my brother a few years ago."

"I'm sorry to hear that," Tara and I said, almost in unison. Beth cracked a smile, and Tara continued, "I'm not sure what I want, but start with Anna while I think about it."

"No way," I said. "I go first, and you'll back out."

"Fine. Give me a banana with muscles, in honor of my best friend here."

I burst out laughing. "What?"

"Well, nothing rhymes with Anna. But ba-NAH-na's close enough, and you're one of the strongest people I know, and I'm totally messing with you." She pulled a sheet of paper out of her messenger bag and handed it to Beth. "Actually, I'd like a lotus on the back of my shoulder. To remind me of inner peace even when waters are murky."

"That's beautiful," Beth said. "We can do you both at the same time. My partner's in the back. No one's escaping."

She led us behind a curtain, where a tall, muscular man she introduced as Chad waited. Tara showed him the drawing she'd brought, then whipped her shirt off to allow access to the back of her shoulder. Beth pulled over a stool and took my right hand.

Chad moved behind Tara and pulled a tray of instruments over. "You ladies ready?"

"Ready," we said.

My left hand stretched out toward Tara when I saw the needles. She squeezed it. "You can do this. We can do this, together."

"Uh-huh." I shut my eyes when Beth started swabbing my wrist with wet cotton balls. Tara convinced me to get the tattoo, but she couldn't make me watch.

"So last night, I went to the bar with Jen and Chris," she said. A couple we went to graduate school with. "We're sitting there, and I'm telling them about that time we found the pelican on Jersey Beach, caught in those plastic rings from soda cans, remember?"

"Yeah."

A buzzing sounded to the right, and a light

pressure touched the inside of my wrist. Warm and firm, but not painful. Not nearly as bad as I feared. Still, my eyes remained closed.

"So, I've just gotten to the part where we're checking to see if the bird's wings are okay, and this guy sitting on the other side of Chris butts in. Says he heard our story and it reminded him of this one time he shot a bird for chirping outside his bedroom window."

My eyes flew open. "What?"

"Exactly! So I'm looking at him with total horror written across my face. And then he asks for my number!"

"He didn't!"

"Swear to Buddha, he did. Like, dude, what about my story made you think 'the best way to hit on this chick is to talk about killing poor defenseless animals'?"

Laughter shook my body.

"Hey," Beth said. I jumped. Thanks to Tara's story, I'd nearly forgotten where we were. "No laughing while I'm inking you. You'll wind up with a wonky semicolon."

"That's okay," I told her. "Life can get pretty wonky sometimes. As long as I have my best friend here, everything will be okay."

Beth looked from me to Tara and back, then grinned. "Life *can* get pretty wonky. But sometimes, things turn out better than you expected."

Before we left, I studied the inside of my wrist. The tattoo sat next to the nearly invisible scar. A perfect black circle above a comma. A promise that I'd always put a semicolon at the end of my life instead of a period. No matter what happened in court tomorrow, life would go on. I would go on.

Chapter 15

The ancient stone building rose against a gray backdrop, making it more depressing than imposing. Enormous concrete pillars reminded me of how small and insignificant I was in the grand scheme of things. Only the red, white, and blue on the flagpole cut through the dreariness.

Here's to truth, justice, and the American way.

Whoever built the Monmouth County Courthouse put a space between "court" and "house," reminding me that this particular building likely stood in this spot for about three hundred years. I wondered what our forefathers would say about the internet and revenge porn. Did they make nude drawings of their wives and girlfriends that they shared with friends when angry? Somehow, I suspected not. Maybe advances in technology were impeding, not enhancing, social progress.

A shiver ran down my spine. A goose walking over my grave, as Mamá used to say. Maybe a courthouse should be depressing. People relived a lot of pain and sadness within this building. Marriages were severed, children taken from families, fathers sent to jail.

I hadn't set foot in a courtroom in twenty years. The only time I'd been called for jury duty, the state later told me not to come in after all. This building seemed smaller than the one I'd entered at thirteen, when the lawyers decided to settle at the last minute after seeing the way prospective jury members gazed at a pitiful teenage girl who lost her foot and tried to kill herself when doctors told her she'd never be able to live a "normal" life.

The memory made my palms sweat. I'd been terrified of testifying then, too. The night before opening arguments would begin, nightmares kept me up until nearly sunrise. Visions of the rubber tip of my crutch catching as I made my way toward the jury stand, of falling in front of everyone. Again. Fewer people, lesser risk of injury. Same shame.

My phone beeping with a text from Meili shook me out of my reverie. I'M HERE, SO COME IN WHENEVER YOU'RE READY.

I chuckled, a dry humorless laugh. Would I ever be ready? When I was younger, the thought of testifying in court gave me nightmares for weeks. I'd been so relieved when the lawyers approached my parents with an offer they couldn't refuse, I cried.

Now, things were different. I'd never let Eric off the hook by allowing him to settle. I was much stronger at thirty-four than at thirteen. It was up to me to hold him responsible so he'd never treat another human being the way he'd treated me. Maybe a verdict would make other men think twice before doing the same thing to their ex-girlfriends.

With effort, I threw my shoulders back and steadied myself with a deep breath. The little girl who'd cried in her mother's arms outside the courtroom had long since grown up, and Mamá wasn't here to help me through this time. Time to put my big girl panties on.

A throng of reporters stood outside the main entrance. Meili had warned me this might happen. This case would be news even if Eric and I weren't both fairly well-known. I walked around to a side entrance, head down, hiding behind the scarf wrapped over my hair and large sunglasses. A couple of reporters waited there, as well. Seeing them stopped me in my tracks, although I shouldn't have been surprised.

For a long moment, I stared at the semi-colon on the inside of my wrist. Then I forced myself not to hear the media, not to see the flashing cameras, as I strode into the building. No one tried to stop me.

This won't be that bad, I told myself on the way to the elevator. *You're not the bad guy here. You're a strong, successful woman. Eric may be able to take away your job and your boyfriend, but he can't change who you are. You'll be successful again.*

The chant carried me through the crowd at the elevators, up three floors, and down the hall. Then my resolve faltered. For a long moment, I stared at the wooden double doors, tracing the lines with my eyes and wishing I were anywhere else. Inwardly, I cursed Eric for destroying the confidence I'd worked my whole life to build.

I am a strong, successful woman. I was a junior executive for a corporation worth a quarter of a billion dollars, on the path to Chief Financial Officer someday. I can bring down one entitled, spoiled asshole.

The inside of the courtroom looked like what I expected from TV. A waist-high, wooden partition divided the room into two sections, with rows of benches in the half nearest the door. The judge's bench dominated the front half of the room, a massive wooden structure flanked by the United States and New Jersey state flags. Two wooden tables for the parties stood in front of the barrier, with two chairs at each. Meili waited at the table on the left, which sat nearer the jury box. She reviewed her notes, but I barely registered her, because my brain had finally processed who the figures sitting at the table on the right were.

A short orange-skinned man with the tiniest ring of gray hair seemed far less imposing than he had on the phone or via emails. The terrible blond toupee he wore made him appear downright comical. For a moment, I wondered if he'd worn such a ridiculous mop to induce the jury to pity him. But Mr. Carter wasn't what caught my attention, either. He wasn't the one who made my breath catch and my heart pound when I entered the room. When my eyes fell on the man next to him, I gasped as if someone sucker-punched me in the gut. None of the time I'd spent thinking about this moment prepared me for how I'd actually feel when I faced him again.

Eric sat in the far right chair, his back to me. He'd once told me he could sense when I was nearby, but he didn't stir. I took advantage of the opportunity to examine his lanky form. Some part of me had expected he would've sprouted horns in his absence or vibrated a red aura to let others know of the evil within. Instead, eighteen months of house building made him more muscular, leaner. If I didn't know what a dick he was, I'd have said he grew more attractive. Appearances certainly were deceiving.

His hair had grown a bit, but he'd pulled it back into a man bun for court. Of course he had. Instead of one of the thousand-dollar, tailored suits probably still hanging in the closet of the loft apartment we'd once shared, he wore an ill-fitting navy blue jacket and khaki pants. He'd dressed down for court, presumably because he realized the jury may be less sympathetic toward a trust-fund baby born with a silver spoon in his mouth than some do-gooder whose girlfriend cheated while he went off building houses for the homeless in a foreign country. Oh, no. The blackness began to close in on me.

I choked, wanting to embrace the darkness. What was I thinking? Why did I imagine I'd ever be able to take him on? Everything was hopeless.

No, it's not. The voice in my head sounded like Tara's, a white light cutting through the depression bearing down on me.

With effort, I lifted my chin even higher, dragged my gaze away from my ex-boyfriend, and focused on my lawyer. Meili was the bright, shining spot in this room. I took deep breaths and banished the negative thoughts to a locked vault in my mind where they couldn't consume me. Then I dumped kerosene into the vault and set the negativity on fire.

Out of the corner of my eye, I sensed movement, but I resisted the urge to turn my head to the right. Eric hummed under his breath, a low rumbling once as familiar as my own voice. A tiny, traitorous part of my heart flip-flopped.

I told myself the turmoil was normal. Most people felt some mixed emotions when encountering an old lover face-to-face for the first time. Once, I'd thought we'd get married, have children. Still, I loathed the tiny part of me that still loved the person who put me in this position.

Beside me, a chair scraped against the floor, and I held my breath. *Don't let it be him, don't let it be him.*

A voice murmured, higher than Eric's. I couldn't make out the words. But a moment later, the chair scraped again, and something thudded onto the table.

I'd asked Meili if the judge would allow me to skip jury selection, the way I'd skipped most of the pretrial motion hearings. Even after all this time, the thought of being face-to-face with Eric again made me want to crawl back into bed and hide under the covers. She'd pointed out I needed to face him sometime. Better to get the first meeting out of the way during jury selection than moments before opening arguments.

Her logic made sense, but my sweaty palms begged to delay this moment forever. If only Eric could undo what he did and magically give my life back, I cheerfully would've given up every penny. But he wouldn't, even if it were possible. Everywhere I went, there he was. His pictures, the comments they generated, emails, texts—and the shame. The shame never went away, no matter what I did. Holding Eric accountable might give me back some measure of self-respect. I hoped it hurt him for the rest of his life.

The bailiff instructed everyone to rise, and our judge appeared at the doorway. *Here goes nothing.*

Judge Patel was a short, thin man whose unlined face made his salt-and-pepper goatee seem premature, but he must be in his fifties, at least. His robe and aura of authority dared people to underestimate him due to his baby face.

"Good morning, counselors," he said after the bailiff instructed us to sit. "Ms. Guerra, Mr. Rutherford. We're here to pick a jury for your case. Before we get started, are there any other matters up for discussion?"

Meili remained on her feet. "Your Honor, we move to suppress all evidence of the plaintiff's sexual history, both before and after the distribution of the pictures."

The judge squinted at Mr. Carter, who was already jumping to his feet. "I assume you object to this request?"

"Yes, Your Honor. Part of a defamation suit is

to show reputational damage. That means letting the jury see the plaintiff's reputation before and after the incident in question."

Meili said, "Your Honor, no one is going to try to claim my client's reputation before this incident occurred isn't relevant. But after? Is the defendant going to be allowed to benefit from making my client so depressed, she acted out of character?"

The judge rubbed his chin for so long before speaking, I expected a genie to pop out. Then he set down his gavel and leaned forward. "I'm going to allow the evidence, to let the jury weigh how these things affected her. They deserve to get a full picture of events. For one thing, your Amended Complaint alleges additional damage when the pictures were reposted a couple of weeks ago. The jury will need to see Ms. Guerra's reputation to determine what additional damages might be relevant."

My heart sank. Silently I cursed Caitlyn for spotting me at the mall, for reaching out to Eric. I cursed myself for going to the mall in the first place. I should've changed my name and moved to a foreign country or something. Or dyed my hair blonde, hidden in the house, and gained a hundred pounds or so before showing my face in public.

I thought Meili said this judge seemed sympathetic. Ruling against us so early seemed a bad sign. She squeezed my hand under the table and wrote something on the legal pad sitting between us. *In every case, motions go both ways. No one wins them all. It doesn't mean the judge is against us.*

The judge continued, "If her behavior was brought on by depression, then you'll have the ability to bring in medical experts who can testify to that."

"In that case, Your Honor," Mr. Carter said, "We'd like to move for a continuance while we have the plaintiff examined by a neutral third-party expert."

Meili was halfway to her feet when the judge spoke. "Absolutely not, counselor. The discovery deadline expired a month ago. Expert witness information was due in September. You even submitted the name of a medical witness. The plaintiff's depression and need for psychiatric assistance can hardly be considered a surprise sprung on you on the eve of trial."

:-), Meili wrote on the pad. Then she added, *Time to focus on picking jurors. Whatever happens, act like it's exactly what you want to happen. Smile. Try not to look so terrified.*

The corners of my mouth tilted upward in what I hoped looked more like a smile than a grimace.

Jury selection took up the rest of the day. A parade of people, all genders, shapes, sizes, and colors, came and went. Some were dismissed because they couldn't afford to take as much time off as we needed for the trial. Three of the younger male jurors were dismissed for admitting to having uploaded pictures to revenge porn sites in the past or texting them to the girl's friends and family. We let an additional one go for viewing revenge porn sites, despite not uploading any pictures. Five prospective jurors admitted seeing the pictures and recognizing me.

Juror after juror left the room. An hour after lunch, I started to fidget, wondering if we'd ever find six New Jersey citizens who would promise to be unbiased.

Beside me, Meili scribbled something on the legal pad. *Relax. The first round always thins the herd. We don't want people who resent being called to jury duty. We'll get there.*

Finally, a group of nine individuals sat in the box. In a civil case, six jurors deliberated to reach a verdict; the remaining three served as alternates in case someone left before the trial ended. According to Meili, two alternates were more common, but in a case expected to last weeks or even a month, Judge Patel preferred not to risk starting over due to lost jurors. Considering how badly I wanted this to be over, we didn't argue.

I studied the faces in the box, remembering

what Meili told me about who we wanted to decide the case.

"We want primarily women in their late twenties to mid-thirties," she'd said. "Liberal if possible, non-religious. Fathers with teenage daughters might be okay. They'll be outraged at the idea this could happen to their girls. What we want to avoid are older, more conservative women who will judge you instead of Eric, or young men who think it's funny to post naked pictures of someone online without consent. And anyone who supports Trump."

Comparing her words to the faces staring back at me sent my heart plummeting all the way to the tips of my shoes. Nine sets of eyes returned my gaze from the box: one silver-haired woman with her lips pressed tightly together; two guys who barely seemed old enough to serve, one in a YOLO cap turned sideways and the other dressed like a member of the Young Republicans club; an elderly man who admitted hoping for a long trial because his wife wanted him out of the house; and two stay-at-home moms with perfect hair, spray tans, and diamond rings nearly the size of my head. Between them sat a guy in his late twenties, with a buzz cut and "Semper Fi" tattooed on his left bicep. Only the remaining two jurors gave me any hope - a blue-haired college-aged girl with a pierced nose and a man with bulging muscles and a gray goatee. I prayed he had a daughter.

"Luck of the draw," Meili murmured. "Don't worry. We still get our challenges."

"What?"

"After we toss out all the jurors who are biased or can't afford to miss work to hear the case, then each side gets to remove jurors without giving a reason." She cast a glance at the other table, where Eric conferred with his lawyer. "Each side gets three, plus an extra one for the alternates. We're keeping an eye not just on who's already there, but who we might get as replacements. The brunette in the second row's been making doe eyes at your ex since we walked in the room."

Poor thing. If only I could warn her about what she'd get if she walked down that path. "So what do we do?"

She leaned forward, lifting one hand over her mouth and turning away from the jury box. I did the same, giving us the illusion of privacy in this crowded room.

"Jurors 4 and 7 should be okay," she said. The blue-haired girl and the dad-type. I nodded. "Retired folk usually are happy to serve on the jury, so at least he won't get antsy if the testimony goes on for a while. We might luck out if he's got a granddaughter. So, I think we can keep 7.

"A marine may be sympathetic to your ex,

being away from loved ones for a long time while off trying to help people. If he ever served overseas, and he or a friend got a Dear John letter while away, we're screwed. Also, military types who get dumped are known for passing pictures of the exes around. It's not the same as posting them online, but—he's the number one guy Carter's going to want on this jury, and the first one I'm striking."

That made sense. The more Eric and his lawyer liked a prospective juror, the further I wanted that person from the courthouse. "Okay. What about the rest?"

"The rest are a crapshoot. The Real Housewives of New Jersey over there seem like the type to band together, vote the same way. We need to convince one. If either of them has a cheating husband or an old sex tape from college, we might get them both on our side. So, I think we're going to strike the young George Bush over there, the marine, and the woman who looks like Barbara Bush."

"What about the guy in the YOLO cap?"

She shrugged. "The sheet says a student, poor. He may be inclined toward being sympathetic toward you, someone who's self-made, rather than a rich yuppie. Plus, he's Latino. There's a chance the other side will strike him because they think he'll be on your side."

"Can they do that?"

"Not really. We could raise a constitutional race discrimination challenge. In a criminal case, we probably would. In this case, since he's young and has been raised in a culture a little more accepting of this stuff, letting him go could benefit us."

I appreciated Meili keeping me in the loop. As the lawyer, decisions regarding jurors were one hundred percent up to her, but her explaining things gave me the illusion of some control. Feeling like I had some control over my destiny let me sit up straighter, keep the depression at bay. During the trial, I couldn't afford to lie in bed all day and night staring at the walls. I needed to be present in the courtroom, pay attention, and review the case every night when we left.

Meili gave the judge three juror numbers, and the judge excused them. The youngest of the three appeared relieved, like he struggled not to cheer on his way out of the courtroom. A middle-aged paralegal and a fifty-year-old ophthalmologist in a "Keep America Great 2020" hat replaced them. Neither looked terribly happy to be there, but we couldn't do anything about it. More prospective jurors were dismissed for cause. The judge sent the Trumpeter away, which is probably why he wore the hat.

Mr. Carter dismissed the man in the YOLO

cap, bringing in a permed brunette who kept adjusting the neckline of her sweater when she glanced at Eric. Then he sent the blue-haired girl out of the room, leaving me facing the nine strangers who would decide what justice meant. We'd run out of challenges.

The jury box now contained eight frowning faces and one set of red, lush lips aimed at the defendant. Eight blank expressions, hard eyes. I felt them judging me already. A chill ran down my back. Jury selection often came down to luck of the draw, and my luck had run out. I was screwed.

Chapter 16

The next morning, we returned to court for the opening arguments. Too nervous to eat breakfast and afraid of being late, I found myself at the courthouse nearly half an hour early. I texted Tara from a bathroom stall, afraid of running into Eric or a juror outside the courtroom. Finally, though, I couldn't delay any more—time to start.

I forced my legs not to shake as Meili and I walked together to our table. She squeezed my hand, a gesture hidden by the backs of our chairs. A peek at Eric showed him in another ill-fitting suit. The gray plaid jacket clashed horribly with the horrid yellow shirt, which gave him a sallow complexion, and a lime green tie. He certainly wanted the jury to think he had no money. If I got lucky, Juror No. 9 wouldn't find him nearly as appealing in such an unflattering combination.

As soon as we got settled, first the judge then the jury entered.

Show time. I steeled myself, determined not to let my nerves show. I would do this.

The judge greeted the jury, and everyone sat. Then, he turned to our table. "Good morning. Would the plaintiff like to make an opening statement?"

I pinched my elbow surreptitiously but didn't wake up. No turning back now.

"Good morning, Your Honor. Yes, we would. Good morning, Counselor." Meili rose to her feet and nodded at the men in the room before approaching the jury box. "Ladies and gentlemen of the jury, this is a simple case. My client, Anna Guerra, used to date the defendant. She loved him desperately. In fact, she thought they would spend the rest of their lives together. On their first anniversary as a couple, he told her he had special news, and they went to dinner at a five-star restaurant. My client fully expected the night to end with congratulations and champagne. She wanted to marry him."

Perhaps she was laying it on a little thick, but Eric never knew about my doubts about our relationship. He definitely loved himself enough to believe I'd been positive he was The One.

"Instead, he told Ms. Guerra he was moving to a foreign country for several months. My client painted on a brave face. She agreed to stand by him until he returned. She took care of his home. She wrote to him frequently. But, when one partner says he's going to South America for a few months and stays away for over a year, with minimal contact, it's going to take a toll. The relationship deteriorated. They eventually broke up via email. When the defendant returned to the United States and discovered my client had started seeing someone else, that she wasn't still pining for him, he plastered nude pictures of her all over the internet."

Beside me, the innocent expression on Eric's face made me itch to punch him. If I didn't want to strangle him in a white-hot rage, I needed to keep my eyes away from my ex as much as possible.

"Not only did he post pictures on the internet, but to ensure that everyone Ms. Guerra knew viewed the photographs, he hacked her email account and sent them to her friends, family, coworkers, boss, and current boyfriend. He hacked her social media accounts and posted the pictures for the public to see: Facebook, Twitter, and Instagram. He created a fake resume, attached the pictures, and sent them on LinkedIn to potential employers. He vandalized billboards near her work and boyfriend's apartment, posting pictures that offered advertisements for prostitution services."

A couple of jurors gasped. One of the Real Housewives held her hand to her chest. Maybe Meili was right, and we'd lucked into someone with a cheating husband. The married retiree appeared to be saying a prayer. The rest of the jury nodded along as Meili spoke, seemingly enchanted by what she had to say.

"There is no legal justification for the defendant's actions. He made untrue statements about her, destroying her formerly-pristine reputation. She lost her job as a junior executive for a well-known company, on track to reach the top. Before this happened, Ms. Guerra's bonuses gave her an income of more than a quarter of a million dollars a year."

A couple of the jurors looked at me with new-found respect when she said that. If they thought this case was all about hurt feelings, they'd soon realize how much I'd lost.

"The evidence will show he did this for the sole purpose of hurting my client, and he did, in fact, hurt her. The New Jersey legislature stated that this type of behavior should not be tolerated when they made it a crime to distribute nude pictures of someone without their permission. You'll be left with no doubt when we finish here. My client did not consent to this distribution.

"Ms. Guerra has suffered greatly, and all because the defendant abandoned her, then couldn't believe she had the temerity to start dating someone else. I know what you're thinking, right? 'Poor thing.' When this is all over, the only two words you'll be thinking are 'punitive damages.' Thank you."

As Meili walked back to our table and took her seat, I wanted to clap. She winked at me, and I struggled to suppress a smile. I knew, of course, everything she said would be good for me, and everything the other side said would be bad. But seeing her in action was a thing of beauty, like watching a pride of lions take down a gazelle.

When she sat, Meili passed me a note. *Remember: You are going to disagree with everything Carter says in his opening. Try not to react. It's usually better not to object during opening/closing. He's going to try to get a rise out of you. Don't look at Eric. Don't scribble notes to me. Sit, fold your hands, and dream of the beach house you'll buy when we win this.*

None of this information was new or surprising, but the reminders gave me some much-needed bolstering. I played her words in my head over and over as opposing counsel addressed the jury.

Mr. Carter rose to his feet slowly and waited

until everyone in the jury box met his eyes before beginning to speak. "Ladies and gentlemen of the jury, this has all been a terrible, terrible mistake. We do not dispute there are nude pictures of the plaintiff all over the internet, and if that's something she didn't want to happen, we are very sorry for her. But there is no evidence—zero—my client had anything to do with it."

No evidence, my ass. Meili patted my knee. She'd warned me they might take this approach, especially when they didn't ask for any discovery. They had no idea we'd seen Eric's Facebook posts. Or printed them. I couldn't wait to see Eric's face when we produced them.

"My client has spent the past year in South America with limited internet access," Mr. Carter said. "He built housing for the poor, trying not to think about the woman he left behind. The woman who promised to wait for him, then cheated on him."

Serenity now, I whispered to myself under the table, recalling the old sitcom episode. *SERENITY NOW.*

"What happens when he returns to the United States? He's accused of violating his ex-girlfriend's privacy by posting nude pictures of her on the internet. One. The plaintiff cannot prove my client posted the photographs, or indeed, that she didn't post them herself. Anyone in the world might have done it, and the law says she needs to convince you my client did it. She has no evidence pointing to him as the culprit."

Meili nudged me under the table, and I forcibly unclenched my jaw.

"Two. To recover for emotional distress, the plaintiff must establish my client behaved in an extreme and outrageous manner. Even if she proves my client shared her photographs, this type of thing is neither extreme nor outrageous in today's society. About ten minutes after the internet was invented, seconds after they started putting cameras on telephones, what were people doing? Sharing naked pictures of themselves and other people. Another way of saying extreme and outrageous is behavior that isn't tolerated by our society—but this type of thing happens *all the time.* It's not just tolerated; it's common."

Rage made my blood boil. If this was the approach the defense took for the next week, I'd never make it. What if the jury believed this garbage?

"Three. The evidence will show the plaintiff was promiscuous long before this happened, and she, to be blunt, had no reputation to preserve. She's what we call 'libel proof,' ladies and gentlemen. Nothing my client allegedly did damaged her reputation worse than the things Ms. Guerra did herself."

My hand shook as I picked up my water glass. I tried to envision my new beach house and swinging hammock but instead started wondering if I'd get enough money to hire someone to bludgeon Mr. Carter with a shovel. No reputation worth preserving, indeed.

"The evidence will also establish the plaintiff's long history of mental illness, dating back to her childhood. She wants someone to blame for her bad luck, and as so often happens when you're a wealthy young man like my client, she's targeting the deepest pockets. The plaintiff failed in her efforts to get my client to marry her, and now, she's looking for another way to access his fortune. The truth will come out, ladies and gentlemen. You'll know Mr. Rutherford did not have anything to do with what happened to the plaintiff. Then you'll rule in favor of the defendant. Thank you."

If only I could stick my legs out into the aisle and kick him when he walked back to the defense table. But I forced myself to take deep breaths to eliminate the red spots dancing in front of my eyes.

"Thank you, counselors," Judge Patel said. "Ms. Chang, call your first witness."

"The plaintiff calls the defendant, Eric P. Rutherford III, to the stand."

When Meili said she planned to call Eric to the stand first, I balked. But then she explained that if we got his version of the story on the record, he couldn't change it later. One of the benefits of being the plaintiff is deciding in what order the jury hears witnesses. If I went first, Eric could listen and then change his testimony based on what I said. We wanted to make that impossible.

At hearing his name, my ex rose to his feet. I felt his gaze on me but kept my gaze planted on the judge. If I met Eric's eyes, I might lose control. When he promised to tell the truth, my nails dug into my palms. I wanted to scream. *You're a liar and a life destroyer.*

Meili cleared her throat and strolled toward the witness stand. "Mr. Rutherford, are you familiar with this picture?"

"Yes, ma'am."

"Can you describe it for the court reporter?"

"This is a nude picture of the plaintiff," he said.

Meili had warned me this part would be difficult. She even offered to let me wait outside the courtroom during the testimony. I'd wanted to be here: to sit in my seat and stare him in the eye and let him see that we both knew he lied. But when the first picture appeared on the five-by-eight-foot screen in front of the jury box, the air was sucked from the room. The ocean roared in my ears. I shoved my chair back from the table, gasping for oxygen.

It had been too long since I'd last forced myself to view the images, and they hadn't been nearly so large on my computer screen.

A million miles away something banged against wood. Panic muffled the noises. My hands covered my ears and I slammed my eyes shut. I leaned forward, bringing my head between my knees.

Something rancid touched my nose. My head cleared. Smelling salts. I coughed and wiped my eyes. Beside me, Meili dropped a small vial into my lap. I clutched it like a life raft.

"Ms. Guerra?" The judge spoke to me from the bench. "If you can't handle yourself, I'm afraid I'll have to ask you to wait outside. It's not fair for you to distract the jury."

My heart stopped. It's not like I controlled when depression swooped down on me. How would he feel if his naked body had been posted up there?

Words utterly escaped me, but Meili intervened. "I'm sorry, Your Honor. I'm sure it won't happen again."

Mr. Carter stood. By only the second day in court, he reminded me of a jumping jack, hopping to his feet whenever he had something to say. Maybe because he was only five feet tall, he thought jumping around made him seem bigger to the jury. "Your Honor, I'd like to move that Ms. Guerra be removed from the courtroom until my client has finished testifying."

Meili opened her mouth to respond, but I shook my head at her.

"It's fine, Your Honor," I said. "I'll wait outside until she's done showing the pictures."

A moment after I settled onto a bench in the hall, the door swung open. The last person I ever would've expected to see entered the hallway.

"Detective Egan? What are you doing here?"

"Your lawyer asked me to come in and testify about the police reports we got, and the ads we saw. I thought about sending Detective Stern intead."

My eyes narrowed. "You wouldn't!"

"Luckily, she's on vacation. I didn't have to make the call. But I won't be needed for a few days, so I'm headed back to the city. Ms. Chang's going to call me."

"You certainly go above and beyond, Detective. 'To serve and protect,' right?" I sniffled and swiped and my eyes. A tissue appeared in front of me as if by magic. "Thanks."

He shuffled his feet, then cleared his throat. "You're welcome. I'm sorry I can't stay for more of the trial, but I'll be back next week. Just remember—you didn't do anything wrong. This is something he did to you."

"I know. I thought I was prepared to see the pictures on the big screen, but I didn't realize how horrifying it would be." I shrugged. "It'll all be over soon, right?"

"Right. The reason I wanted to talk to you is, I figured out where I know you from. Told you I'd get it eventually."

I tilted my head and raised an eyebrow at him. "Oh, yeah? Remembered you do read *Forbes*, after all?"

He chuckled. "No, but it finally hit me. When I was a teenager, my kid sister loved horses. She worked in the stables in exchange for lessons twice a week. Then Mom remarried, and she and my stepdad suddenly could afford to let her enter shows."

Before my family moved from New Jersey to North Carolina, my parents owned a modest house in a nice neighborhood not far from where I currently lived. One of our neighbors had a full stable and a soft spot for the starry-eyed little girl who loved to ride them. Maybe the detective and I had crossed paths at some point.

"Hmmm. What's your sister's name?"

"Amira."

"Amira Egan? Doesn't ring a bell."

"No reason it should. I changed my name

when my stepfather adopted us. She's Amira Malouf."

That name sounded very familiar. "You mean Mira?"

"Yeah! That's her." Apparently Detective Egan hadn't investigated my history with his sister or he wouldn't sound so excited. This wasn't something I particularly wanted to relive, especially moments after witnessing my worst humiliation on the screen in the courtroom.

"You remembered my name from twenty years ago?"

"The accident was a big deal when it happened. It was in the papers, but I didn't recognize you. But it's been twenty years, and you no longer wear glasses and braces. What I remember—"

The heavy double doors swung open. The bailiff beckoned me back into the courtroom. Saved by the bell.

"Sorry, Detective. We'll catch up later."

He grinned. "Count on it."

Grateful to have been released from our conversation, I followed the bailiff back to my seat. The giant screen facing the jury had been moved to the corner. The eyes of the jury had been on me since the beginning, but now they felt less like pinpricks than daggers. I kept my eyes focused on the ground, trying to will the blood to keep from rising into my face.

Not my fault. Keep it together.

As soon as I settled in my seat, Meili addressed Eric. "Mr. Rutherford, did you show the printouts of those pictures to anyone?"

"No, I didn't. They were under my pillow, for the long, cold nights working for Habitat, if you know what I mean."

Meili ignored the single entendre. "Did you forward the emails with the pictures attached to anyone else?"

"No."

"Did you upload those pictures to the internet?"

"What do you think I am, a monster?" From the smug expression on his face, Eric didn't expect Meili to answer. The laughter in his eyes died at her response.

"Yes. Yes, that's exactly what I think."

Mr. Carter shot to his feet. "Objection, Your Honor! I move for a mistrial."

The blood drained from my face. Mistrial meant everything we'd done meant nothing. We'd have to go back, get a new trial date, wait another three months at least, pick a new jury, and Eric would avoid paying for several more months, at least.

"On what grounds?" Meili shot back at him.

"Your Honor, she's insulting the witness. She's trying to bias the jury against him, making it impossible for my client to get a fair trial. Misconduct substantially impairing the rights of a party is grounds for a mistrial."

"No, your witness asked me a question. I answered it. Perhaps someone should explain to him how court works," she said to Mr. Carter. Then she turned to the judge. "Your Honor, the complaint details some pretty monstrous things. Mr. Carter admitted in his opening statement that something terrible happened to my client. It's no secret I believe Mr. Rutherford is the one who did it. Therefore, it's no stretch for the jury to conclude I might possess a rather low opinion of Mr. Rutherford. It shouldn't impact how they view the evidence. Each of those jurors promised to make a decision based on the testimony, not based on whether I personally like the defendant."

Whispers swept the courtroom behind me. I prayed she could convince the judge not to dismiss this case. The thought of having to start over made me want to give up entirely.

The wooden gavel cracked against the bench. "That's enough," Judge Patel said. "I'll see you both at sidebar. Jurors, take a minute to stand and stretch."

Sidebars were held on the other side of the bench, making it impossible for me to catch the conversation. Meili wore a sardonic smile; Mr. Carter's face turned beet red. Judge Patel looked like he wished he'd taken early retirement. After a moment, both attorneys returned to their tables. Meili poured herself a glass of water while the members of the jury returned to their seats.

When they were settled, the judge spoke. "Mr. Rutherford, I'd suggest you not ask Ms. Chang any questions you don't want her to answer honestly. Please remember, her job is to ask the questions, and your job is to answer them." He raised his voice. "The jury will disregard Mr. Rutherford's question and the response, and they'll be stricken from the record. Also remember that only testimony from the witnesses is evidence. Counselor's questions and statements are not."

Had the jury noticed Eric never answered the question? Maybe this was part of his plan to avoid a judgment. Misdirection, smoke and mirrors, creating a sideshow.

"Allow me to repeat the question, Mr. Rutherford. I'm looking for a yes or no. Did you upload those pictures to the internet?"

"No, I did not."

I snuck a peek at the jury box, then immediately wished I hadn't. Several of them leaned forward, heads turned toward my ex-boyfriend. They appeared to be eating up his every word. Juror No. 9 angled her cleavage at the witness stand; apparently, the bad suit didn't bother her. Maybe calling Eric to the stand first was a tactical mistake. We didn't want the jury to go home thinking about poor Eric, the golden boy who's being used as a scapegoat by his evil ex-girlfriend.

"Are you familiar with Facebook?"

"Yes, of course."

"Do you have an account?"

"Doesn't everyone?"

"Objection, Your Honor. Move to strike as non-responsive."

Judge Patel said, "The witness will please answer the question."

"Yes, I have a Facebook account. I also have Twitter, LinkedIn, Tinder, Clout!, Bebo, Deviant-Art, Tumblr, Instagram, Ello, and an old Live Journal. There may also be an old MySpace account out there with my name on it."

"Do you recall posting to your Facebook account on November 9, 2018?"

"Not specifically, but I post frequently when I have internet access. It's possible."

"Excellent. Allow me to refresh your memory." Meili strode to the table and collected a sheaf of papers before returning to the witness stand. "These are screenshots taken from a Facebook page. The first one shows a post dated November 9. Is this your Facebook wall?"

"It could be."

"Yes or no, please."

Eric glanced at his lawyer, who nodded. "Yes, it is."

"Thank you. Could you please read the post to the jury?"

"I'd like to invoke the Fifth Amendment and refuse to answer on the grounds that the answer might tend to incriminate me." The lips of Eric's mouth turned up, but the smile didn't reach his eyes. If his attorney told him to smile to cater to the jury, he should've suggested making some effort not to look like a serial killer.

Meili returned his smile with a tight-lipped one of his own before address the judge. "Objection, Your Honor. All criminal charges against the witness have been dismissed."

"They could be refiled at any time before the statute of limitations expires," Mr. Carter replied promptly.

"No they can't. The case was dismissed with prejudice," Meili fired back. She turned to the judge. "This is ridiculous, Your Honor. I'm asking the witness to read a statement, and I can easily bring in any number of his Facebook friends to read it instead. It's impossible for him to go to jail at this point."

"We would, of course, object to having any of Eric's friends called as witnesses due to their lack of personal knowledge. Also, these posts are irrelevant."

The juror's heads swiveled between the attorneys like they followed a ball at a tennis tournament.

"In a defamation and intentional emotional distress case, the idea that the defendant's own words aren't relevant is hilarious. I find myself wondering if Attorney Carter picked up his law degree on the internet."

Judge Patel banged his gavel. "Enough, counselors! Mr. Carter, since the defendant is on trial for defamation of character, his own words are relevant to the action. Ms. Chang, you will refrain from disparaging opposing counsel or showboating for the jury. Do I make myself clear?"

Meili nodded, then turned back to Eric. "Tell me, Mr. Rutherford, is it true you posted online the following, 'Revenge is a dish best served cold.'?"

"Yes," Eric said through gritted teeth. "I think I was talking about a movie. I don't remember which one."

Liar.

"So the post wasn't about my client?"

"Of course not."

"What about this one?" She handed him another page. "November 10, 2018. Would you like to read the post, or should I?"

Eric gritted his teeth. "'A storm is brewing… Spending the evening thinking about a certain someone on the east coast.' I was thinking about my father. He lives in Manhattan, and we'd had an argument."

"So this post wasn't referring to my client, either?"

"No." His eyes dared her to defy him.

Undeterred, Meili pressed on. "Here's another post, dated November 29. Please read it to the jury."

"'I hear there's quite a storm up in the northeast. Putting a lot of lights out. Someone's going to get a big surprise when she gets back on her feet...er... foot.'" Eric's smile faltered, and many of the jurors now craned their necks to gawk at my legs.

"Is that post about my client, Mr. Rutherford?"

"Of course not."

"Do you know many females in the northeast who only have one foot?"

"I'm a popular guy; I have a lot of friends of all types."

Meili shot him a withering look before turning to the judge. "Move to strike as non-responsive to the question."

Before the judge could respond, Mr. Carter shot to his feet. "Your Honor, this is ridiculous. Surely Ms. Chang doesn't expect my client to remember every thought he ever had before ever posting on social media."

"It's not a stretch to suggest Mr. Rutherford would be able to recall any one-legged friends he cared enough about to be concerned for their welfare during a hurricane."

"That post says nothing about concern for anyone's welfare."

"Touché," Meili said. "Because, as we know, he wasn—"

"Enough!" Judge Patel said. "Mr. Rutherford, please answer the counselor's questions as asked. Mr. Carter, your objection is overruled. Ms. Chang, you *will* refrain from adding your own commentary for the jury or you'll be held in contempt. I won't warn you again. Let's hurry up with this line of questioning."

"I'm sorry, Your Honor," Meili said. "Only one more question. Mr. Rutherford, please read this last post aloud for the jury."

For a split second, Eric's smug mask slipped when he read the page. He recovered so easily, only close friends—or close, bitter enemies— would notice the momentary lack of composure. "The post is dated November 10, 2018. It says 'Hehehehehehehehe. Pretty icy in some parts of New Jersey, huh?'."

In the jury box, one of the Real Housewives gasped and leaned backward, fanning herself. Her theatrics almost made me giggle, but I appreciated the sentiment.

"What does that post mean, Mr. Rutherford?"

"I have no idea. It was almost a year ago." He returned smoothly.

"Is this post about Ms. Guerra?"

"Of course not."

Nothing. Not a crack. We'd lost our chance to get him to confess to the jury. My heart sank. My lawyer pressed her lips into a thin line.

"Hmmm." Meili studied Eric for a minute, then took a step back. "You're a good-looking guy, Mr. Rutherford. Charming."

"Thank you," he said.

Mr. Carter raised his hand. "Objection. While I'm sure my client is flattered, opposing counsel's opinion of his looks aren't relevant to the proceeding."

"I'm getting to the point, Your Honor."

"Get there fast, Counselor. I tend to agree with Mr. Carter."

"Absolutely. Thank you." Meili strolled over to the jury box, almost casually. "You probably have a lot of female admirers, don't you?"

Eric made a face he must've thought made him appear humble; in fact, he looked constipated. "Well, I don't like to brag, but I've dated my fair share."

"I bet women fall in love with you pretty easily right?"

He coughed. "You know how it is. A gentleman doesn't kiss and tell."

"And when the time comes, it's usually you who ends the relationship, right?"

"Yes," Eric said. "It's not uncommon for a woman I date to want to get serious before I'm ready. Especially now that I'm older, a lot of them seem to expect a proposal pretty early on. It doesn't seem right to string them along, so I cut them free."

"How noble of you," Meili said. She cleared her throat before firing her next questions. "So would it be fair to say, Mr. Rutherford, you don't get dumped often? And to say, a woman breaks up with you, you don't like it at all?"

Eric's face darkened. "No—"

"So, when my client dumped you, when a woman had the nerve to fall out of love with you, you wanted to show her she'd made a big mistake, right? You wanted to make her pay, didn't you?"

"Objection, Your Honor!" Mr. Carter remained seated, but color rose in his face.

Meili raised one hand. "Withdrawn."

Eric smiled at her, every inch the entitled little Prince, and rose to his feet. "If that's all you wanted to know…"

"Don't move," Meili ordered.

He paused, raising one eyebrow.

Meili said, "I'm not finished yet. You can get up when I say so."

Eric settled back into his seat, fuming. He wasn't the only one—we weren't getting anywhere. He'd admitted nothing. Without his confession, our entire case was circumstantial, and he knew it.

Chapter 17

The next day contained more of the same: Eric sat on the stand while Meili did her best to show the jury what a vindictive creep he was. He stalled us at every turn. Mr. Carter had prepared his client well. If I didn't know Eric did this, even I'd wonder if he might be telling the truth.

Out of desperation, Meili even tried to bring up the hot sauce incident.

"Objection, Your Honor. Relevance?"

"This evidence shows a pattern of vindictive behavior on the part of the defendant. It's relevant to showing a predisposition toward this type of behavior. We're building a circumstantial case to show the jury, more likely than not, he's the one who did this."

Judge Patel wasn't impressed with Meili's reasoning. "Objection sustained. Next question, counselor."

My heart sank. Meili designed this entire line of questioning to make the jury wonder about Eric's character, to show he was exactly the type of person who would post naked pictures of his ex-girlfriend on the internet to destroy her life. We needed the jury to see his true self: a narcissistic, self-important creep.

"Mr. Rutherford, do you remember Tina Catania?"

Another ex, long before we met. After they broke up, someone smashed the windows of her car. I wished with my whole heart I'd spoken to her when she first called, so long ago. Maybe some of this could have been avoided. But I'd stupidly believed Eric when he said she was pissed because he'd dumped her. Until I'd talked to her and got the full story. Eric had a history of "punishing" girls who'd broken up with him.

Tina's new husband had been stationed on a military base in Japan, where we couldn't subpoena her. But we could make the jury wonder who she was and why Meili brought her up.

Mr. Carter interrupted again. "Objection, Your Honor. Relevance?"

"We believe the defendant's prior behavior toward ex-girlfriends is probative of how he acted in this specific case, sir." Meili spoke as if she weren't aware we stood on quicksand, sinking fast.

"Sustained. Move on. Talk about something other than the defendant's character."

Meili consulted her notes. She lifted one page, dropped it. Lifted the next, skimmed, dropped it. Slowly, lazily, like she had all the time in the world, she went through every page in her legal pad. Mr. Carter shifted impatiently at the next table, eyes on the ticking clock above the judge's bench. When she'd examined several pages in this manner, he spoke. "Excuse me, Your Honor, but is there a reason for this delay?"

My lawyer raised her head, smiling slightly. "I'm looking for a question that doesn't address your client's predisposition to do this type of thing."

The jury tittered. I hid a smile behind my hand. Mr. Carter roared. "OBJECTION! Move to strike."

Meili raised one hand. "My apologies, Your Honor. I withdraw the statement."

"I move for a mistrial."

"Ms. Chang's statement will be stricken from the record," Judge Patel said. "Mr. Carter's motion is denied, and I'll see you both in my chambers. This bickering is ridiculous. Bailiff, take the jurors out for an early lunch. We'll reconvene at two."

The clock read a few minutes after eleven. Too nervous to eat and not wanting to sit around for three hours, I snuck out a side door of the courthouse and went home. There, I settled into a chair in my living room and stared out the window, thinking. Waiting. Hiding from my life. Wondering how it would all end. How could we possibly win the case now? What would I do if we lost?

After lunch, Meili told me the judge warned them both that there would be sanctions for any more argumentative or hostile statements in front of the jury. My spirits sank. If we couldn't keep picking away at Eric until he exploded and showed the jury his true character, proving the case could be impossible.

"Hey, this is a good thing," she said. "It means when you take the stand, Carter can't harass you without getting sanctioned himself. All I did was ensure that the judge will look out for potential issues. He's put us both on a short leash."

"What's on all those pages of notes you flipped through?"

She grinned. "My shopping list, calls to return later, and a reminder to ask my housekeeper to pick up my clothes from the dry cleaner. Super important lawyer stuff."

"So none of it was about Eric's character?"

"Not a word."

AFTER LUNCH, Meili called Detective Egan to testify about the defaced billboards around the city and the complaints the police department received. The ads themselves contained no fingerprints, so we unfortunately couldn't prove Eric put them up. I sincerely doubted he did the dirty work himself, so it didn't matter.

Mr. Carter popped up long enough to ask if my ex-boyfriend had been charged with any crimes relating to the billboards or vandalism, then excused the witness.

At the end of the day, after Judge Patel sent the jury home, Meili and Mr. Carter went into chambers to advise that no progress had been made toward settling. I ignored Eric, sitting at the table beside me. My phone buzzed and beeped several times as soon as I turned it on, sending a wave of panic through me. Surely he hadn't posted more—

But no, the texts were all from Tara.

Tara: How's court going? Did Meili make him cry yet?

Tara: Do you need someone to come in and testify as to what a pompous jackass Eric always was?

Tara: I could make time in my schedule to talk about how much I hate him.

Me: Court wasn't very interesting, but your Detective Hottie came in to testify. Sorry you missed him.

Tara: If Det. Hottie was there, it's interesting.

When I exited the double doors with Meili a few minutes later, Detective Egan waited in the hall.

"Hey. Thanks for helping out." Since Detective Egan lived and worked in New York rather than New Jersey, we didn't have the power to subpoena him. He came down voluntarily to help, which meant a lot to me. Another officer may not have been willing to take the time. His partner certainly wouldn't have been.

"Not a problem." He shoved his hands in his pockets. "I'd like to continue the conversation we started the other day. If you're not doing anything, would you be willing to have dinner with me?"

Meili glared at me, and her warning against dating rang through my head. This wasn't a date, though. It was dinner with the police officer worked on my case and wanted to see if I was okay. Or reconnecting with the brother of an old friend.

"One moment, please, Detective," she said, pulling me aside.

He moved down the hall in the other direction, stopping around the corner from the elevator bay.

Meili waited until he moved out of earshot, then turned to me. "Anna. What did I tell you about dating during the case?"

I met her gaze without flinching. "It's not a date. His kid sister and I were friends twenty years ago. He's looking out for me because of what happened."

"I've been lied to by some of the best, you know. You're not the best."

"I know," I said. "I promise, no physical contact. No romantic restaurants. I just want to be around someone who treats me like a normal person for a while. He's nice. I could use a friend these days."

"I'm your friend."

"I'm paying you a lot of money to be my 'friend.' This is different."

She studied my face for a long moment before she finally nodded. "Okay, fine. But no nookie—I mean it."

I laughed. "Don't worry about that. I promise."

"Okay, fine." We reached the elevator bank, and she nodded to the officer. "Good evening, Detective. Good night, Anna."

She disappeared behind the stairwell door.

"Sorry to make you wait. We were talking strategy."

"No problem." He shoved his hands into his pockets, shuffled his feet. "There's a coffee shop right down the street."

"The media's been camping out in that coffee shop since the case began. Most of them are gone, but can we head in the other direction? I can walk surprisingly long distances before my prosthetic starts to make my leg ache."

"Absolutely. If we see any media, I'll arrest them." I grinned at him. His return smile made something flutter, low in my belly. I shoved the feeling aside, and he continued, "Like I was saying, I was there, the day of your accident. My sister, Mira, finished competing in the pre-teen dressage competition earlier, and we were waiting for them to announce the winners."

"She came in second, right?" ...*and never spoke to me again.*

When we reached the cafe, Sayid held the door open for me. I couldn't remember the last time a man did that, but I liked it. "Right. You came in first. Did you ever get your medal?"

"Yeah. Someone brought it to the hospital later."

"That's good. So what happened?"

"Well, our neighbor was some kind of big shot.

I don't remember what he did, but he liked the attention his company got when his horses did well, so he let me ride them in competitions. He got the publicity and the money, I got the ribbons and the thrill. Win-win. At first." The waiter brought menus, and we made small talk until we placed our orders. Then I sipped my coffee, gathering my courage to return to the topic he wanted to discuss. The liquid scalded my tongue. When my vision cleared and I could breathe again, I asked the million-dollar question. "Did you see the accident?"

"Yeah. The pre-teen hunter over fences event, the one with the jumps, started in the main ring, and Mira was up about halfway through the lineup. I sat in the stands with my parents, watching. Mira's face went white when you fell. You were so still, and then the crack echoed over the speakers when the horse landed on you. People thought…" He swallowed. "Well, we were all relieved to hear you were going to recover."

I smiled ruefully. "At the time, I wished I hadn't. Junior high's painful enough without unwanted fame and a disability."

"I know." He squeezed my hand where it lay on the table. "She ran to help, but someone held her back. One of the judges, I think. I'd never seen her so terrified, before or since. She refused to ride again for three months after it happened. Did you know that?"

"No. She never called, never visited. Her and the rest of my friends." My voice cracked. So many years passed, but bitterness lingered well beyond the time when a more reasonable emotion evaporated. I waited while the server delivered our food, then continued. "Only Tara stood by me, even after my parents moved to North Carolina. We sent letters back and forth every week." I blinked back tears, wondering why I was sharing so much with this stranger.

He touched my chin, and I met his eyes. If I'd seen pity, I'd have run out the door and never turned back, but only empathy gazed back at me. "Hey. Mira didn't abandon you. She was thirteen, too. Before the competition, my parents bought a house in Connecticut. We moved a few days later. Hardly anyone had cell phones, limited internet, you remember. You were in the hospital, and by the time she got up the courage to visit, you were gone. She'll be thrilled to hear I found you."

"Somehow, I doubt that. People aren't exactly rushing to befriend me these days."

He cleared his throat, ducked his head. Redness rose in his cheeks as he smiled shyly at me. "I'd befriend you, if you'll let me."

My stomach fluttered again. I smiled at him. "I'd like that, Detective. Lord knows I need a friend these days."

"Call me Sayid." He took a bite of his burger.

"So what happened? I mean—we never found out what caused you to fall."

Eric's words haunted me, a knife twisting in my gut. *You never would've made anything of yourself without affirmative action and someone else's money.* I shook my head, trying to clear them.

"You don't have to talk to about it, if you don't want to," Sayid said.

"No, it's okay. It's been twenty years. After my parents moved to the States, Papá opened a private practice and Mamá went to school to get her CPA license. We lived in a nice area. Not super ritzy, but nice. Our next-door neighbors had a stable in the backyard. Their twins were about my age; we did everything together. When they learned to ride, I learned to ride. When we got older, Paula and Andy started taking other lessons, but I still worked in the stables. Mamá and Papá wanted me to learn the value of hard work, so I helped out in exchange for continued access to the horses. For the competition, their dad agreed to let me ride a beautiful black creature named Sir Maxwell."

"Interesting name for a horse," Sayid said.

"Horses always have weird names. You get used to it." I sipped my no-longer scalding hot coffee. "I did the dressage competition that morning—killed it, as you saw. I was so excited to have won. When I sat in the ring, waiting for Sir

Maxwell and me to get the signal to begin, I thought it was the best day of my entire life."

These memories had been suppressed for so long, I wasn't prepared for how I'd feel unburying them. A wave of despair hit me. I ate a French fry slowly, trying to regain my composure. Sayid motioned to the waitress to refill our coffees but waited for me to continue.

After a moment, I continued. "Sir Maxwell fidgeted a bit, but I chalked it up to anxiety caused by the buzz of the crowds, thought maybe he sensed my nerves. When the signal came, I took off, cantering around the ring.

"Something was wrong. Sir Maxwell wasn't acting right. But I figured we'd be in the ring for two minutes, finish the event, and then I'd give him some extra treats when we got back to his stall. Stupid, I know, but I was only thirteen and we were both nervous. Anyway, we rode around the ring a few times, and I aimed him for the first jump. This was something we'd practiced a thousand times. We were approaching head-on, perfectly placed."

I was no longer recapping the moment so much as reliving it. Air rushed past my face, hooves thundered against the dirt floor of the ring. The fresh scent of the flowers braided into Sir Maxwell's mane touched my nose.

"And then, at the spot where he should've

taken off, I rose in the saddle, like we'd practiced a thousand times. My form was perfect. But something went wrong. Instead of pushing off the ground, Sir Maxwell stopped dead, throwing me off balance. He bucked, and I went flying. Nearly hit my head on the jump. When I hit the ground, I instinctively rolled—but Sir Maxwell reared, and I didn't make it out of the way. He came down on my ankle. Shattered nearly all the bones in my ankle and my foot. Ironically, my pinky toe was fine."

Sayid's eye's filled with sympathy. "Wow. I'm sorry. It must've been horrible, especially as a teenager. What went wrong?"

"We found out later. The mother of one of the other contestants—the one who came in fourth in dressage—paid one of the stable hands a lot of money to put something under my saddle to make the horse throw me. I guess neither of them thought through the consequences of a fall like that. Or maybe they didn't care since I wasn't one of them."

"Holy shit! That's literally insane. She could have killed you."

"Yeah. Well, she spent about a year in jail, and the settlement paid for my house and college. I guess it's better than the Texas cheerleader thing that happened a few years earlier, but still, it changed my life." I cleared my throat and blew on my fresh coffee to cool it. "At the time, I blocked it all out. Remembered nothing after pointing Sir Maxwell at the jump. What I told you is what my parents said they saw, and bits I got from Tara, but it still feels like recapping an old movie. The doctors said I might never regain the memory of what happened. Apparently, the brain sometimes erased traumatic events to protect us from having to relive them." I laughed hollowly. "If only my brain could wipe out the memory of this past year."

"Even though it means you wouldn't know who I am, I wish there were a way to make that happen."

I forced myself to swallow the negative feelings brought on by the memories and focus on the present. Decent coffee, a good sandwich, incredibly good-looking police officer, and something so long forgotten, it seemed foreign. Hope. "Maybe the entire year hasn't been completely terrible, after all."

Chapter 18

The trial continued. Using what seemed like an endless parade of former coworkers, college friends, and even the teenage kid who worked at the Starbucks on the ground floor of my old office building, Meili showed the jury how thoroughly Eric trashed my reputation. Those weeks felt like years. She could've called more, but I figured it was overkill to bring in my kindergarten teacher or the doctor who amputated my left foot. By the time Mr. Carter finished cross-examining the second-to-last witness on our list, I'd nearly managed to numb myself to hearing over and over how little people now thought of me. Almost.

Knowing what came next, I wiped my palms on my skirt, took a deep breath, and stood.

"The plaintiff calls Anna Guerra to the stand."

The jurors leaned forward, some of them showing interest for the first time in several days. I stood, hands on the table, waiting for my legs to stop shaking while I walked up to the stand. When I'd dressed in the knee-length charcoal skirt Meili chose, I also slipped my right foot into a slightly heeled ballet flat. The shoe pinched enough to make me limp after a couple of hours; I never wore it. But after nearly two years in the back of my closet, this overpriced shoe's time had come.

My left shoe scratched and thumped against the floor. The resulting ominous echo reminded me of walking toward the execution chamber. I forced myself to walk slowly, per Meili's instructions, letting the jury get the full impact of my injury. It wasn't something they'd necessarily notice on their own, always being brought in after I'd been seated and being led out before the parties. During trial, I sat at the table most of the time after my dramatic exit the first day. A couple of jurors peered at me from the box, but the front of the table blocked them from checking out my legs. All things considered, that may have been a blessing in disguise.

I reached the box and turned to face the bailiff. "Do you swear to tell the truth, the whole truth, and nothing but the truth, so help you God?"

I no longer believed in God, but wisely refrained from mentioning that fact. Instead, I nodded. "Yes, I swear."

"Thank you. Please take your seat. State your name for the record?"

"Anna Guerra. A-N-N-A G-U-E-R-R-A."

I smoothed my skirt and sat in the wooden chair, which squeaked. The microphone attached to the witness stand pointed at the air above my head. When I reached to adjust it, my shaking fingers sent it clattering to the floor. I jumped. "Sorry, Your Honor."

"Don't worry about it." The judge nodded to the bailiff who'd barely made it back to his post. While the officer fixed the microphone, Meili brought me a glass of water.

Before she started, I ran her instructions through my head. Head up, shoulders back, eyes forward. Talk to the jury, not the judge, not the lawyers. Try to make eye contact with each of them, personalize the testimony. Don't look at Eric if I could avoid it. Ask if I needed to take a break for any reason.

I wouldn't break. Not here, not again.

We practiced these questions, but Meili didn't want to practice reading the texts and emails over and over. I asked if she worried I get desensitized to the content, and wanted the jury to see my reactions as I read them. She said she didn't see any reason to torture me unnecessarily, which never occurred to me. How sad.

"Can you tell us what happened, in your own words, the morning of November 11, 2018?"

I quickly gave an overview of the morning I returned to work after the hurricane, right up until I got to the bathroom and remembered to turn my phone on.

"Do you ordinarily wait to check your phone until you get to work in the morning?"

"Usually, no. But we lost reception for a couple of days after the hurricane, and the storm knocked out the power at my house so I didn't have Wi-Fi. The network was so jammed, the phone was constantly trying to reconnect, doing nothing but draining the battery. I turned it off early the next morning and left it off."

The jurors nodded sympathetically. Hurricane Harriet hit everyone hard. Meili wanted this bit out to immediately make the jury feel sorry for me. She'd argued that the timing played into how much I suffered. Mr. Carter argued the hurricane wasn't Eric's fault and he couldn't be responsible for the weather. Personally, I suspected he timed the bomb to drop when I had no way of trying to reduce the damage before it got out of control, but we had only the Facebook posts to prove it, and our efforts there flopped.

The judge surprised me by allowing the testimony, but Meili said the defendant in a court case "takes the victim as he finds him." If circumstances in my life having nothing to do with the photographs made the damages worse than they would've been otherwise, Eric still bore the responsibility.

The whole thing sounded weird to me, but I wasn't about to argue the judge out of ruling in my favor.

"Thank you, Anna. So what happened when you got to work after the hurricane?"

"I turned on my phone when I entered the building to see if the network was back up and I could download my messages. It had been years since I took three days off work, and being unplugged against my will made me antsy. While I was in the restroom, the phone started vibrating constantly."

"What happened when you checked your phone?"

"More than three hundred text messages poured in, mostly from unknown numbers. While I held the phone, more popped up."

Meili held up a sheaf of papers. "Your Honor, I hold Plaintiff's Exhibit A. Anna, do you recognize this document?"

"These are my cell phone records from last November and December. My old phone number."

"Thank you. If you flip ahead to page ten, I've starred a text for you. Can you read the date and time of the first text?"

"November 10, 2018. Nine forty-seven p.m."

"Thank you. Do you know what you were doing at that date and time?"

"Hiding in my basement with my roommate's cat, Hermione." One or two of the jurors smiled at me. Good to know we had some animal lovers. "It was the middle of the hurricane, around the time a tree fell onto my car."

"Objection, Your Honor!"

"We covered this in pre-trial, Your Honor. It's all relevant to my client's emotional suffering."

"Overruled."

"Thank you, Your Honor." To me, Meili said, "Anna, would you please begin at the starred message and read each text?"

I swallowed, sipped my water. "Nov. 10, 2018. 9:47 p.m. 212-555-3298. 'Slut.' Nov. 10, 2018. 9:47 p.m. 617-555-9084. Whore."

"That's the full content of those two texts?"

"Yes, it is."

"Do you recognize either of those numbers?"

I shook my head before remembering all responses needed to be verbal for the court reporter.

"No. 212 is a New York area code. I think 617 is in Boston. But I don't know who sent the texts."

"Thank you. Please continue."

I glanced at the jurors, several of whom were leaning forward, and cleared my throat before reading the next message. "November 10, 2018. 9:47 p.m 203-555-4112. 'You're hot. I'd fuck you, even if you are illegal'—all the 'you's' and the 'are's are misspelled, by the way."

Mr. Carter stood. "Objection, Your Honor."

My heart pounded. They weren't going to let us read our best evidence?

The judge raised an eyebrow. Meili snorted into one hand. Her amused reaction calmed me slightly. "Surely you're not suggesting these messages are irrelevant to the question of whether my client suffered emotional harm? Perhaps the defendant is so used to getting texts that cast aspersions on his morality, these wouldn't bother him?"

The jury whispered. The galley buzzed.

Judge Patel banged his gavel, and the courtroom fell silent. "That's going to cost you $100, Ms. Chang. You've been warned about making those comments in front of the jury. We'll try this case on the facts, not on sniping." He turned toward Mr. Carter. "What is your objection, Counselor?"

"It is my understanding, Your Honor, that the plaintiff intends to read several hundred emails and text messages into the record. We believe this evidence is unnecessarily cumulative and unfairly prejudices the jury against Mr. Rutherford. Although we've been in court for days now, there is still no evidence he sent any of the texts or caused someone else to send them. We will stipulate that the texts Ms. Guerra received are substantially similar to the ones already read, but object to taking up the court's time reading all of them into the record. The jury can review the texts at their leisure during deliberations."

"That's a great idea, Your Honor!" Meili said. "Why introduce evidence in the courtroom when the jury can read it themselves later?" A few titters came from the jury box, but I worried she was setting herself up for another fine from the judge. "This evidence goes directly to how my client suffered. The impact of receiving these messages, the emotions Ms. Guerra felt—That's all directly relevant to the question of whether she was emotionally distressed, which is a required element of the tort. It also speaks toward her damages. The jury needs to hear these messages to understand their full impact. Much of their effect will be lost if my client isn't allowed to read the messages, and it's unfair to put the burden on the jury to review the evidence once they're in the deliberations room."

I watched the jury while the judge considered the arguments. Other than Juror No. 9, who inspected her fingernails, I'd never seen them so interested. Not for the first time, I thanked all the fates that she was an alternate and prayed we wouldn't need her to deliberate. The rest of the jurors were desperate to know what was in those text messages. At that point, it didn't matter if the judge let me read them or not: the jurors would spend hours poring over these pages in the deliberations room. Exactly what we wanted.

"You bring up an excellent point, Mr. Carter," Judge Patel said. "However, when the question on the table is the outrageousness of the defendant's behavior and how it affected the plaintiff, I'm afraid I agree with Ms. Chang. Objection overruled."

The messages went on and on. In addition to the texts I found that morning, there were emails, Facebook posts, and the LinkedIn profile (not to mention the responses that one generated). I read until my voice went hoarse, stopping only for sips of water or the occasional objection that a message was irrelevant. For two days I continued. When my voice shook, I paused, but otherwise soldiered on.

Finally, near the end of the second afternoon, my voice gave out and my eyes filled with tears. The message that got me said simply, "I'd fuck you and your mother, you filthy little sluts."

We expected this moment to come: when I

broke down in front of the jury. Meili wagered it would arrive early in the trial, but in my naïveté, I swore to get through the entire stack of messages. Not so much.

Instead of prompting me to read the next message, my lawyer studied me. From our prior conversation about this moment, I knew she'd count to thirty before saying anything, so I sniffled, sipped my water, and quelled the urge to fill the silence.

Finally, she tilted her head to the right, away from the jury box, her eyes still locked on my face. "Anna, how many messages do you have left?"

Wordlessly, I held up the stack of papers from which I'd been reading.

"I'm sorry, Ms. Guerra," the judge said, "but we need a verbal response for the record."

I cleared my throat. "It's okay. The stack of papers is about two inches thick, Your Honor."

In response, Meili glanced from me to the jury, and back, then turned to the bench. "Your Honor, at this point, I'd like to accept Mr. Carter's stipulation regarding these messages. It's not fair to my client to put her through any more grief. We'd like to move them all into evidence to spare my client the stress of having to relive those that remain. The jury can review them privately."

Mr. Carter sputtered a bit but didn't object. After all, with every message I read, the potential damages went up. The judge told me I could step down and take a break until morning.

The court clerk handed me a tissue, and I dabbed at my eyes while the jury filed out of the room. Through the haze of my tears, one thing was clear: the jurors couldn't take their eyes off the pages still clutched in my lap.

ON THE THIRD MORNING, we moved from the aftermath to the pictures themselves.

"To your knowledge, did anyone have nude pictures of you before these photographs appeared on the internet?" She'd skated around the issue as much as she could, but at the end of the day, if we didn't introduce evidence Eric possessed pictures of me, no matter how he got them, our case evaporated.

"Yes. The defendant, Eric Rutherford."

Wood creaked as several jurors leaned forward. A gray-haired man pursed his lips at me and a woman about my father's age swiveled her head between me and Eric. The expression on her face suggested I'd lost some points.

"What did those pictures show?"

"They are the same photographs the jury saw on the first day of the trial. My body, naked."

Meili held up each picture for me to identify.

After each one was introduced into evidence, she passed the photograph among the jury. Once the jurors examined each picture and returned them to the clerk, we got down to the heart of the dispute.

"Anna, did Mr. Rutherford understand that these pictures were private?"

"Objection, Your Honor. The witness can't possibly know what my client thought over a year ago."

"I'll rephrase. Did you give Mr. Rutherford permission to share these pictures with anyone else?"

My head high, I met the gaze of each juror for a second before I answered. "No, I did not."

"Did you give anyone permission to distribute nude pictures of you?"

"No, I did not."

"Did you ever tell him you'd like to be a prostitute?"

Before I answered, I took a moment to survey the jury box again. Meili said making eye contact could help establish a connection with the jurors. This testimony was so embarrassing but so important. Although part of me wanted to run and hide under the plaintiff's table, I understood the importance of getting the jurors on my side. "No."

"Have you ever traded sexual favors for money?"

"No."

"Did you ask Mr. Rutherford to post advertisements for you, offering sexual favors for money?"

I looked directly at Eric, whose eyes were glued to the wooden surface in front of him. "Of course not."

"Did you ask or allow him to post nude pictures of you on the internet?"

"No."

"Did you ask him to create a LinkedIn profile for you?"

"No."

"Did you ask or allow him to submit resumes in your name?"

"No."

"Did you give him permission to access your social media accounts and email?"

Another glance at the jury box, where a few jurors leaned toward me, two watched the clock, and one picked at her cuticles. "No, I did not."

As planned, Meili spent a long moment reviewing her notes to allow me to compose myself for cross-examination. "Thank you, Anna." Meili said, "No further questions, Your Honor."

Before she made it back to our table, Mr. Carter bounded out of his seat. He approached the witness stand, grinning like a hyena stalking his prey. "Good afternoon, Ms. Guerra. May I call you Ann-a?"

"No, you may not." Over the lawyer's shoulder, I recognized the wrinkling of Meili's eyes that signaled her amusement. She'd told me I didn't have to be nice to this parasite. "My name is Ahna. You may call me Ms. Guerra."

My rudeness might lose me half a point with the jury, but it was worth it to throw him off his game, even a little. Even knowing he was just doing his job, I loathed Eric's lawyer with every fiber of my being. My fingers itched to slap the permanent self-satisfied smile off his face.

"Yes, my mistake." Mr. Carter paused to take a sip of water, and I did the same. "Now, Ms. Guerra, how did Mr. Rutherford get the naked pictures of you?"

Meili surged to her feet. "Objection, Your Honor!"

The judge peered at Mr. Carter over his glasses. "Didn't we cover this with the pretrial motions?"

"It did come up, sir. However, I just thought the jury has a right to know Ms. Guerra sent—"

"OBJECTION, YOUR HONOR." Meili shoved her chair back. "Permission to approach?"

The judge banged his gavel. "Order in the court!"

"—the pictures to the defendant," Mr. Carter said at the same moment.

Pandemonium broke out. A buzz filled the

courtroom, and the jurors whispered among themselves. Everything blurred into a sea of activity.

The gavel slammed against the wood a second time. "I said, ORDER!"

I leaned forward, bringing my head between my knees and forcing myself to take deep breaths. The buzz of activity made my head spin. In a heartbeat, I was right back in my office, packing my desk while the rest of the office whispered and tried to pretend they weren't trying to peek through the blinds covering the glass walls.

The bang of the gavel penetrated my hysteria. "EVERYBODY, QUIET!"

Silence descended. I tried to force air into my lungs, with limited success. The judge barked orders from the bench.

"Bailiff, clear the audience. Another outburst like that, and I'll close the courtroom for the remainder of the proceedings. Take the jury out to get some air. We'll reconvene in about half an hour. Counsel, I'll see *both* of you in my chambers."

I shot a questioning look at Meili, and she shook her head. The judge nodded at Eric, then leaned toward me. "Mr. Rutherford, Ms. Guerra, you're welcome to join us in chambers, but if you want to take a walk, visit the restroom, that's okay.

One of the bailiffs will let you know when we're ready for you."

My fingers twisted in my lap. "Thank you, Your Honor. I could use a break."

In the restroom, I splashed water on my face, brushed my hair, then reapplied my make-up. I told myself I wasn't hiding, but before I came up with somewhere else to go, my phone buzzed.

THE JUDGE OFFERED US A MISTRIAL, Meili texted. WHERE ARE YOU?

IN THE RESTROOM. BE RIGHT THERE. I thought for a moment, then sent another message. MIS-TRIAL MEANS THE CASE IS OVER, RIGHT? WE START AGAIN WITH A NEW JURY?

Meili: THAT'S RIGHT. OR, WE SETTLE.

Me: FUCK THAT.

Chapter 19

Ten minutes later, I sat back on the stand while the jury filed into their seats. They avoided looking at me. I forced myself not to let my shoulders slump. This was a setback, yes, but I couldn't let the jury see how much Eric and his lawyer upset me. They couldn't think they'd won this battle. Besides, Meili had a plan.

As soon as the jurors sat, the judge addressed them. "Members of the jury will disregard all comments made this morning. You may not consider anything you heard while evaluating the evidence. We're going to restart cross-examination from the beginning. Am I understood?"

Twelve heads bobbed in agreement. We all knew it wasn't true. Some things are so prejudicial, it's impossible to un-hear them. But Meili thought we could do some damage control, and I didn't want to reset this trial. We couldn't allow Eric's lawyer to force a mistrial, knowing that's what he wanted.

The thought of reading all those texts and emails again, of more weeks on the stand, made my skin crawl. I couldn't start over. The strain would send me back to the hospital.

We wouldn't settle. We wouldn't let Eric win. I'd finish this case or die trying.

The judge informed Mr. Carter that he would be held in contempt of court if he made any further comments of that type and fined one hundred thousand dollars—which he was prohibited from billing to Eric. The judge also hinted he wasn't above locking Mr. Carter up overnight until he learned to show some respect for the court's rulings. Meili was under the same prohibition, but she looked delighted about it.

We decided to continue on those terms, rather than cave and let my ex-boyfriend win yet again. No matter how much Eric was paying his lawyer, Mr. Carter wasn't likely to risk that kind of money now that we'd shown we weren't willing to accept a mistrial.

Once the jury re-entered the courtroom, I took the stand again and waited for Mr. Carter to speak.

"Hello, Ms. Guerra."

In response, I glared at him.

"Your Honor, do I have permission to treat the plaintiff as a hostile witness? Can you direct her to please answer me?"

Meili rose halfway out of her seat. "Your Honor, Counselor hasn't asked my client a question. I'm sure, if he does, she'll respond."

"Fair enough." Mr. Carter tapped his fingers together, one at a time. My demeanor couldn't have thrown him; he was stalling for time. I wondered why.

Behind him, Eric stared at the table, rolling a pen across his fingers. He'd seemed amused, almost gleeful, when witness after witness testified as to what they'd thought of me before seeing the pictures, and how that opinion plummeted after. I hoped the jurors spent as much time watching his body language as I did. Now, he seemed bored, as if he had an important meeting to get to and the entire courtroom put a major inconvenience on his important schedule.

I'd inconvenience him, all the way to the bank. Hopefully for seven figures.

"On second thought," Mr. Carter said, rubbing his chin, "I have no questions for this witness. Ms. Guerra, you may step down."

Meili popped out of her chair while Mr. Carter's words still hung in the air. She crossed the floor to the podium in a heartbeat. "Anna, why did you send Mr. Rutherford those pictures?"

Mr. Carter rose. "Objection, Your Honor. Since my entire cross-examination was stricken from the record, there is no testimony for Ms. Chang to redirect."

"You can't be serious." If looks could kill, Meili would've vaporized opposing counsel on the spot.

Judge Patel closed his eyes before he spoke. "Under the circumstances, Mr. Carter, I strongly suggest you withdraw your objection. My court-room is not a circus."

"Your Honor, my client——"

"You are about three seconds away from being held in contempt of court. Is that what you want?" Mr. Carter shook his head. "The next words out of your mouth can be 'I withdraw the objection,' or you can spend the night in lock-up. Your call."

I snuck a peek at the jury box, where most of the jurors seemed as amused by the exchange as I was.

He shifted, rubbed his terrible toupee, then finally spoke. "I withdraw the objection, Your Honor."

"A wise choice, Counselor. Ms. Chang, please continue."

"If I may repeat the question?" The judge nodded.

"Thank you. Anna, why did you send Mr. Rutherford those pictures?"

I shrugged. "He'd been in South America for months. We barely got to talk. I had a lot of extra time, I wanted to give him something to remember me while he was gone—and at the time, it seemed like a good idea It was a fun thing, a way to entice him to come home soon."

"How did you feel about Mr. Rutherford when you sent those pictures?"

"I loved him. I thought we were getting married someday. I never dreamed he would show the pictures to anyone, that he could be this vindictive."

"How did you feel when you realized he wasn't coming back?"

"Angry. Frustrated at first, and then hurt."

"Did you post nude pictures of him on the internet or set out to destroy his reputation?"

"Of course not."

"Why not?"

For the first time, I met Eric's eyes. "Because I loved him. I was hurt when he left me, but those feelings don't evaporate. Sometimes, relationships don't work out, and it's sad, but it's not anyone's fault. I wouldn't dream of punishing someone just because I wasn't his Ms. Right."

Meili cleared her throat, drawing my eyes back to her. "Thank you. That's all."

It felt like I'd been on the stand for a lifetime. When Mr. Carter stood, I wished I could curl into a ball on the floor. Luckily, the cross-examination was brief.

"Just one question. Ms. Guerra, did you ever tell my client he *wasn't* allowed to show the pictures to anyone else?"

He had me there. It never occurred to me to tell the man I planned to marry not to share the sexy photographs I sent him with the entire first world. Not that it would've made any difference.

"No, I—"

"Thank you. No further questions."

"—didn't think I had to."

Mr. Carter chose not to ask me any more questions, which felt like a thousand-pound weight lifted off my shoulders. My role in this ordeal had almost ended.

"Next witness, Ms. Chang?" Judge Patel asked.

"Your Honor, the plaintiff rests."

At the next table, Mr. Carter surged to his feet. "Move for a directed verdict, Your Honor."

I didn't remember what that meant, but it didn't sound good for us.

The judge glanced at the clock. "It's nearly time for lunch, counselor. Why don't we let the jury go early, and then I'll hear your arguments?"

"That would be fine, sir."

"No objection," Meili stated. She turned to me and lowered her voice. "You could go, too, if you want, once the jury leaves. Get some air. This could be long and boring."

"What is it?"

"They're going to try to convince the judge we failed to meet the basic requirements for proving the case, so there's no need to continue with the rest of the trial."

My lawyer seemed much too calm for someone who might be about to lose our case. "Do you think they'll win?"

She squeezed my hand under the table, watching the jury file past us. "I don't think so. This is a standard motion, made in almost every case. To win, Judge Patel has to find that no reasonable juror would believe Eric uploaded the pictures or that he did it on purpose, or that you were upset. I'd be shocked if the judge allowed the motion."

Sure enough, the moment the doors closed behind the last juror, the judge spoke. "This should be a pretty quick hearing. I see no reason to grant a directed verdict at this point."

Mr. Carter's face turned red. "But, your Honor, there's no evidence——"

"'A brick is not a wall,' counselor." Judge Patel said. I smiled, recognizing the words as taken from a famous case Meili quoted me during one of our meetings. "I see plenty of bricks of evidence, and it's up to the jury to determine whether they form a wall of proof. Motion denied."

Unable to contain my joy, I clapped. Eric shot me a dirty look, but I ignored him.

After lunch, I steeled myself for Eric's defense. Watching my ex claim he was the wronged party would be no less upsetting than sitting through the parade of witnesses explaining how their opinions of me went into the toilet. For a moment, I wished I'd thought to down a couple of glasses of wine with lunch. But I needed to be clear-headed for this.

Mr. Carter moved to the middle of the courtroom and gestured toward the audience. "The defense calls Doctor Ayesha Simmons to the stand."

The tallest woman I'd ever seen strode through the gate and took a seat. With her flawless ebony skin, erect posture, and gleaming white teeth, she looked more like a supermodel than a psychiatrist. The jurors leaned forward, heads swiveled toward the witness stand in anticipation.

Mr. Carter gave the jury a brief overview of the doctor's credentials. I stared at the tiny silver diamonds on Dr. Simmons's manicured nails, trying to clear my mind. This was another witness I preferred not to watch, but Meili told me to sit and try not to react if I could help it.

Eric's lawyer wasted no time in getting to the heart of his defense. "Dr. Simmons, have you reviewed Ms. Guerra's psychiatric records?"

"Yes." The doctor held up a slim folder. "I brought the records with me for reference."

"What did you conclude after reviewing those records?"

"These records show a patient who suffered from depression for more than two decades. Someone who tried to take her life more than once."

"Objection!" Meili said.

"Overruled," Judge Patel responded. "The jury should hear this."

Dr. Simmons continued, "In my expert medical opinion, Ms. Guerra's depression is a genetic condition which spiraled out of control after she stopped seeking treatment. She was able to control it for a while with medication, but in time, the depression simply overwhelmed her. Her emotional state led to Ms. Guerra's break-up with Mr. Epstein and her job loss. These things are the direct result of allowing a psychiatric condition to fester untreated for years, and likely would have happened even if the pictures never made their appearance on the internet."

My hands clenched reflexively into fists. Spots swam across my vision, but I shoved them back. This wasn't the time or place to lose control, not when everyone watched me for signs of mental illness. I breathed slowly, counting until my rage dissipated.

One, two, three, four, five…

Mr. Carter returned to the defense table, drawing my attention back to the courtroom. I hadn't even noticed when the examination finished. Probably for the best.

…Nine hundred forty-seven, nine-hundred forty-eight, nine-hundred forty-nine…

Meili approached, smiling at the doctor in a gesture that more conveyed the image a mother wolf protecting her cubs than any sort of warmth. "Good morning, Dr. Simmons."

"Good morning," she said.

"Let me ask you. Did you ever examine my client personally?"

"No, I did not."

Hopefully the jury would find her opinion less impressive given that I'd never actually met the doctor. Meili had explained that a doctor could give an opinion based on medical records, but we could argue it wasn't strong evidence.

"What are the dates on those medical records?"

"The first set of records is from 1994. The second set is from March of 2019."

"Do you have any records showing my client's mental state in October of 2018?"

"No, I don't. However, I can tell you that—"

"Just answer the question, please," Meili interjected.

Dr. Simmons shot daggers at Meili for a moment before smoothing an invisible thread on her crimson shirt. She crossed her long legs and waited.

"Is there anything in the records to suggest my client suffered from mental illness in October of 2018?"

"Depression doesn't go away forever. It comes back," Dr. Simmons said. "The lack of any records whatsoever for nearly two decades suggests Ms. Guerra made no effort to control her condition. Which makes it unsurprising that she suffered a relapse."

My breath caught in my throat. We'd never considered that they might try to use my lack of medical records against me. But Meili pressed on, apparently undaunted.

"Can depression flare up due to external factors or problems in a patient's life?"

"Yes, it can. Things like losing a job or a break-up or high-stress situations can all make depression worse. All of those things happened to Ms. Guerra before she filed this lawsuit."

"Yes, they did. After the pictures were posted." Meili paused to consult her notes, but Dr. Simmons didn't take the bait. "Is it common for people suffering from depression to be delusional or vindictive?"

"No, it isn't."

I breathed an internal sigh of relief. Maybe this doctor's testimony wouldn't hurt us quite as much as I'd worried. After all, there was nothing in my medical records to suggest I'd attack Eric without cause.

"Are you familiar with the symptoms of narcissistic personality disorder?"

"Objection!" Mr. Carter called from his seat. "What does this have to do with anything?"

My lawyer addressed the bench. "If opposing counsel is going to claim my client's depression caused her to make everything up, don't you think we should be allowed to show that his client's personality is consistent with someone who would do something like this?"

I snuck a peek at Eric, whose face matched Dr. Simmons's lipstick. Seeing him sweat for once brought the ghost of a smile to my lips.

From the bench, Judge Patel said, "I'll allow this line of questioning for now. But tread carefully, counselor."

"Of course, Your Honor." Meili turned back to the witness. "Dr. Simmons?"

"Yes, I've treated a number of patients for narcissistic personality disorder." Her smile did not reach her eyes, and her demeanor told me in no uncertain terms that this expert wouldn't give an inch if she could avoid it.

"Can you share those traits with the jury?"

"Certainly. Symptoms vary by patient, but many narcissists are extremely charming and confident. They frequently make grand gestures and may be perceived by others as elitist or arrogant."

The members of the juror now eyed Eric, in his cheap suit, with his long hair and a day's worth of stubble. I wanted to scream at them, show them a picture of the old Eric, with his perfect hair and manicure, wearing suits costing more than many of them paid for their mortgages.

At the front of the room, Meili said, "Is it true, Dr. Simmons, that some narcissists see themselves as 'fixers'? They reach out to people with perceived weaknesses and latch on, making themselves seem indispensable?"

"In some cases, yes. Every case is different."

"Have you ever seen narcissists who were drawn to relationships with those who have physical disabilities?"

Dr. Simmons shifted in her seat. "It is possible. But plenty of non-narcissists aren't bothered by disabilities. It would be unfair to say only a narcissist would date someone with a disability."

Meili said, "We're not implying that at all. But it is possible?"

"Yes."

"Thank you. And is it true some narcissists can be sensitive when someone challenges them?"

Beside me, Eric snorted. Dr. Simmons shifted in her seat, but her smile didn't falter. "Yes, it's possible."

Meili consulted a sheet of papers in her hand. "Some narcissists may act out in anger, correct? Behave rashly?"

"Yes, that's true," Dr. Simmons said. "But I wouldn't classify the systematic destruction of the plaintiff in this case as rash behavior."

Meili turned to the judge. "Move to strike the last sentence as non-responsive."

"Granted," Judge Patel said. "We'll let the jury decide how to classify things, Dr. Simmons. Please stick to the facts."

The psychiatrist nodded but did not respond.

"It's okay, I'm done with this witness," Meili said.

Mr. Carter jumped to his feet. "Dr. Simmons, did you ever treat my client for narcissistic personality disorder?"

"No, I did not."

"Were you asked to review any medical records for Mr. Rutherford in connection with this case?"

"No, I was not."

"And have you ever seen him display any behavior suggesting my client needs psychiatric treatment?"

"No, I have not. I have never met with Mr. Rutherford professionally, but in our interactions, I spotted no red flags."

Across the aisle, Eric smirked at me. I forced myself to keep my breathing steady. Meili may have gotten the jury thinking, but I wasn't convinced we had the evidence we needed to get a judgment. I kept going back to what Meili said at our first meeting: If Eric wouldn't admit what he'd done, we could have a hard time convincing the jury. The Facebook posts didn't seem to be enough.

Eric handled himself masterfully on the stand. Without a confession, he was untouchable, and he knew it. But maybe, if I could get him alone, I'd be able to put a chink in his perfect armor.

WHEN COURT ENDED for the day, I took the train into the City, then hailed a taxi up to Central Park. Without thinking, I let my legs carry me down the familiar paths, in and out of trees, past landmarks I'd seen a thousand times. Eventually, I veered off the path, took a shortcut, and emerged between two trees to find myself at the duck pond.

A familiar old bench about ten yards away faced the pond.

It wasn't empty.

On some level, I knew Eric would be there, although we hadn't spoken in more than a year. Two years had passed since the last time we met face-to-face. In court, I walked in with Meili, refused to acknowledge him, and never gave him a chance to approach. A million times I'd thought of calling, but I couldn't let him have my new phone number. Emails were evidence; I started and deleted half a dozen messages that couldn't adequately convey anything I wanted to say to him, even if I were allowed to say it.

Although his back was to me, I suspected he knew I was there. After rummaging in my bag for a moment, I pulled out a mirror and smoothed my hair before approaching the bench.

"I've been waiting for you," he said without turning.

Instead of responding, I sat at the far end of the bench, setting my bag between us as a buffer. The cold of the wood penetrated my winter coat, and I shivered. There were no ducks this time of year, so the two of us sat, staring at empty ice. Occasionally, someone would cross the bridge above, riding a bike or on foot.

Finally, I found my voice. "I loved you, you know."

"I loved you, too. Once."

"You were this great force, my knight in shining armor." My voice cracked, but I ignored it. "That night, when you told me you were leaving—I thought you were going to propose. I stupidly dreamed about us spending the rest of our lives together."

"Then you shouldn't have cheated on me."

I glared up at him. My hands itched to slap the face that once seemed so handsome. "Did I? Did I really, Eric? Because you abandoned me. You left the country, with hardly any notice, and all I got was a stream of emails delaying your return. Anyone in my position would've thought you ended it."

"Then why were you still living in my apartment?"

"Because I was an idiot. As soon as I realized it was over, I left."

"Is that why you're here?" He smirked, and I visualized my palm connecting with his cheek. Repeatedly. "You came to find me at our spot so we could reunite? You wanna suck my dick to apologize?"

My fingers curled into a fist. "Don't be crass, Eric."

"Then why are you here?"

"Why are you here?"

"It's peaceful."

He was lying. After sitting on the stand for two days, lying through his teeth, he wanted to gloat. He wanted someone to listen to him talk about how much the jurors loved him, and he hoped I'd be fool enough to seek out an apology by following him here.

Maybe I'd sought him out, but I was no fool, and it wasn't an apology I wanted from him. "Why'd you do it?"

"Why do you think?" His gaze held mine.

I held my breath, praying he'd continue. When he didn't, I said, "So you're not denying it?"

"Why would I?" He laughed, a humorless sound that child me to the bone. "The jury is eating out of my hand in there. They'll never believe you if you tell them I admitted to posting the pictures. I'm a Rutherford. People don't believe someone like you over someone like me."

"You seem awfully sure about that."

"Years of experience," he said. "Say whatever you want, but you cheated on me. Women don't cheat on Rutherfords. Women line up, happy to spread their legs—like Juror 9, who sits there all day, panting for me."

"That's it? I hurt your feelings, so you ruin my life?"

"You say that's it like it's no big deal. I'm the heir to a multi-national corporation. People bow to my every whim. No one gets the better of me," he said. "Especially not some Jersey girl who only got her job because of Affirmative Action."

My blood boiled, but I remained silent.

"You're nothing. And you're delusional. Never, in a million years would I have ever married you, Anna. You're good in bed, but you're not Rutherford material."

He walked away, whistling a tune. My entire body trembled with rage, but I forced myself not to respond.

I watched until he was out of earshot, then reached into my bag and pulled out my phone. At the movement, the screen lit up. "Tara? Did you get that?"

"You bet your ass I did."

Chapter 20

The next morning, I entered the courtroom with a spring in my step and beamed at the members of the jury while they filed in. Across the aisle, Eric cocked one eyebrow at me, clearly wondering what I had up my sleeve. My smile widened, and I kept my gaze locked on his until the bailiff told us to take our seats.

That smile died when Mr. Carter called his next witness. Although Meili had given me a copy of his witness list, the first name on the list hit me like a sucker punch in the gut. I hadn't seen him since I threw my glass at his back in the hotel room. What I had seen was a notice in the engagements section of the newspaper I still couldn't think about without getting upset.

"Your Honor, the defense would like to call Jason Epstein to the stand."

Oh, no.

We intentionally hadn't called Jay, because his testimony wasn't needed to show what I'd lost. I focused on a pen lying on the table, concentrating on inhaling and exhaling until the pounding of my heart in my ears slowed.

"Mr. Epstein, how do you know the parties?"

"Ms. Guerra is my ex-girlfriend. I only know Mr. Rutherford by name."

"And how did you meet Ms. Guerra?"

"I met her at a networking event, a couple of years ago. She was being underutilized at her current organization, and my company needed an executive."

"What do you do for a living?"

"I'm Head Legal Counsel for Li'l Tots Corp. We design and manufacture clothing for toddlers."

"When did the two of you start dating?"

Meili stood. "Objection. Relevance?"

"This case is about whether certain statements about Ms. Guerra's sexual behavior damaged her reputation," Mr. Carter said. "If she was promiscuous before the photographs appeared online, it suggests that the pictures did not, in fact, damage her reputation."

"Objection," Meili said. "Move to strike.

There's no evidence my client is or was promiscuous."

My face grew warm despite my efforts to keep cool. I wasn't exactly the Virgin Mary.

"Objection sustained as to the promiscuity comment," Judge Patel said. "The jury will disregard that statement, as there's no evidence regarding Ms. Guerra's sexual history. As to the original objection, overruled. I'd like to hear this."

I snuck a peek at Eric, who grinned like a child on Christmas.

"Mr. Epstein?" Mr. Carter said, "Can you tell me when you started dating the plaintiff?"

He thought for a minute. "I'm not entirely positive. Sometime around October or November maybe? A couple of years ago."

I resisted the urge to roll my eyes at him. He talked like our relationship was so unimportant, he didn't even know our anniversary.

"Was that before or after Ms. Guerra started working for your company?"

He cleared his throat. "I'm sorry, but I'm going to have to refuse to answer the question on the grounds that the answer may tend to incriminate me."

Mr. Carter turned toward me. "There are no pending charges against Mr. Epstein, are there?"

Meili put her hand on my arm and stood. "Your Honor, the plaintiff and I have not yet discussed the possibility of pursuing any sort of sexual harassment charges against the witness."

This was more lawyer talk. Nothing but smoke and mirrors. I'd never sue Jay for what happened between us, and he knew it.

Judge Patel leaned forward. "Sexual harassment is a civil issue, not criminal. I'm going to allow it. Mr. Epstein, please answer the question."

Jay cleared his throat, stalling for time. "Will Mr. Carter repeat the question please?"

"Certainly. Did you and the plaintiff start your romantic relationship before or after she started working at your company?"

"Before. And I wasn't the one who hired her."

Mr. Carter waited to see if Jay would elaborate, but the only sounds were the ticking of the clock and a squeaking from one of the chairs in the jury box.

"Was Ms. Guerra seeing anyone else at the time you started dating?"

"Objection," Meili said. "Lack of personal knowledge."

"I'm asking what he knew."

"Overruled," Judge Carter said.

"I'm afraid you'd have to ask Ms. Guerra. I have no idea whether she was seeing anyone else at the beginning of our relationship."

"Do you know when she broke up with Mr. Rutherford?"

"No. I wasn't there when it happened."

Mr. Carter flipped a couple of pages of notes, whether searching for something or stalling for time, I didn't know.

My heart swelled. Jay was doing his best to protect me. He'd known all about Eric—I told him the morning after our first date. We'd agreed to put our relationship on hold until I'd broken things off. Which took about eleven seconds via email. Thinking about it now made me realize how cold I'd been, and I cringed inwardly.

Then I shook it off. Eric didn't deserve my compassion. It wasn't like he'd left me any alternative. You can't break up with someone in person when they're avoiding you.

Mr. Carter looked up from his notes and addressed Jay again. "Can you describe your last meeting with the plaintiff?"

"Objection, Your Honor. Events that occurred after the pictures were posted are irrelevant."

"The key question is whether it was my client's alleged behavior or the plaintiff's own actions that destroyed her reputation. I'd say that's relevant, especially if we get to the question of damages."

Judge Patel rubbed his chin for a minute. I held my breath, waiting. Finally, he nodded. "I see your point, Counselor. Objection sustained."

Meili casually wrote something on the tablet

between us and tilted it for me to see. *It's okay. All he's doing is letting the jury see how badly Eric hurt you.*

I blinked furiously to clear my vision and forced a neutral expression back on my face. On the stand, Jay spoke. "It was about two weeks after Ms. Guerra took a leave of absence from the company."

"Were the two of you still dating at that point?"

Jay met my eyes before answering. At least he had the self-awareness to look embarrassed. "No, we weren't."

"What was the purpose of that meeting?"

"I went to Ms. Guerra's hotel room to tell her that she'd been fired."

"And how did you find her?" Mr. Carter asked.

"She'd told me where she was staying. The hotel was near the office, so I walked."

"Yes, of course. I meant, what was her condition when you arrived?"

Jay hesitated. "She was drunk."

"Objection. The witness is stating a conclusion."

"I'll rephrase." Mr. Carter said. "What did you see when you got to the hotel room?"

"A bottle of half-empty whiskey sat on the coffee table. Anna's speech slurred when she spoke, and she was staggering."

"What time was it when you arrived?"

"Around nine o'clock in the morning."

The housewives gasped. The brunette wrinkled her nose and put one hand over her ample cleavage; probably more to get the onlookers to turn their gaze to her than due to actual disgust. She looked like the type who wasn't opposed to the occasional morning drink.

For the rest of Jay's testimony, I watched the ticking clock above the judge's head. Scenes from my favorite childhood movie played in my head. No matter what he said, Jay couldn't hurt me anymore. Eric couldn't hurt me anymore. I wouldn't let the jurors see me break down again.

When Mr. Carter turned the witness over to Meili, I prayed she could reverse some of the damage Jay caused. Jurors who once gazed at me sympathetically now wore identical expressions of distaste, as if I'd fallen in their esteem to no better than the dog walker who slept with their husbands.

"Mr. Epstein, how long did Ms. Guerra work for you?"

"About a year."

"During that time, were there any allegations of sexual misconduct?"

"You mean before the pictures were distributed?"

"Yes, before."

"None. She had no disciplinary record of any kind. Ms. Guerra was an exemplary employee."

"Thank you. No further questions."

I'd hoped the judge would allow a recess to give me a break before the next witness, but he decided instead to power through until the end of the day. Mr. Carter swore his next witness wouldn't take long. As Jay walked out of the courtroom, I forced myself to hold my head high. But then the next witness was called: My friend from the club. The one with the happy pills. Silently, I cursed the rules of discovery that prevented parties to a lawsuit from keeping some things private.

My face flamed, but I stared straight ahead. The jury needed to see that I wasn't ashamed of my sexual history. No man would be expected to be ashamed. And if the jurors thought it mattered, hopefully they would see that Eric drove to me to uncharacteristic actions by dragging me to a pit of despair and shoving me over the edge.

An eternity passed before he was excused, and Mr. Carter told the judge that he rested his case.

Judge Patel turned to us. "Have you any additional witnesses?"

"Yes, sir." Meili stood. "The plaintiff calls Tara Fisher to the stand."

Mr. Carter hadn't even made it back to his seat yet. His entire body swiveled toward the bench. "Your Honor, this witness wasn't on the list."

Tara paused where she stood, one hand on the partition that separated the audience from the place we sat.

"Rebuttal witness, Your Honor," Meili said, "called specifically to refute testimony presented by the defendant."

"She can't have anything relevant to say, unless the plaintiff wants us to believe her best friend was with my client in November of 2018."

"I think," Meili said, "that the relevance of Ms. Fisher's testimony will be quite clear as soon as she is able to give it."

Judge Patel took in Tara's burgundy hair and the nine jurors swiveling their heads from me to her to Eric. The wheels turned in his head as if he wondered what she could possibly add to the conversation. "I'll see both counselors at sidebar, please."

I leaned forward to see if I could catch their conversation, trying not to laugh when three members of the jury did the same. Eric inspected his fingernails. His obvious disdain for the judicial process made me want to toss a pencil at him.

The whispers at the front of the room were undetectable, but I watched Mr. Carter's face turn nearly purple. Meili must have mentioned our conversation. A second later, everyone returned to their seats.

Judge Patel said, "I'll allow the witness."

A little thrill went through me. If Tara wasn't allowed to testify, I would've gone back on the stand, and I didn't think I could handle it. The eyes, the snotty comments from opposing counsel, everything.

My best friend shot Eric such a hate-filled look as she strode past in her gray pin-striped suit, I wanted to burst out laughing. But when she took the stand, she was smooth and emotionless.

"What is your relationship to the parties, Ms. Fisher?"

"Anna's been my best friend for more than twenty years," she said. "We went to grad school together, and we've been roommates ever since."

In light of the psychiatrist's testimony on personality disorders, the judge reversed his earlier ruling and agreed to let Tara recount the hot sauce incident. Two of the jurors actually chuckled, the sound slashing through my gut like a knife. But one of the Real Housewives sat back and crossed her arms. Another wrinkled her nose and exchanged glances with the other two. The three of them no doubt imagined the horror of having to throw out expensive clothes stained with Fire Sauce.

Watching the jurors and trying to guess what they might decide was going to give me a stroke.

"When was the last time you spoke to Mr. Rutherford?" Meili asked when Tara finished describing my birthday party.

She thought for a minute. "Oh, it's been ages. Probably at his going-away party? But he was drinking and talking to his friends, so I mostly hung out with Anna."

Mr. Carter started to rise, but Meili held out her hand. "I'm getting there." He sat, and she continued. "So what do you have to tell us?"

"After the trial started, I overheard a conversation between Anna and Eric."

At the other table, Eric stiffened. "She's lying."

Judge Patel banged his gavel. "Mr. Carter, control your client."

"But you weren't there," Eric said.

"Do you want to go outside, young man?" The bailiff took a step closer to the table. Anticipating what was coming, I found myself grateful he stood more or less between us.

Eric clenched his jaw before shaking shook his head.

Meili turned back to Tara. "How did you overhear this conversation?"

"Anna called me before she approached him, and I recorded the conversation with her consent."

Beside me, Eric surged to his feet. Rage twisted his once stunning good-looks into something grotesque. "You little bitch!"

His arms stretched out as he lunged toward my table. If I didn't move, his fingers would lock around my throat.

He wanted to kill me.

For the first time in ages, death didn't sound like an escape.

A shriek escaped me. I shrank back, falling across Meili's chair right before the bailiffs grabbed him. He continued to yell, but I couldn't even hear the words.

Pandemonium broke out. Judge Patel banged his gavel repeatedly as two of the bailiffs wrestled Eric out a side door. I could hardly believe I'd ever loved him.

A third bailiff cleared the audience from the back of the courtroom. The moment the doors shut behind my ex-boyfriend, the judge ordered the jury out of the room.

"Are you okay, Ms. Guerra?" he asked once they left.

I pulled myself back up. Before I could say anything, Meili spoke up. "Your Honor, if we could, I'd like to request a ten-minute recess for my client to compose herself."

"Yes, of course," he said. "And I want to see

your client back in here, Mr. Carter. He's about to face contempt of court charges."

One of the court officers escorted me and Tara into the hall, where we waited in a corner until Eric returned to the courtroom. Then, I threw my arms around her. "That was brilliant! You just won our case."

"No, you won your case. I could never have gotten him to admit to anything. That was all you."

"Still, I don't know what I'd do without you."

She squeezed me tighter. "Let's hope you never have to find out."

The bailiff appeared at the courtroom door and beckoned at us. When I returned to my seat, I spared a glance at the defense table. Eric's hands lay folded in his lap, knuckles white. The vein in his forehead throbbed, but he was silent.

A smile exploded out of me. I folded my hands on the table to cover my face, not wanting my reaction to provoke another outburst.

After the jurors returned, Tara played the tape. The voices were clear. We'd both spent enough time on the stand, there could be no question who spoke. The conversation was unequivocal. Mr. Carter didn't even bother to object when Meili moved the recording into evidence.

When cross-examination began, he looked deflated. "Is it true you've never liked my client, Ms. Fisher?"

"Yes." She didn't elaborate.

"And you never approved of their relationship?"

"I wouldn't say 'approved' is the right word. I didn't think he was the right guy for Anna. Apparently, I was right."

"Move to strike. Argumentative."

Judge Patel leaned forward. "The jury will disregard the witness's last sentence. And the witness will only answer what she is asked."

"Yes, Your Honor." Tara winked at me, not the least chagrinned.

After consulting his notes, Attorney Carter apparently decided it wasn't worth asking my best friend any more questions. Meili chose not to redirect, and Tara squeezed my shoulder on her way out of the courtroom.

"No more witnesses," Meili said. "The plaintiff is prepared to make closing arguments."

Mr. Carter stood. "We are also ready to give our closing, Your Honor."

Judge Patel glanced at the clock, then at the jury box. "It's been a long trial, counselors. We'll start fresh next week. Closing arguments begin Monday at nine."

Chapter 21

After the judge dismissed us for the weekend, I got a text from Sayid inviting me to his parents' home in Connecticut to be reunited with his sister and meet her horses.

I thought maybe it would be good for you to get out into the fresh air for a bit. Take your mind off the trial.

He was right, of course. Meili told me before we left the courthouse not to spend the entire weekend on the couch, watching *Legally Blonde* or a Grisham movie marathon. Especially not Grisham—too many cases where the bad guys won. I'd been home from court for an hour and was already binge-watching *Law & Order: SVU* when the text rolled in. Still, I wasn't sure what was happening with Sayid or if I was ready for it.

Was he genuinely just a nice guy? Did I want to hang out with someone because he pitied me? Or was he hoping for something I was in no state to give him?

Before I could decide, my phone buzzed again. No pressure. Not a date. Amira would like to see you.

I remembered his sister. A short girl with braces and long, dark brown hair the rest of us envied. She'd probably grown up to be a supermodel, whereas I'd grown up to be accused of being a prostitute. Still, Sayid had been nothing but nice to me. And a day in the country away from everything might do me some good.

Me: I haven't been on a horse in almost twenty years. I'll think about it. What's the address?

The reply was instantaneous.

Sayid: I'll pick you up. Tomorrow morning at 9, ok?

Not a date, huh?

Tara looked up from the other end of the couch, where her notes for the exam spread across her lap, the middle cushion, and the end table. "What are you smiling at over there?"

"I'm not sure." I read her the texts.

"Go," she said.

"But—"

"Go."

"I'm not—"

"Don't argue with me," she said. "Go. Is it a date? Who cares?"

"I haven't exactly had the best luck with men recently. Meili doesn't want me to date until after the trial is over."

She leaned over and grabbed my phone. "Maybe your bad luck comes from dating pretty trust fund babies instead of smoking hot police officers. Besides, who brings their sister on a first date? You have three seconds to tell him you're going, or I'll do it for you."

"You can't go for me. What about Beth?"

Tara stuck her tongue out at me. "We're not exclusive, and you're stalling. That's not what I meant."

"Fine." I held out my hand. "Give me back my phone."

The next morning, my hands shook as I brushed my now too-long bangs over my eyes, pulling the rest of my hair back into a low pony-tail. My old glasses were in my hand, halfway to my face before I changed my mind. In went the contacts, and my hair went back. No more hiding. I didn't need a disguise.

I didn't know if the butterflies in my stomach were due to seeing Sayid or getting back on the horse for the first time in two decades.

A little of both, honestly.

By 8:59, I stood in the entry wearing my coat and gloves, ready to bolt the second a car pulled into the driveway. Riding clothes hadn't been a part of my wardrobe since the accident, but stretch jeans and knee-high leather boots would be fine. Tara hovered. I glared at her.

"I just want to say hello," she said.

"It's not a date, remember? When have you ever come to meet a friend before I spent time with them?"

"In seventh grade, you let me vet all your friends. Especially the cute ones."

I grinned at her. "I'll put in a good word for you, okay?"

"Put in a good word for *you*, silly. I'm seeing someone." Tara pointed over my shoulder. Outside, a red Toyota stopped in front of the house. "Go. Have fun."

Seeing Sayid out of uniform was weird. I almost didn't recognize him, but his forest green hoodie brought out the gold flecks in his eyes. We spent most of the drive to Connecticut talking about the trial, with me filling him in on the bits he missed. I didn't mention how much Meili asked the jury to give us, and he didn't ask. Before I knew it, we'd arrived at the stable.

A beaming woman with a friendly face stood outside. Mira looked more or less the way I remembered her—like some girls, she'd apparently hit her peak height before she reached her preteen years. The primary difference was the straight, gleaming white teeth that replaced her braces. We'd once worn matching metal mouths.

"Anna Guerra," she breathed. "I never thought I'd see you again. Your fall gave me nightmares for weeks."

"I know."

She flushed and looked at the ground. "Sorry. Of course you know. You were there. But you also know how important it is to get back on the horse. And not to wait twenty years to do it. I can't believe you."

"Look at the bright side. You'll definitely be a better rider than me this time."

"Oof." She laughed. "Guess I deserved that."

Mira led us through a side door, to the end of a row of stalls. When I crossed the threshold, I stopped and inhaled deeply. The familiar scents of leather, horses, saddle soap, and sweat carried memories I'd buried twenty years ago. Riding, running, being free. Jumping, flying. Falling.

Maybe this was a bad idea. My breath hitched. Beside me, Mira squeezed my hand. "It's going to be okay," she said.

A bay horse stuck his head through the window in the stall door at her words. She rubbed his nose. "This is Noor. It's Arabic for 'light.' She does a lot of work with autistic kids."

I held my hand out for the horse to sniff and waited. A moment later, she allowed me to rub her nose. "Autistic kids and amputees?"

"For your first time on a horse in years, she's a good choice. Gentle, not too skittish. But when I give her her head she really flies. I'm not sticking you on some old nag who's nearly out to pasture. I think you'll like her."

"Okay." I tried to sound braver than I felt. "Let's get her saddled up."

It took a few minutes to remember what to do with all the straps and buckles, but I refused help. By the time Noor and I reached the ring, Sayid and Mira waited for me, already on their horses.

"You ride, too?" I asked him.

"Of course I do. We're a horse family." He handed me a riding hat and a pair of battered gloves. "I'm going to assume you want to mount by yourself."

In answer, I smiled at him. He directed me to the mounting block. For a long moment, I stared over the top of the saddle, gathering courage. The last time I mounted a horse, I stood on two feet and mountains of self-confidence. I closed my eyes, shutting out everything but me and the animal in front of me.

"If I fall on my ass, you won't laugh, will you, girl?"

The look Noor gave me suggested she was

making no promises. Wiping my sweaty palms on my jeans, I wished I'd made it to the ring earlier, so no one would be watching me.

Something jingled behind me. A glance over my shoulder showed Sayid and Amira had walked their horses to the other side of the ring. They couldn't help if I needed them, but they weren't watching, either.

The normal way to mount a horse means placing your left foot in the stirrup and swinging your right leg over. My prosthetic had served me well for years, but I wasn't sure I trusted it to balance all my weight while I found my seat. Yet I also wasn't sure I even knew how to mount a horse backward.

Oh, well. Here went nothing. I could do this. With one more deep breath, I grasped the saddle with both hands and placed my right foot in the stirrup. It took two tries to swing my left leg over, and I nearly kicked poor Noor, but once my butt finally hit the leather, I settled into the saddle as if I'd been born to it.

I couldn't help myself. I gave a little cheer. Noor flicked an ear at me but otherwise stood patiently while I maneuvered my left boot into the stirrup. When I straightened, I raised my arms over my head in a "V" for Victory. Amira and Sayid clapped, and I beamed like Noor and I had won the Olympic Grand Prix instead of mounting a horse the wrong way.

Something I hadn't felt in months flared within my chest. It took a moment to recognize pride and hope for what they were. Pride not only at getting back on the horse, finally, but also for taking my life back. Hope that things would get better. I was invincible. Never again would I let someone take my sense of self away from me.

Being back in the saddle after so much time away felt weird, but I was determined to make it work. After finding my seat, Noor and I went through the paces: walking, trotting, walking, trotting. The inside ring wasn't big enough to go faster, but my fingers itched to let the horse run.

When I slowed Noor to a walk for the third time, Sayid pulled up beside me.

"Having fun?" He studied my face. "Actually, you don't need to answer that. There's this expression on your face I've never seen before."

I rearranged my features into the scowl I'd worn perpetually since the hurricane. "Is this better?"

"No! I liked it the other way." He beamed at me and I rewarded him with the smile that twice graced the pages of *Forbes* magazine. "Seriously, though, I'm glad to see you having a good time. You deserve it."

Something stirred inside me. When did joy become such an alien emotion? "Thank you so much for bringing me here. I haven't had this much fun in years."

After two decades away from riding, my thighs ached pleasantly after only a few trips around the ring. Still, once I found my seat, Amira let us take the horses outside to a trail that wound through the woods. We marveled at the red and gold of the leaves, beauty that rarely went noticed in New York City. The two of us chatted about television and current events, avoiding more serious topics until Sayid pleaded fatigue. I moaned about stopping, but since my butt and thighs were on fire at that point, I really shouldn't continue.

Despite the discomfort, I wouldn't have traded the experience for anything in the world. When we returned to the stable, I swung to the ground like days had passed, not decades, since my last ride. And then my knees buckled.

Sayid stepped up and caught me before I fell, sending a flush through my body that wasn't entirely due to embarrassment. I buried my face in Noor's mane to regain my composure.

"I, um, guess I may have overdone it," I said sheepishly.

Amira laughed. "We probably should've made you stop a while ago. But you'll get used to riding again soon enough."

Would I? I'd assumed when I arrived at the

stables that this would be a one-time thing, but I'd forgotten how much I loved riding.

"Thank you so much, both of you. I can't believe I ever gave this up."

"You're such a natural," Amira said. She and Sayid exchanged a glance, and he led all three horses back to their stalls. "You know, Noor hasn't been getting enough exercise lately."

"Oh, yeah?" I raised my eyebrows at them, recognizing the setup for what it was. Still, no reason not to listen.

"Yeah. Parents don't want to bring their kids out here and sit in the cold while they ride. The girl who used to exercise them got a scholarship to Northwestern. She moved at the end of the summer. She said she'd be home for breaks, but I could still use a hand."

"You want me to work at the stable?"

My inner CFO-in-training bristled. The bored woman who sat at home all day desperately seeking anything to do with her time perked up. And a balloon of hope swelled within the chest of my inner thirteen-year-old girl, whose parents never let her near a horse after she lost her leg.

"I know you'll be getting a full-time job soon. Working at a stable is a huge step down for someone like you. But if you have a few hours a week to help out, clean some tack, muck out a stall or two, especially on the weekends, you can ride Noor anytime you want."

Her offer gave me exactly what I needed: something to take me out of the house, but plenty of time to work once I found another job. My cheeks ached with the force of the smile stretching across them.

"That would be absolutely amazing. Thank you so much!" Reality prickled at the back of my mind. "But… well… I'm not sure I can accept your offer right now."

Her face fell. "Anything I can say to convince you?"

"I'm not saying no," I said. "It's just that, we don't know what's going to happen with the trial, and I don't want to bring negative publicity to your stables and the work you do here. Would parents of autistic children bring them to the stable where someone accused of being a hooker works?"

"Fair enough. After the verdict?"

I glanced at the door through which Sayid vanished with the horses. "Is this some scheme to hook me up with your brother?" My pulse quickened at the thought, but I tried to act casual.

She laughed. "Not at all. He brought it up, but I'd never make the offer if you weren't dependable and good with horses. Besides, I think the work will do you a lot of good. Using horses for rehabilitation and therapy isn't only for kids. My brother can find his own dates."

"Sorry, I had to ask. We'll see. It's been a hell of a year. After the trial, win or lose, I want to take a long vacation. No idea where or how long or where I'll eventually settle."

"I can understand that." She pulled out her phone. "Give me your number. I'll be checking in with you in a few months."

I recited my new phone number and email address. "Thanks, Mira. We should stay in touch either way."

"Don't thank me. Thank my brother."

The drive home was quiet, with me mulling over the offer and Sayid giving me time to think about it. When we arrived back at the house, he opened the car door to let me out but didn't move to walk me to the door.

"I know you've been through a lot," he began. The understatement made me laugh, but he continued. "We didn't exactly get off on the right foot. No pun intended. Sorry."

"It's no problem," I assured him. "You were fine. Your partner was the problem. I'm grateful you were there when Detective Stern started giving me a hard time. For weeks, I worried she would call again. I suspect you're the reason she didn't."

"Yeah. I don't know what her problem is."

"She's a racist."

"You don't know that."

"She's a Birther, which means she's probably a Trump supporter."

"I—" He swallowed hard. "I never asked her, but of course you're right. I didn't want to make things more difficult at work. We don't talk about politics."

"You're a good man, but you don't have to protect racists," I said.

"No, I don't. I won't apologize for her again," he said.

As I stared into his eyes, Sayid's pupils dilated. I knew exactly what he was thinking, because I was thinking it, too. All I wanted was to step forward, to run my fingers across his shoulders, to press my lips against his. Kiss him long and hard, right there on the sidewalk beside his car. But I couldn't.

"I like you," I said.

"I like you, too." He leaned forward, and I leaned back. Confusion crossed his face.

"You're a great guy and I like spending time with you. You wouldn't believe how attractive I find you—Tara calls you 'Detective Hottie.'"

He blushed, but his smile faltered. "Why do I feel like there's a 'but' coming?"

"Because I've hopped from one bad decision to the next for years. I don't think you're a bad decision, but getting involved with you right now would be. So much has happened. I'm barely starting to claw my way out of this pit of depression, and if things went wrong, I don't know if I could handle it. I'm sorry."

The words broke my heart. Sayid was exactly the kind of guy I should be involved with—but it wouldn't be fair to use him to put myself back together.

"I understand. You need to take care of yourself first."

"Thank you." His acceptance of my decision without question made my heart ache more.

"No need to thank me. Good luck tomorrow," he said. "When you figure things out, give me a call. Either way, call Mira."

"I will, thanks. I'll let you know what the jury says." I wondered if it would be too familiar to give him a hug, too awkward to shake his hand. The answer to both questions was yes. Instead, I gave a little wave before getting out of the car. Just as awkward as a handshake, and possibly weirder.

Good job, Anna.

Tara went to the library while I was out, so the rest of the afternoon was spent soaking in my glorious new bathtub, trying not to wonder if I made a mistake. A dozen times, I stopped myself from picking up the phone.

To keep my mind off the upcoming delibera-

tions, Sunday passed in a flurry of activity. I un-
packed the remaining boxes from the storage unit,
color-coded the clothes in my closet, reorganized
the pantry, and was seriously considering re-
painting the tiny office before Tara returned from
lunch with Beth, saw what I was doing, and made
me stop.

She moved the coffee table into the corner,
spread a blanket on the floor of the living room,
and brought me a carpet picnic, like we used to do
before my family moved away. Unlike in middle
school, she also brought me a bottle of red wine.
We gorged on baguette slices with tomato and
mozzarella, shrimp cocktail, and spinach dip, followed by a carton of Ben & Jerry's garnished with
three spoons. It was after eleven when I went to
bed, tired, full, and happy.

Chapter 22

The sun shone brightly as I walked into the court-house on Monday morning, which I took as a good sign. As the plaintiff, our side got to talk to the jury first. Meili and I'd discussed this part at length. She planned to review the evidence, discuss how much I made before this happened, harp on my pain and lost wages, and make the jury pity me.

"This case is pretty simple, ladies and gentlemen. You're not here to judge my client's conduct after the defendant posted nude pictures of her. You're not here to judge her for the fact that the pictures exist. The questions you are here to answer are: did the defendant have a legal right to distribute the pictures, did he distribute them, did he ruin her reputation with false statements, is that why Ms. Guerra lost her job. How much should the defendant pay?"

I examined the nine individuals in the jury box. The back of my neck prickled, but I refused to turn to see if Eric watched me watching them. Most of the jurors stared at Meili, sympathy etched on their faces. A couple glanced at me, but I lowered my eyes to avoid meeting their gazes.

"My client never told the defendant he could publish nude pictures of her on the internet. No one else has the right to make that decision for her. You've heard—from his own mouth—that he posted them, anyway. You've heard the text messages she received before she changed her phone number. You've seen with your own eyes how distressed she became as a result of those messages. If you want to judge my client's conduct after November 2018, then you also need to judge the person who drove her to that behavior—the defendant, Eric Rutherford.

"You read the posters, advertising sexual favors from my client in exchange for money. You listened to the police officer who received complaints about someone distributing prostitution ads with Ms. Guerra's face, name, and phone number on them. She didn't post those ads—the defendant did. A dozen coworkers testified Anna was fired after these pictures went live, another dozen individuals showed you what happened to her reputation.

"There can be no question that Mr. Rutherford legally wronged Anna by intentionally, maliciously, and without justification or excuse, posting nude pictures of her on the internet. There can be no question that he made false statements and damaged her reputation. There can be no question that she suffered. The evidence is clear on those points. The only real question is, how much?"

Meili turned her attention to a whiteboard placed near the witness stand, picked up a marker, and wrote a number.

"Seven hundred and twelve. That is how many text messages Ms. Guerra received calling her a slut, whore, dirty, disgusting, prostitute before she disconnected her phone." She wrote another number. "Seventeen hundred and ninety-two. That's how many comments appear on the blogs containing Ms. Guerra's pictures. Three hundred and fifty-nine. That's how many posts people made to Ms. Guerra's social media pages after Mr. Rutherford posted the password without her knowledge and consent before we got the page shut down. Those posts received a total of twenty-three thousand, two hundred sixty-four comments while the page was visible. Sixty-three. That's how many employers received Ms. Guerra's fake resume through LinkedIn. Two hundred twenty-six people viewed the fake profile before it was deleted."

I'd worried the jurors would be turned off by someone speaking math to them, but several leaned forward as Meili wrote more and more numbers on the board. A few of them seemed to be doing the math in their heads. They needn't have bothered; Meili was happy to provide the calculations.

"What else? Oh, right—emails! Two thousand, six hundred and eighty. That's the number of emails received threatening Ms. Guerra or calling her names. More appear in her inbox daily. She also received four hundred fifty-three emails from people offering to pay her for sexual favors or expressing desire to have sex with her. Flattering? Nope. Insulting, demoralizing. Humiliating. You saw her reaction to receiving these messages. Her doctors testified as to how this type of situation affects someone, mentally and physically. How would you feel?"

All heads on the jury turned toward me, sitting at the table, with my hands folded in my lap. Meili advised me to minimize my makeup for closing arguments, let the jury see the shadows under my eyes. I glanced at them from under lowered lashes before returning my attention to my attorney. Hopefully, the members of the jury were as riveted by this display as I was. I could practically hear Eric sweating more with each number she wrote.

She set down the blue marker and picked up a red one. An angry slash appeared beneath the list of numbers, followed by a much bigger number. "So, what's the total, ladies and gentlemen of the jury? Twenty-nine thousand, nine hundred seventy-seven texts, emails, insulting comments, profile views. Sounds like a huge number, right?"

Throughout the jury box, heads nodded in agreement.

"We can't ever know the number of people who walked by those billboards. New York City has a population of more than eight million people. There are an estimated 54.3 million travelers to New York City and beyond, not only from the United States, but from the entire world. Let's assume one-tenth of those people noticed the billboards. That's 620,000 people, give or take. What's that worth?

"If we were to include damages for every single person who potentially saw the billboards, that's an astronomical amount of money. We're not going to do that. All we want is one hundred measly dollars for each of the personal attacks, texts, emails, blog comments, and profile views. That's less than three million dollars in punitive damages. Then we're asking you to take that amount and add it to the lost wages, past and future, that Ms. Guerra should've made over the next few years. It sounds like a lot of money, but it's a tiny fraction of the defendant's trust fund. He can afford to pay a small judgment without blinking. Make him pay enough that he'll think twice before doing this to someone else, ladies and gentlemen. Thank you."

When the closing argument concluded, I felt good, confident. As my lawyer walked back toward our table, she flashed a small thumbs-up, blocking the jury's view with her body.

That serenity left me as soon as Mr. Carter started speaking to the jury. I already knew I wouldn't like what he said, but I wanted to stay in the courtroom to hear him. Sticks and stones may break my bones, but words will never hurt me.

"Listen, guys," Mr. Carter said, "I'm going to be completely honest with you. What happened to Ms. Guerra was highly unfortunate. No one could've anticipated the pictures going viral like that. But my client, Mr. Rutherford, is a scapegoat. He's not the cause of what happened. There's no lawsuit here, and Ms. Guerra knows it."

My blood boiled, but Meili cleared her throat and sipped her water. I unclenched my fists and reached for my own glass.

"To win in court, a person has to be able to

prove the elements of their claims. Ms. Guerra has to show that my client engaged in extreme and outrageous behavior. Nude pictures have been around since cameras, ladies and gentlemen. Heck, nude paintings existed back in the Middle Ages. I'd go so far as to say viewing pictures of naked ladies is commonplace. Most of you men on the jury have done it, I'd wager."

A couple of heads nodded, and bile rose in my throat. Red spots swam across my vision. Meili wrote something on her legal pad and tilted it toward me. *This is his job. Don't let him get to you. Don't even listen—that's MY job.*

"This isn't extreme and outrageous. Sharing pictures of naked ladies has been done for many years, and it's not to hurt the woman in them. It's to enjoy the woman in their glorious fertility, to share in her beauty. That's a legitimate reason to share a photograph—people share photographs on social media all the time for mutual enjoyment. That's what happened here."

My jaw clenched so hard, I worried one of my fillings would pop out. If my tongue had been in the way, it would've been bitten in half.

"So when it comes time to vote, ladies and gentlemen, don't think about how you'd feel in Ms. Guerra's position. Think about whether they proved my client intentionally and knowingly engaged in a course of conduct that served no legitimate purpose and served only to embarrass her. He did not. Thank you."

Meili stood and walked straight to the jury box, put her hands on the railing, and leaned forward as if about to tell a secret.

"Maybe there's something wrong with my hearing. I guess I could be getting old." Several members of the jury chuckled, and she held each of their gazes for a heartbeat before continuing. "But I could've sworn Attorney Carter said you should not find his client's behavior extreme and outrageous because, well, *this kind of abominable behavior happens all the time.*

"He's saying it is *okay* for his client to have ruined my client's life, because, after all, it happens to plenty of other young women in this world. Why not Ms. Guerra? Who cares if she lost her job, making six figures a year, plus bonuses? Who cares that she can't get a new job, that's she's getting constant harassment?

"Isn't that what she deserves for being female?"

The matron on the jury turned bright red. I could've kissed Meili for insisting we keep her.

"Let me tell you: No, it's not. For one thing, Mr. Carter neglected to mention that it's a crime in New Jersey to distribute intimate pictures of someone without their consent. The legislature has already spoken, and they've said, 'This is not commonplace. This is extreme and outrageous and should not be tolerated, and we're going to make it a crime.' That's what crimes are, right? Behaviors that aren't acceptable? Why should it be common or acceptable to post nude pictures of someone online without their consent?"

She gave such an exaggerated shrug, I half expected her to fall over. "Because, well, when relationships don't work out, you should be allowed to destroy the other person, right? Is that what you want America to be about? Are we all so privileged, so *entitled* that we have a right to be in a relationship with someone who doesn't love us anymore? Should Ms. Guerra have waited patiently to see if Mr. Rutherford ever returned from South America, if he *deigned* to lower himself to be with her? Look at that man!"

Meili turned, pointing at Eric, who stared at the table and shifted in his seat, his ears pink. "He hasn't even apologized. Worse, he said she deserved it. You heard him on the tape. 'No one gets the better of me.' I didn't say it—he did. Why? Because he thinks he did nothing wrong. He thinks, in his attorney's words, 'this kind of thing happens all the time.' He didn't like when she took control over ending their relationship.

"But you can have the control, right here, today. Power over the men you might date in the future, to men who might date your daughters and sisters that this is *not okay*. This behavior is extreme and outrageous, and it's not okay to punish someone for breaking up with you. You have the power, ladies and gentlemen of the jury, and that's why I ask you to hold Mr. Rutherford liable for his behavior, for the first time in his life. It's well past time someone did. Thank you."

As she strode back to our table, I had to refrain from clapping. Under the table, I picked the skin between my thumb and forefinger to keep from grinning. It wouldn't do to let the jury see me react to her words.

Judge Patel broke the silence. "Thank you, counselors. Court is adjourned. Jury deliberations start tomorrow."

Chapter 23

The jury reached a verdict Tuesday shortly after lunch. Tara took the day off to wait with me. The two of us sat at a table in the courthouse cafeteria, playing poker for five cents a hand. Neither of us kept a tally.

I didn't realize how tense I'd been until Meili sent a text informing me they'd come to a decision. My shoulders sagged, and panic rose in my chest. I'd been waiting for this for so long, wanted it to be over, but such a quick verdict—how could it be good for me?

"I can't do it, Tara. I can't go back in there."

"Of course you can." She took my hand and pulled me to my feet before wrapping me in a hug. "The only thing better than the verdict will be the expression on Eric's face when they read it.

There's no way in hell, I'm missing that, and nei-ther are you."

"But Meili said a quick verdict could be bad news—"

"Waiting here won't make it any better. You can do this. You're strong, remember?" She touched the inside of my right wrist. "I'll be sitting right behind you. Plus, I'm prepared to trip Eric on the way out of the courtroom, win or lose."

Laughter eased the knot in my chest. "You're a good friend. Let's go."

Ten minutes later, I stood beside Meili as the jurors filed silently into the box. Tara sat in the front row behind me, packed in with reporters from New Jersey, New York, and a few nationwide blogs and news sources. Even Fox News was there; part of me desperately wondered at their cover-age, but I'd never give in to the temptation to listen to how they portrayed me.

Jurors 1 and 2 kept their eyes glued to the floor as they entered, which told me nothing. The third snuck a peek at me before stumbling over a step and returning her attention to the space in front of her. The rest stared at their feet.

Oh, no. Why would none of them meet my eyes? My heart sank, and I knew they'd ruled against me.

Meili cleared her throat, drawing my atten-tion. She nodded her head a fraction and lifted the corners of her lips. I forced myself to look less petrified; a smile seemed beyond my abilities. Weeks of trial didn't prepare me for the realization that the rest of my life hinged on this one moment.

Finally, the judge and jurors sat. The bailiff motioned for me to remain standing. I clasped my hands in front of me, knotting my fingers together to keep from fidgeting.

The foreman, the middle-aged juror with tattoos, rose and cleared his throat. Behind him, the three housewives glared daggers at Eric from underneath identical haircuts. I hid my amusement beneath one hand, pretending to stifle a yawn.

"Mr. Foreman, has the jury reached a decision?"

"We have, Your Honor."

"How do you answer the first question?"

"We the jury find that the defendant, Eric Rutherford, did commit an extreme and outrageous act and violate the plaintiff's privacy by posting nude pictures of her on the internet and public billboards."

With every word, I felt lighter than I had in ages. Although my lawyer told me to keep calm no matter what happened, a smile exploded across my face. I kept my eyes glued on the jury box. Smirking at Eric wouldn't help me. Behind me, a low cheer broke out. The judge banged his gavel.

"Quiet, please!" He stared into the galley until the whispers ceased. "Mr. Foreman, how do you answer the second question?"

"We the jury find the defendant knowingly and maliciously caused substantial emotional distress to the plaintiff, without legal cause or excuse, through his extreme and outrageous behavior."

The pit living in my stomach for the past year and a half shrunk. Finally, someone was holding Eric accountable for his actions.

The foreman said, "We find the defendant made untrue factual statements about the plaintiff: First, that she is a prostitute, and second, that she entertains fantasies of being raped by strangers."

Even though I was winning, those words still sent a chill down my spine. I tried to focus on the foreman's words.

"The jury finds that the plaintiff incurred medical and therapy bills in the amount of $45,947.23."

A decent start, but that was to reimburse the insurance company. I'd only paid about a thousand bucks out of pocket.

"The jury further finds, at the time of relevant events, the plaintiff was working as a mid-level executive for a world-renowned children's clothing company. The defendant's behavior cost the plaintiff approximately $300,000 in lost wages and bonuses to date. The defendant's behavior will make it difficult for the plaintiff to find a new job in her field. We find that the plaintiff would probably earn additional raises throughout her career, so the jury also orders the defendant to pay two million dollars to offset her future lost wages."

"Holy shit!"

The exclamation came from behind me, but Tara's voice mirrored my thoughts exactly. Did I hear the foreman correctly? The jury awarded me millions of dollars in compensatory damages alone? Even knowing from the outset how much we asked for, my brain couldn't compute that much money. Never did I truly think we'd win this kind of award. Too many ways for things to go wrong.

The judge peered at the gallery behind me. "Ms. Fisher, if you can't contain yourself while the verdict is read, I'm afraid I'll have to ask you to wait outside. That goes for the rest of the spectators, too.

"And the final two questions, Mr. Foreman? What did the jury say about punitive damages?"

"Your Honor, the jury finds the defendant knew that statements he made about the plaintiff were untrue and that he, therefore, acted with actual malice. We find that he posted the pictures with the intent of hurting the plaintiff, and he had no legitimate purpose in doing so. In addition, we find that the defendant possesses sufficient resources to pay a large judgment. A light fine in this scenario would be a mere slap on the wrist and would not discourage future conduct of this type."

He read directly from the jury instructions we'd submitted. That was a good sign. Finally, I allowed myself to sneak a peek at Eric. The bastard somehow still had the audacity to look smug, standing there, hands in his pockets. But the spreading wet spots beneath his armpits betrayed his true emotions.

Judge Patel said, "Did the jury assign a dollar amount to the defendant's behavior?"

"We did, Your Honor," the foreman said. "We the jury award the plaintiff punitive damages in the amount of fifteen million dollars."

It's only after we've lost everything that we're free
to do anything.

- Chuck Palahniuk, *Fight Club*

Epilogue

After the verdict, I tried to buy Papá a new house, but he said if I was strong enough to stand up against the world, he could handle a few busybody neighbors. Instead, he accepted some of the money I offered him and joined me on a trip around the world. I got some new glasses, cut and dyed my hair, and the two of us hopped on a plane headed east from Charlotte. For several months, we traveled the world, losing ourselves in the crowds of Venice, Cairo, Sydney, Sao Paulo. Papá showed me places he'd been with Doctors without Borders and the village where he'd met my mother.

Throughout dozens of countries and hundreds of cities, I wore large sunglasses and ate everything in sight. About twenty pounds later, the old

Anna vanished from the mirror, replaced by someone with fuller cheeks and a lot more sparkle in her eyes.

My new pink and purple shock do turned out to be the perfect disguise. Papá didn't have much hair left, but he proudly sported a neon green punk wig wherever we went. We followed the sun, moving between locations where the weather allowed me to wear skirts year-round. My prosthetic sat on display to everyone I encountered. People noted our hair, my disability. No one paid any attention to me.

Strangers, both fellow tourists and residents, avoided eye contact. No one yelled, "slut," "whore," or any of the other insults I'd become used to hearing. Instead of ogling my breasts, strangers averted their eyes from my hair to my foot to my father, then stared right past us into the crowd.

Being invisible was freeing, but I couldn't hide forever. Seven months, three weeks, and two days after I left the United States, I received a text from Tara.

It's ready. Are you?

For a long moment, I stared out the window of my hotel room at the ocean below, timing my breath to the rolling of the waves. Papá and I had explored thirty-four countries on six continents. It was time.

I'm ready, I typed. I'll be home next week.

Papá and I said our good-byes. I repeated my offer to buy him a new place, maybe somewhere closer to me. He declined but extracted a sworn statement to visit more often, helpfully notarized by a man sitting beside us at Charles de Gaulle airport.

When my flight landed, Tara and Beth greeted me, wearing matching sapphire and ruby engagement rings and identical smiles.

———

TWO WEEKS LATER, Tara and I finished settling into our new office. In the mornings, I called local schools to set up talks while Tara worked on the legal and business sides of things. In the beginning, all was quiet. On the third day, however, people started to get the message that we were open for business.

"You've got three messages," Tara said when I arrived that morning with a bag of croissants and two lattes.

"Already? We just opened."

"Well, one was your dad, wishing us luck." We exchanged a smile, and I set the food on her desk. "Anyway, *Forbes* wants to do a follow-up to their Couples article, sort of a 'Where Are They Now?' They're calling you 'The Face of Revenge Porn.'"

"I'll absolutely do it. What's the third message?"

"A pharmaceutical company called. They're doing a series of articles on living with depression and want to know if you're willing to be interviewed."

I thought for a minute while hanging up my coat. "That might be interesting. I'll talk to Dr. Bracken and see what she thinks."

She handed me a package. "And we got something from Meili, which looks promising."

The manila envelope must've weighed three pounds. I tested it in one hand, almost afraid to open it. Tara sighed and held out one hand at my indecision, but I ripped the tab off the envelope and pulled out a sheaf of papers.

Random words jumped out at me: "foreclosure…appeal…abuse of discretion…" I blinked, closed my eyes, and started at the beginning. Then, a squeal escaped me.

"What is it? What does it say?"

"Eric lost the appeal! The court says the judge didn't abuse his discretion, and he has to pay me."

Tara whooped.

No one had been remotely surprised when Eric refused to pay and filed a Notice of Appeal and Motion to Stay instead. The judge's decision was a huge load off my mind.

"Also," I said, "she's registered the judgment in

New York and scheduled an auction on Eric's loft."

Now that the appeal had been denied, we could try to collect the money, and the easiest way to start was to sell the loft to the highest bidder. I would've felt bad for taking the place he loved, but, well, he didn't live there anymore, and he'd brought it on himself. Plus, the sale should cover at least half of what he owed.

Tara jumped up and down, clapping. "Awesome. That's such a relief."

"I know, right?"

"This calls for a celebration! Drinks are—"

A jingle sounded above the door, cutting off her words. Our first client. Tara glanced over my shoulder, then sat and started typing furiously.

"Can you help our guest? I've got to set up interviews for our new secretary."

Her desk was about eleven inches from the door, and she'd been about to bust out the champagne a minute ago, but I guess she wanted to look professional. There was no point in arguing while a potential client stood directly behind me.

When I turned around, my heart skipped a beat. "Why, hello there."

"Hello. I heard someone was starting a business to help people go after jerks who post private pictures of them online without consent."

It was tough to keep my voice even while my

pulse tap-danced in my throat. "Yes. Yes, we are. Welcome to Lotus." I swung the door open and gestured. "This is my associate, Tara Fisher."

Tara popped out of her chair suspiciously fast for someone who was supposed to be frantically setting up secretary interviews. "Nice to see you again, Detective. I was just leaving." She gathered her coat and swooped out the door so fast, I wondered if she'd disapparated.

"Why don't you come on in?"

Sayid twisted his cap nervously in his hand while he hovered near the wooden chair we'd found for our clients. "I can't stay too long. I wanted to let you know, I've got a new partner these days."

"Oh, yeah?" Weird. I wondered why he felt the need to inform me he started seeing someone new. We hadn't spoken in months.

"Yeah. The brass thought someone with Detective Stern's, uh, people skills would be better off in Internal Affairs."

Oh! That kind of partner. Duh. A smile crossed my face, and my hopes soared. "So, tell me about this new partner."

"Trent's a great guy. Helping me put away the real criminals. We're doing a new community outreach program. We go around to high schools and talk about things like how it's a crime for a minor to text naked pictures of themselves and what happens if those pictures are distributed, and even if the person is an adult, why you shouldn't do it. We're planning to talk to the New York Legislature soon, too, about things we've seen. Statistics. Changing the law."

"That sounds fascinating, Detective. Your idea?"

He shook his head, his eyes never leaving mine. "No. Yours. And I was thinking, I know you're busy, but maybe if you can take a break, we could go get some coffee and discuss the possibilities?"

I swallowed, hoping he didn't see how he made me feel like a schoolgirl. "I'd like that."

Also by Laura Heffernan

The Reality Star Series
America's Next Reality Star
Sweet Reality
Reality Wedding

The Oceanic Dreams Series
Time of My Life

The Gamer Girls Series
She's Got Game
Against the Rules
Make Your Move

Finding Tranquility

Acknowledgments

First and foremost, thank you so much to my agent Michelle Richter for your unfailing patience and your tireless dedication to improving my books. Thank you to each of my critique partners and beta readers for your essential feedback. I did my very best to represent Anna positively, and any mistakes are my own.

Thank you to Kirsty McManus, not just for designing this beautiful cover but for all the hours you spend online holding my hand when I wavered about entering the world of indie publishing. You're amazing, and this book likely wouldn't exist without your help.

Always and forever, thank you to my amazing husband for believing in me. And thank you to my readers for your support.

I hope you enjoyed this book. If so, please consider leaving an honest review on Bookbub or with your favorite retailer.

Looking for more? Keep reading to get a sneak peek at

FRICTION
a moving and insightful look at first love

Coming Soon!

Chapter 1

When I was eight years old and still believed in happily ever afters, I swore I'd grow up and marry Tommy Devereaux, the cutest boy in third grade. I stared at the class photo, painstakingly tracing the letters of his name and repeating them to myself until I knew it as well as my own identity. "Brittany Devereaux" covered the insides of my notebooks, journals, any scrap of paper I could find in clumsy, childish script.

Fourteen years later, I sat in a coffee shop, doodling my first name in the margins of my term paper notes when someone approached my table.

"Is this seat taken?" Hello, green eyes. The guy appeared to be about my age. One hand rested on the top rung of the empty wooden chair in front of him. Between the din of the coffee shop and my music, I barely heard his question.

I nodded. He let go of the chair. I pulled out an earbud and realized what he'd said. "Wait, sorry. No, it's not taken. Yes, you can sit."

"Thanks. I'm Colin Devereaux."

All those childhood dreams rushed back, and a response tumbled out of my mouth automatically, like when I was eight. "D-e-v-e-r-e-a-u-x."

Smooth, Britt.

I wasn't the most suave at talking to members of the opposite sex. That's probably why I could count the number of dates I'd had in the past four years on my right hand, not including hookups.

What? I said I wasn't suave, not that I'm a nun.

Hooking up was easy, dating carried the pain and misery of sitting by the phone, texting yourself to see if the phone still worked. That's what my friends did during high school. Not me, though. High school boys never seemed to want a relationship with me. I was too self-assured, too good at math and science. It was easier for me not to get attached.

Colin laughed as if impromptu spelling was a perfectly normal response to introducing himself. A single dimple and crooked teeth flashed at me before he settled into the chair.

"Do you always greet people you don't know

by spelling their names at them? Is that your secret super power?"

Warmth flooded my cheeks. Avoiding his eyes, I mumbled, "Something like that."

He pulled out his laptop, still chuckling. "And you are?"

"Brittany."

"B-r-i-t-n-e-y? Like Spears?" He winked at me.

Usually, I didn't like winkers. They tended to fit into the same category as men with mo-lestaches. Creepy. But it worked for Colin. Maybe it was the laughter in his green eyes or his wide smile. Yes, men can wink when they're totally hot.

"Like Alvin and the Chipmunks." He looked confused, but I waved a hand at him. "Apparently it started as a cartoon in the '80s. Most people call me Britt."

With that, I replaced the earbud I still held in my right hand and returned my attention to my laptop. This guy was good-looking, sure, but I had a twenty-page paper on gram-positive bacteria due in three days and had written about two para-graphs. "Hot" wouldn't pass my classes.

I wondered if he was flirting with me, but shared tables were common at Buzz's Caffeinery. Despite the pretentious name, Boston University students packed into Buzz's at all hours of the day and night. The shop sat on the edge of campus, making the tables prime real estate. Also, they sold beer after dinner and to-die-for Mexican mochas all day (made with sweetened condensed milk, espresso, cocoa, and cinnamon, for approximately two thousand calories per serving).

Thanks to the crowds, strangers ignored each other at two- and four-person tables. No one sat alone. The walls created by our laptop screens gave an illusion of privacy. The seat Colin currently occupied had been vacated four minutes earlier when my roommate Amber left for a lab. I didn't have class on Tuesday mornings. I had a deadline and a pending nervous breakdown.

That's what you get for lying on the beach instead of doing homework during spring break.

Shut up, I told myself. I hated when I was right.

After leaving a stack of papers next to mine to stake his claim, Colin stood. He waved to catch my attention. I removed my earbud again, despite not having restarted the music since he sat. He didn't need to know that.

"Can I bring you anything from the coffee bar?"

I raised my now lukewarm, half-full Mexican mocha. "I'm good, thanks." Without making eye contact, I replaced my earbud and hit "play." Depeche Mode filled my ears.

It might seem like I was being rude, but strangers at Buzz's liked to talk to me. Amber said they flocked to me because I had such a pleasant face, but I told her she didn't need to suck up to get my help on her chemistry. Anyway, if I didn't discourage interaction, I'd never get anything done. Once, a woman sat down and launched into a detailed explanation of how to make simple syrup. Another guy poured out a full break-up story within thirty seconds of settling into a chair at my table. Self-preservation—and the fact that I needed a good grade—dictated I do whatever I needed to focus.

Except, you know, go to the library.

A few minutes later, something made me glance up in time to see steaming brown liquid headed for me…And my stuff.

I jumped up, ripping my earbuds out in the process. My laptop managed to avoid disaster when I plucked it off the table with seconds to spare. Colin grappled for the overturned cup, but the damage was done.

Coffee covered the surface of the table, including the page of handwritten notes I'd been copying all morning.

My heart skipped a beat. That paper was three-quarters of my grade. I couldn't move. Just stood at the table, holding my laptop at chest level, mouth open.

Two employees materialized out of the wood-work with rags. They made quick work of the sopping mess on the table, while I remained frozen to my spot. I hadn't even recovered enough to look for another table or pick up my now-ruined notes.

"Oh, my God. I'm so sorry."

Colin stood on the other side of the table. Coffee dripped from the empty mug in his hand. Horror covered his face. Behind him, a skinny brunette wearing a Vera Bradley backpack smirked at him over a latte gripped with perfectly manicured fingernails.

She smirked at him. "That's what you get for trying to take my seat. I told you I needed to sit there."

Colin seemed unsure what to say. He eyed me apologetically, then glared at the girl like she was some kind of alien being.

Before he made his decision, I turned on the girl. With each word, my voice rose. "Are you saying you poured Colin's coffee on the table and ruined my term paper *on purpose?*"

"He was taking the last seat!"

"He was ALREADY SITTING HERE."

The girl's fingers curled; the cup in her hands dented. I narrowed my eyes at her, but otherwise didn't move. After a moment, she stormed out.

I snorted.

"Is everything okay?" Colin asked. "Your computer?"

I accepted a dripping piece of paper from the

barista. "I think I'm okay. Most of these notes were already on the computer."

"I'm so sorry."

"Thanks. It's not your fault some girl pushed you out of your seat."

The employees finished wiping down the table and vanished.

Colin said, "I know, but I feel terrible. Can I do anything?"

Finally, I gave this guy my attention. Like I noticed earlier, totally hot. Spiky brown hair above clear green eyes and well-groomed eyebrows. Delicate cheekbones made him seem innocent. He had full lips and a quick, easy smile. A couple of days worth of scruff dotted his jawbone. The incongruity with his otherwise clean-cut look added to his appeal.

Ah, well. Cute guys come and go. Failing grades are forever. I sat in my thankfully-dry chair and opened my computer.

"You can buy me a coffee later or something." I didn't mean it, but he relaxed. "It's fine. I can fix this."

Two hours later, my stomach rumbled. I stretched and sipped the last of my drink—now a half-melted iced coffee. The hoodie I'd huddled into earlier hung off the back of my chair. When I lifted one hand to rub the back of my neck, the movement pulled one of my earbuds out. I craned my neck from side to side, before turning to stretch my back.

When Colin spoke, his voice made me jump. I hadn't realized he still sat across from me. "Is that a chipmunk tattoo?"

My cheeks warmed as a flush rose into my face. I remained turned away to give him a better view of my left shoulder. Not to wait until the flush faded, returning my skin to its normal bronze color. "Oh, um, yeah. That's my namesake. Brittany."

"I like it. A whimsical contrast to the purple hair and the black Docs." He winked. "Like a hint at your softer side."

Usually, I told people I didn't know well that I'd been drunk when I got it or I lost a bet, but I wasn't comfortable with the direction this conversation was going. Better to let it end. This stranger shouldn't be able to see me so well within minutes of meeting.

"Thanks," I said.

To distract myself, I put my mouth around the end of my straw. The slurping that reached my ears made me wince.

Manners, Britt. Look into it.

Colin chuckled at my faux pas. "What's $F_1 = -F_2$ mean? The other tattoo."

Self-consciously, I touched the back of my neck. "It's Newton's third law of physics. For every reaction, there is an equal and opposite reaction, you know? Positive and negative friction cancel each other."

He nodded, but may have been hiding a blank stare. "You like science?"

"Yeah."

Understatement of the year. Still, I didn't feel the need to elaborate.

"Cool," Colin said. "Is the food here any good?"

"The muffins are okay, but they're not lunch. I usually get a sandwich across the street."

"Want to come with me? Buying you lunch is the least I can do, after spilling coffee all over your notes."

I smiled, the morning's disaster shoved to the back of my mind. I'd gotten enough done that I could afford to take a break to relieve some tension. Nothing relieved my tension like banging it out with a total hottie. Hanging out for a few hours might help me refocus my energy later.

I shrugged, trying to seem cool. "Sure. It would probably be a good idea for me to get out of this chair for a while." My stomach growled again, destroying my nonchalant illusion. "Also, I'm starving. Do you want to go somewhere we can hit the books?"

His gaze was direct, steady on mine. My

stomach flip-flopped. "No. The words are blurring together. Let's take a break."!

A FEW HOURS LATER, I wondered if I'd misinterpreted his interest. This had become the weirdest hook-up ever. Colin bought me a sandwich for lunch. We sat outside in the grass, eating under the bright blue sky. He told me that he grew up in Northern California. While chewing on a lobster roll, I'd asked Colin what he thought of Boston.

"The winter was brutal," he'd said, "but the city is beautiful. I love looking at the old buildings."

"Yeah, I'm used to the weather, but the architecture is amazing. What's your favorite?"

"Well, my favorite structure in Boston is Fenway Park. Unfortunately, I haven't managed to make it inside yet. Too bad."

I'd wiped mayo and lobster off my hands. "Why don't we go now?"

"I can't get tickets."

"Have you tried going right before the game?"

Colin had glared at me. "That's not funny. I've been trying to see a game since I got accepted to BU. I can't afford scalper prices, though."

I bit back an angry retort only upon remembering he wasn't from Boston. "No, I'm serious. Season ticket holders turn their tickets in if they're not going, and the ballpark sells them. Plus, you can buy standing room before the game starts." I glanced at the display on my phone. "We can go now, if you want. Game's at four."

Colin had sat up so fast, the top of his head almost collided with my elbow. "You're not joking? You'll take me to a game right now?"

Standing, I brushed off my skirt and extended my left hand to him. "Sure. No guarantees we'll get in, but only one way to find out."

Together, we walked to Fenway to see if they had any seats left. We commiserated over beers when the couple ahead of us bought the last standing room tickets, at a price no rational person would pay to stand for three hours. Especially not a college student.

Colin had yet to make a move on me. He didn't try to kiss me while we lay back in the grass. When my fingers brushed against his while we stood in line outside Fenway, he didn't hold my hand. His words contained no innuendo. What if I'd blown off half a day of studying to hang out with a guy who needed a friend?

Oh, well. He was a nice guy, anyway. And it was one of those rare spring days with perfect weather, not a hint of rain. Afternoon turned to evening, and we stopped at my favorite burrito place to load up on carbs and guacamole. It was nothing compared to what my Tata made, but for a quick fix I didn't have to cook myself, this place was perfectly adequate.

Halfway through the meal, Colin tilted his head at me and set his burrito down.

"What's wrong?"

He leaned forward. Was he going to kiss me in the middle of the dining room? My lips parted as I gazed up at him. Colin's face neared mine. I smiled and brushed a lock of hair out of my eyes.

Our faces were only inches apart. Unconsciously, I leaned forward.

Colin picked up a napkin. "Don't move. You've got something…" He dabbed my chin.

Oh, right. Never mind.

"Thanks." How awkward.

Our eyes met. He was so cute. My tongue darted out to moisten my lips. At the table behind us, a middle-aged man coughed. The spell broken, I flushed and sat back in my seat.

But something definitely sparked between us. I hadn't imagined his interest. We rushed through the rest of the meal. I couldn't wait to get Colin back to my place.

About the Author

Laura Heffernan writes fun, witty romantic comedies and more serious women's fiction. After a few years of practicing law, she realized that she much preferred arguing with her characters rather than other people. It's easier to win that way.

When not watching total strangers get married, drag racing queens, or cooking competitions, Laura enjoys board games, travel, board games, baking, and board games. She lives in the northeast with her husband, the world's most active toddler, and two furry little beasts.

Laura loves connecting with readers. Find her on at http://www.lauraheffernan.com/, on Facebook, or on Twitter, where she spends far too much time tweeting about reality TV and Canadian chocolate.